October 2013

Donated by

Still Star-Crossed

Still Star-Crossed

MELINDA TAUB

DELACORTE PRESS

Text copyright © 2013 by Melinda Taub
Jacket photographs: girl © 2013 by Holly Broomhall; gravestone © 2013 by Mark Sadlier/Trevillion Images; fabric and rose relief © 2013 by Shutterstock

Visit us on the Web! randomhouse.com/teens

Educators and librarians, for a variety of teaching tools, visit us at RHTeachersLibrarians.com

Library of Congress Cataloging-in-Publication Data
Taub, Melinda.
Still star-crossed / Melinda Taub. — First edition.
pages cm
Summary: "After the deaths of Romeo and Juliet, mysterious figures in Verona are determined to reignite the feud between the Montagues and Capulets, so, for the sake of peace, the Prince orders Romeo's best friend Benvolio to marry Juliet's cousin Rosaline"—Provided by publisher.
ISBN 978-0-385-74350-1 (hc) — ISBN 978-0-449-81665-3 (ebook) — ISBN 978-0-375-99118-9 (glb) [1. Characters in literature—Fiction. 2. Families—Fiction. 3. Vendetta—Fiction. 4. Love—Fiction. 5. Verona (Italy)—History—16th century—Fiction. 6. Italy—History—1559-1789—Fiction.] I. Title.
PZ7.T21142145St 2013
[Fic]—dc23
2012032626

The text of this book is set in 11-point Latienne.
Book design by Stephanie Moss

Printed in the United States of America

10 9 8 7 6 5 4 3 2 1   FICTAUB   10/13   #17

First Edition

For my sisters,
Amanda and Hannah,
who got me across
the finish line

Dramatis Personae

The Montagues and kin

Lord Montague, head of one of two houses once at variance
    with each other, now in truce
Lady Montague, wife to Montague
Benvolio, nephew to Montague, and friend to Romeo
Orlino, Truchio, and Marius, Montague youths

The Capulets and kin

Lord Capulet, head of one of two houses once at variance with
    each other, now in truce
Lady Capulet, wife to Capulet
Rosaline, niece to Capulet, once beloved of Romeo
Livia, niece to Capulet, sister to Rosaline
Duchess of Vitruvio, mother to Lady Capulet, kinswoman to
    Lord Capulet, guardian to Rosaline and Livia
Gramio, Valentine, and Lucio, Capulet youths

The royal family of Verona

Escalus, Prince of Verona
Isabella, Princess of Arragon, sister to Escalus
Don Pedro, Prince of Arragon

The newly dead

Juliet, a Capulet, beloved of Romeo
Romeo, a Montague, beloved of Juliet
Paris, a young count, kinsman to the prince
Tybalt, cousin to Juliet
Mercutio, friend to Romeo and Benvolio, kinsman to the prince

Others

Friar Laurence, Franciscan monk
Lucullus, steward to the Duchess of Vitruvio
Penlet, chancellor to the prince
Nurse to Juliet
Tuft, a stableman
A gravedigger
Citizens of Verona, gentlemen and gentlewomen of both houses,
    maskers, torchbearers, pages, guards, watchmen, servants,
    and attendants

Part 1

⁊

Come away, come away, death,
And in sad cypress let me be laid.
Fly away, fly away, breath;
I am slain by a fair cruel maid.

—*Twelfth Night*

IN FAIR VERONA'S STREETS, the sun was hot.

Late summer was upon the city, and the sun, oh, it beat. It dazzled off the cobblestones so the beggars groaned and burnt their bare dirty feet. It poured down on the merchants so the sweat trickled down their necks on market day. And the great families—well, they were safe in their cool stone houses, cellars deep enough to hold a bit of chill in, but when they did emerge after sunset, the air was still hot and thick.

Yes, the heat hung heavy on Verona. Was it this that bowed its citizens' heads? That quieted the normally bustling city, leaving its people whispering in twos and threes before disappearing in shadowed doorways?

Or was it death?

It had been a bloody summer. Night after night, the streets echoed with the pounding of feet, the scrape of steel. The names of the dead passed from hoarse throats to disbelieving ears. Mercutio. Tybalt. Paris. Romeo. Juliet.

A fortnight and odd days had passed since the flowers of the city's youth had finished cutting each other down. Shaken by the loss of so many of their own, the great houses of Montague and Capulet had sworn to end the bloodshed. Great Montague, to prove his offer of friendship, had just three days before unveiled his gift to his ancient enemy.

The statue portrayed a beautiful young woman just a breath past girlhood. Fashioned in pure gold, it stood over the grave of a lady to whom Montague had never spoken a word in life. His greatest enemy's only child. His son's five-day wife. Juliet of Capulet.

It was a pretty piece of work, Montague's tribute to his dead daughter-in-law. On this Verona morn, the sunrise glittered off her golden face. The cemetery was empty, but had there been any visitors at that moment, they would have noted the skillfully wrought expression of sadness as she gazed on her love Romeo's statue on the other side of the gate. They would note the pretty poem at the base, mourning her untimely death.

And as the first rays of the sun kissed fair Juliet's frozen form, they'd see the word HARLOT scrawled in black paint across her face.

"Just don the gown, I prithee, Livia."

Lady Rosaline blew a brown curl out of her face. She shook the black gown toward her younger sister for what seemed the hundredth time.

Livia wrinkled her nose in disgust and danced out of Rosaline's grasp. "Must we really keep our mourning weeds on, Rosaline? I am sure cousin Juliet would not wish it."

Rosaline gave up trying to catch Livia and plumped down on her sister's bed. "She told thee so, did she? Her shade whispered it from the crypt?"

Livia laughed and snatched the black dress. She threw it on the ground and began to dance on it. Livia never walked when she could instead practice the latest twirl and dip from court. "Aye. I passed by the Capulet tomb and her ghost whispered, 'Cousin, do not put on ugly black mourning for me, for I had rather be remembered with joy than with ugly black that will leave every man and woman of Capulet sweating in the summer heat. Also, I wish thee to have my coral bracelet.'"

"A talkative shade, our cousin." Rosaline picked up the dress, smoothing its wrinkles. "Of course, so she was in life."

The sisters' eyes met in the mirror. Livia, caught mid-twirl, paused. For a moment her gaiety faltered and gave way, like a veil tossed back in the wind.

The orphaned daughters of Niccolo Tirimo did not weep much. It was one of the few traits they shared. Fifteen-year-old Livia had laughed a great deal these last weeks. A stranger might have thought her unfeeling, but her sister knew better. Livia laughed most when she was frightened.

As for Rosaline, the elder at seventeen, her head had not ceased to ache since the bloodbath began. Her temples throbbed anew as she looked at Livia's wide eyes, filled with unshed tears, in the mirror, and the names of the dead began to filter through her mind: Merry Mercutio, sighed over by half the ladies of Verona, slain by Tybalt's sword. Cousin Tybalt himself, so protective of his Capulet kinswomen, fallen to Romeo's blade. Count Paris, kin to the prince, spilling out his lifeblood at the door of his beloved's tomb. Romeo, Montague lordling. And Juliet, flower of the Capulets.

The Juliet Rosaline mourned was not the lovely maiden Verona wept for. The city grieved for a wealthy, beautiful young heiress; Rosaline, however, remembered a sticky hand in hers, a piping voice ordering her to wait so Juliet's shorter legs could catch up, the awed mirth in Juliet's eyes when they accomplished some particularly naughty bit of mischief. When Rosaline was small, she'd been much in the company of her uncle Capulet's only daughter. Though Juliet had been several years younger than Rosaline, Capulet's imperious little heir had preferred the company of the older girls, and Rosaline could not say her nay. Luckily, Juliet had been a witty, openhearted child, so her company was no burden. Rosaline's mother, Lady Katherina, had served Verona's Princess Maria as a lady-in-waiting, and she often took her daughters and niece with her to the palace, where she spent her days. Juliet, Livia, Rosaline, and the princess's daughter, Isabella, had made the palace their playground.

Those days of romping throughout the palace and House Capulet, teasing Isabella's older brother, Escalus, and driving Juliet's nurse to distraction, had been the happiest of Rosaline's life. Her parents had still been alive then. Her mother was a sister to Lord Capulet, and her father a nobleman from the Western coast; she and Livia were not so grand as their little cousin Juliet, but they were assured of their place in Verona.

But when Rosaline was eleven her father died, and everything began to change. All the misfortune she had been spared during her happy childhood seemed to arrive in the space of the next few years. As their father had no son, most of his lands and fortunes had gone to a distant relative, leaving the girls and their mother in greatly reduced circumstances. Princess Maria died giving birth to a stillborn babe not long after, and Isabella was sent away to be fostered with the royal family of Sicilia, ending their family's close association with the palace. Rosaline's mother had never recovered from the shock of her husband's loss, and had followed him into death not two years later. Gone were the days when Rosaline and her family lived in a fine house in the center of town, and counted the richest and noblest young ladies in the city as their dearest companions. Instead, Rosaline and Livia had come to live with Lady Capulet's mother, Rosaline's great-aunt by marriage. The Duchess of Vitruvio's estate was on the edge of the city, but it sometimes felt as though they'd moved to another continent. The ambitious Lord and Lady Capulet no longer considered them fit playmates for their daughter, and had all but banished their nieces from their house. Thereafter, they'd seen Juliet only at feasts a few times a year, and then usually at a distance.

It was in those terrible years that Rosaline had grieved for Juliet. Then that she'd weathered the anger and loneliness as she'd learned to comfort a crying Livia, too young to understand why their friend no longer invited them to call. And so now what pierced Rosaline's heart was that she no longer knew the young lady who'd slain herself in the Capulet tomb at all.

Rosaline sighed, running her fingers over the window's sill, allowing the vision of the sweet, spoiled child Juliet had been to fade from her mind. Despite all her and Livia's misfortunes, their current state was well enough. They shared a small, modest cottage toward the back of her great-aunt's property, and the duchess, who had little interest in the doings of her poor wards, left them mostly to their own devices. If they were ignored by their Capulet kin, Rosaline was not sorry—the summer's events had surely shown that being a member of the Capulets' circle was as much a curse as a blessing. And after their mother's death a rich merchant from Messina had rented their house for a surprisingly generous amount, allowing Livia and Rosaline enough to live on, and to wed when the time came. Well, for Livia to wed, at least. Rosaline's plans for herself were somewhat different.

Rosaline would never breathe a word of it to her family, but her grief for Juliet was no greater than that she felt for Juliet's Montague lover. Every time Rosaline thought of Romeo, she was engulfed in a wave of guilt so great she half wished it could wash her away altogether.

Stop it, she told herself angrily. *Thou knowest that thou couldst not have saved him. Saved any of them.*

But it wasn't true. All Verona knew that there was at least one man she could have saved. For before he loved Juliet, Romeo had loved her. And now the sweet, lovesick boy was dead.

Prince Escalus rode swiftly out from town.

His doublet was stuck to his back with sweat and he could feel his stallion, Venitio, straining beneath him, but he neither stopped nor slowed as Verona's walls receded behind him. His daily ride outside the city was the one pleasure he allowed himself in these troubled times, and of late it seemed he had to ride farther and farther afield to escape the sensation that the city would suffocate him.

He'd awoken that morning shaking from a nightmare in which the former monarchs of the city gathered at his bedside to condemn his failure to prevent the slaughter of Verona's youth. All day it had stayed with him, his mind reflexively mounting counterarguments for his accusing ancestors. *I tried to stop them. Their animosity was too deeply rooted. I have ended it at last.* He tried to bring his mind to bear on that— how he'd induced House Montague and House Capulet to raise statues in memory of each other's children. He'd been there three days prior when the two lords had unveiled them, in an uneasy but determined show of public unity—Romeo and Juliet, golden and beautiful and together forever. Lammas Day, it was, the first of August, and her father's voice kept breaking as he gazed on Juliet's likeness, for it would have been her fourteenth birthday, had she lived. But he'd promised peace as loudly as he could, as had old Montague. None of it seemed to prevent Escalus from imagining his father's disappointed frown.

Well. There was no time for regrets. Both houses had promised an end to the violence; he would do whatever it took to make them keep to their vows, especially since some vicious vandal had already defaced Juliet's memorial. He had a duty to his city.

However much he might currently long to keep riding and riding and leave it behind for good.

With a sigh, he reined Venitio down to a walk at last. The horse complied with a nicker of complaint—his appetite for speed outpaced Escalus's own. The trees threw long shadows on the road, whose orange dust was darkened to a deep bloodred by the late afternoon sun. It was nearly sunset; time to return to the city. But just as he was about to turn around, he spotted a cloud of dust fast approaching down the road. What in the world—

Oh!

Escalus urged an eager Venitio back to a gallop. As they approached the cloud of dust, it resolved itself into a carriage, surrounded by half a dozen well-armed horsemen. The driver shouted a command to halt as he approached.

"Stand down!" the captain of the horsemen called to him. "Are you friend or foe?"

The man must be a foreigner. Escalus dressed simply for his daily rides, but his subjects in and around the city knew his face. He was about to tell the stranger who he was when the door of the coach opened, and a tall, slim lady emerged. Her gown was rich and her golden hair wound about her head in braids in a style unknown in Verona, but her grin was as familiar as his own face in the mirror.

"Peace, good Captain," she said. "'Tis only my brother. Well met, Escalus."

"Well met indeed, Isabella." He moved to help her down

from the carriage and embrace her, feeling a smile spread across his own face—an unaccustomed sensation of late. "I had not expected your party to arrive for several days yet."

"We made good time from Messina, once my husband's friends could be persuaded to let me depart. But I could wait no longer to come home." She laughed in delight. "Verona! How I've longed for it in the years since my departure. You must hold a feast for me, Escalus, so I may reacquaint myself with all our old friends." Escalus smiled but made no reply, and Isabella looked at him quizzically. "I hope I have not arrived in advance of my welcome."

Escalus shook his head. "Not at all. Your visit is the only good news I have had this fortnight."

Isabella frowned. "Why? What has passed in our fair city?"

Escalus looked away. "'Tis too heavy a tale for one weary from travel. How doth His Grace your husband?"

"Don Pedro is all things mild and kind and virtuous. He stayed in Messina to visit friends. Pray do not try to change the subject. What is it, Escalus?"

He winced. His sister might be a woman grown and a princess in her own right, but she still had an uncanny ability to demand he speak of topics he most wished to avoid. "'Tis something touching the Montagues and Capulets."

Isabella rolled her eyes. "Another street brawl?"

Escalus choked back a grim laugh at that description of the death toll. "Among other things. Come, ride with me and I shall tell you of it."

Her men brought her a mount. He helped her a-horseback

and they made for the city slowly, her guards and carriage trailing behind. "Sister, do you remember young Juliet?" he asked.

She nodded. "Rosaline's little cousin, mean you? Old Capulet's child."

Few people would describe the flower of the Capulets as "Rosaline's cousin," but of course Rosaline had been Isabella's particular friend when they were children and Rosaline of Tirimo's mother was a lady-in-waiting in the palace. Escalus himself had spent most days in Rosaline's company, before he'd been sent away to be fostered—his father had thought it best that both his children live and study in other courts, to be better acquainted with the world outside Verona. Except for one or two short visits, Isabella had been absent from Verona for the past six years, and thus had been spared the worst of the feud. He scarcely saw Rosaline now; four years ago when his father died and he'd come home to be crowned, the merry, clever child had been replaced by a solemn, orphaned young maid, and he himself had been too consumed with royal duties to pass the time with childhood playfellows. "Aye, she was. Juliet is dead."

"Dead!"

"Aye. Three weeks ago in high July she met with Romeo, son and heir of old Montague. It seems they wed in secret."

Isabella's eyes grew wide. "A son of Montague, wed to a lady of Capulet? 'Twere wise they spoke not of it."

"Aye." Escalus's jaw was set. "Though rash and unadvised they were in all other things. Impetuous fools. In any case, Juliet's cousin Tybalt took a dislike to Romeo and his fellows, and challenged him on the street to a duel. Romeo's friend took up his part and was slain at Tybalt's hand."

"Romeo's friend? Another Montague, I suppose?"

"Nay, sister." Escalus drew close so he could lay a hand over Isabella's. "'Twas Mercutio."

Isabella pulled sharply on the reins. "Ay me! Mercutio? Our kinsman?"

"Even so."

"I pray you did not let his murderer go free, brother."

"Would I had had the chance to punish him. After he cut Mercutio down, Tybalt was himself slain by Romeo straightaway."

Isabella's hands were clenched tightly on the reins. Her sunny smile was replaced with a frown. How heavily Verona's woes returned to those who escaped them. "Good."

"Isabella! I forbid thee to speak so. Verona must understand that the Crown's justice—"

"Hang the Crown's justice," said Isabella. "And I am a princess now, Escalus; thou canst forbid me nothing. If young Romeo avenged Mercutio's death, I will thank him for that."

"Not in this world, thou shalt not. I exiled Romeo for his part in this bloodshed and he fled Verona, leaving his young Capulet wife in her parents' house. They, unknowing, had arranged for her to wed the county Paris." Isabella shuddered; Count Paris was another of their kinsmen. "Aye, this sorry tale hath many noble souls ensnared. To escape this adulterous union, Juliet enlisted the help of a friar to feign her death so that she could escape and join her love."

"Feign death?"

"Aye. The friar gave her a potion that induced a sleep so deep it appeared that life had fled. We entombed her with all sadness in the crypt of her ancestors, where her love was to find her, but he never received the message that was sent and heard only that she had died. Romeo returned to find what he thought was her corpse, and slew himself. Juliet woke, found him dead, and swiftly followed him."

Isabella sat back in the saddle, staring wide-eyed up at the city walls rising before them. Her hands twitched the reins as though she was having second thoughts about visiting the city of her birth. "In the name of God, a fearful passage. I chose an unhappy time for my homecoming. All those young lives . . . Tell me that cousin Paris at least kept clear of all this."

Escalus shook his head. "Romeo slew him at the gate of Juliet's tomb."

"All this began three weeks ago, you say?"

"Nearly. As best as we can tell, Romeo and Juliet met at a feast of her father's on the fourteenth day of July, and they wed and died within a week."

"And now? Are the houses at peace?"

Escalus gave a heavy shrug. "So they say. The grieving parents have sworn that the deaths of their children have cured them of their enmity. They have even raised statues of the two lovers at their tomb."

Isabella threw him a sharp glance. "But you have little faith in this oath."

"If generations could not cure their ire, will a summer of murder really do so? Old Montague and Capulet mean well enough, but they've little control over the youths of their houses, who walk the streets day and night, their hands hovering at their swords. 'Tis but a matter of time."

"Thou know'st not so. Wilt thou not let them prove their penitence?"

"More likely they will disprove it with the bodies of more of my subjects." Escalus shook his head. "No, 'twill take more than pretty statues to bring peace to my city."

"Your city. You sound like Father."

"Father kept the peace until the day he died."

"After a fashion. Montagues and Capulets aplenty slew each other under his reign. What mean you to do?"

Escalus sighed, passing a hand over his sweaty brow. "I' faith, I know not."

"'Tis strange to think little Juliet could be so rash," Isabella said. "Rosaline would never have done so. The cleverest of my friends, she was. If it had been Rosaline Romeo loved, none of this would have come to pass."

"Actually, he—" Escalus cut himself off. "Ah! Of course."

Isabella blinked. "Of course what?"

"I'll explain anon. Isabella, thou art heaven sent." He squeezed her hand quickly. "I must make haste back to the city." With a flick of his reins, he sent Venitio surging ahead toward Verona's walls.

"Whither goest thou?" Isabella called after him.

"House Capulet," he called over his shoulder.

"Oh, give it here. I'll wear the cursed thing."

Livia pulled the hated black dress from Rosaline's hands. Rosaline looked at her skeptically. "Thou wilt don it?"

"An 'twill stop thee looking like thou smell'st something foul, aye." Livia stood on tiptoes to smack a little-girl kiss on Rosaline's cheek.

Rosaline swallowed, then returned her sister's affections with an embrace, provoking a surprised squeak from Livia. Sorry though she was for Romeo's death, she was also filled with relief that she and Livia had escaped this summer's events unscathed. It all could have been so different, had she encouraged Romeo's affections. It was just this sort of disaster she'd feared when she'd spurned Romeo's love. Apparently cousin Juliet had had none of her caution.

"Ay! Leave off, Rosaline, you'll squeeze me in two."

Rosaline frowned, the effort of forcing her tears back sharpening her headache. What must it be like to love someone so desperately that you cared not what your own death might do to your family? However the poets might praise it, such a love was something she dreamed not of.

What if she had accepted the dreamy-eyed young Montague who had begun to follow her around at the start of spring this year? Instead of barring her door against his visits, refusing to hear his earnest, pretty sonnets, sending back his gifts—what if she had allowed his courtship?

Rosaline had not loved Romeo, but 'twas impossible not to like him. Quick to smile, never pressing the privilege of his rank, he and his two friends were a familiar sight in the city, and even his family's enemies had grudgingly conceded that he was the best kind of youth. Few maids of Verona would have turned down a chance at such a husband. But Rosaline had not wanted any husband, so it had been all too easy to harden her heart against his entreaties.

If she had not, if she had accepted his love and returned it with her own, could they have been married peacefully? She was not the only daughter of Lord Capulet, like poor Jule. Rosaline and Livia were mere nieces, and their name was not even Capulet, but Tirimo. Maybe those cut down would still be alive.

But even guilt could not persuade her of this logic. In the eyes of Verona, she was still a Capulet. More likely, they would still be dead, and it would be Rosaline herself slumbering in the family tomb.

Rosaline smiled and released Livia, who took the black dress and held it out in front of her, wrinkling her nose in distaste before giving a martyred sigh. Rosaline cast her eyes to heaven. "'Tis only for a few more weeks."

"I shall be old by then." Livia stripped off her white linen dress and left it in a puddle on the floor. "'Tis all very well for thee. Black becomes thee so well it will only make thy pack of swains chase thee all the harder."

Rosaline shook her head at Livia's prattle. But there was an undeniable grain of truth to this. Though both were counted among Verona's beauties, the sisters could not have looked less alike. Livia took after their father, with fine, honey-blonde hair, big blue eyes, and fair skin. The kind of face they wrote sonnets about, Rosaline thought, but it was undeniably not a coloring flattered by black attire. Already, holding the dress up to herself in the mirror, Livia looked pale and colorless, like she might fade away altogether.

Rosaline was a different tale. She looked every inch a Capulet, like their mother. Tall and long-limbed, she had the Capulet coloring too: green eyes, olive skin, a rosy mouth prone to pouting. Her tumble of impossibly thick brown curls was pinned back in a twist, but as usual a few strands had sprung stubbornly free and hung round her face. Her own black gown, she noted dispassionately, made her looks stand out all the better.

She was beautiful. There was no point in being modest about it, as all who'd seen her had been telling her so since she left the nursery. But what of that? She'd trade places with the ugliest girl in Verona if she could. Juliet had been beautiful too.

Rosaline bent and retrieved Livia's abandoned white linen. "I suppose you're right," she said. "I'm sure I ought to parade round the cemetery every day in my mourning garb. I would have ten proposals ere I left the gates."

Livia snorted and made a grab for the dress, but Rosaline swung it away, holding it out before her and curtsying to it as though it were a young man. "Of course, sir, I'd be honored to wed thee," she said to it, dancing it out of Livia's grasp, "but only if thou wilt promise to find a husband for my poor, unmarriageable sister, Livia."

Livia shrieked in mock outrage and charged her sister, but long-legged Rosaline easily outran her, laughing. Their chase took them out of Livia's bedroom and down the stairs of the house to the main foyer. "Hast thou a clubfooted bastard brother, my lord? A servant with a harelip, perhaps? Any man who can bear the indignity of a wife who does not look her best in black—"

Rosaline stopped so suddenly that Livia nearly ran into her. Their aunt's steward was in their doorway.

Rosaline had never much cared for Lucullus. He was a large, quiet man who seemed to live for nothing but to do her aunt's bidding. He and the rest of her servants did no more than they had to for her and Livia, and when they did enter the cottage, they did so unannounced—to remind them, Rosaline thought, that this was not their home, that they were but guests reliant upon their aunt's charity. She provided them little but a roof over their heads, leaving them to pay the rest of their expenses out of their meager income, but her household seemed determined they should not forget the paltry aid provided. Though he rarely spoke, Rosaline always thought she saw disapproval in his eyes when they rested on the duchess's poor nieces—especially after Romeo began to hover at her door. The duchess was both mother to Lady Capulet and a Capulet relation herself by birth, and she had never feared to express her scorn for every man, woman, and child of House Montague. Her servant, Rosaline was sure, shared her overweening pride in House Capulet. No doubt he did not think much of two orphan girls from a minor branch of the family galumphing through their house like peasants.

He bowed. "My ladies."

Rosaline nodded as she smoothed her skirt. "Good e'en, Lucullus. What's thy business?"

"Your uncle Lord Capulet would speak with you, Lady Rosaline," he said.

Rosaline frowned. She and Livia were not important enough to be much noticed by their uncle, the head of the Capulet clan. Since their parents died and their fortunes fell, she could count on one hand the number of times they had dined at the great Capulet house without other, grander members of the family. "What is mine uncle's will?"

Lucullus shrugged. "'Tis not mine to know. He'll tell you himself when you see him this evening."

The streets of Verona were not exactly safe for a woman alone these days. She glanced out the window. The sun was already a mere sliver sinking into the western wall. It would be full dark before she arrived at her uncle's house, even if she left now. "Tomorrow morning, perhaps," she said, as politely as she could.

Lucullus shook his head. "Your uncle has said he will see you forthwith. The duchess your great-aunt is at the house already. She sent me to accompany you, and she shall bring you home again when she is done attending to her daughter."

Rosaline frowned in annoyance. It was one thing for her grand relatives like the duchess and Lord Capulet to ignore her; it was quite another for them to order her back and forth like a page when it finally pleased them to notice her. She squashed the urge to stamp her foot and refuse to go. But she could at least escape Lucullus's company. "No need, sirrah. I shall go alone."

"Are you sure, lady?" he asked.

Rosaline felt Livia's worried gaze on her. Perhaps going alone was not the most sensible decision she had ever made, but the prince's men were patrolling the streets to prevent any trouble, and surely the journey was short enough that she had little to fear. Besides, this way she could stop in the graveyard and offer a prayer at Juliet's crypt without Lucullus's eyes on her. "Aye. I thank thee for thy pains."

The man nodded, gave a brief bow, and left. Rosaline closed the door behind him. She and Livia looked at each other. Livia's big blue eyes were wide with confusion. "Rosaline, what in the world can Uncle want with you?"

"I've no idea," said Rosaline.

Benvolio walked, his hand upon his sword.

He ought to be at home, he knew. Ever since the deaths of his two best friends, Mercutio and Romeo, his weeping mother had scarce let him from her sight, as though the shade of that whoreson Tybalt might spring from the shadows at any moment and run him through.

He wanted to stay and comfort her. Truly he did. Perhaps before, he would have. Of the three friends, he'd always been the coolest head, the sensible one. Compared to those other two hotheads, anyway.

Which no doubt explained how he still lived while they slumbered in their tombs.

Benvolio's jaw clenched at the thought. He could feel the anger beginning to scream inside him again. For what good was it to avoid the duels and ill-advised romances of your fellows if they died and left you all alone?

And so this evening he'd fled the stifling walls of his house in favor of the cooler night air of Verona's streets. The city still sang with tension, taut as a bowstring, and it certainly would not help for a young Montague to be seen stalking the streets, but Benvolio didn't care. He, Romeo, and Mercutio had passed many an hour in just this way, wandering Verona side by side, bragging and quarreling and seeking mischief. Benvolio could almost imagine they were there beside him. Mercutio would be to his left, spinning them a tale that was equal shares fanciful and filthy. A cheerfully ugly youth Mercutio had been, tall and lanky with a shock of straw-colored hair and a grin a mile wide.

Not that my looks ever offended the ladies of Verona, Benvolio. Or Venice. Or Padua.

That sort of ribald quip Mercutio would accompany with a waggle of his eyebrows and a devil-may-care grin. Benvolio could just see his cousin Romeo shake his head. *Thou hast never been to Padua.* Romeo had always been the only one with any hope of curbing Mercutio's vast, looping flights of braggery. He'd be ahead of them, deciding whether to point their meanderings up into the hills or down to the city walls. Leading them, as he would one day lead Benvolio's family.

Romeo had not looked much like a Montague. His wavy light brown hair and dreamy, handsome face had marked him more as his mother's son than his father's. Those who met them often assumed that Benvolio, not Romeo, was old Montague's son and heir. With his spiky dark hair and his crooked smile, he took after his uncle far more than Romeo did.

I have been to Padua, his memory-Mercutio announced, flopping idly into a handstand. *For a city is its people, and Mistress Margaret Closenothing the seamstress is from Padua, and I have certainly been to* her.

In that case, the shade Romeo retorted sweetly, *Mistress Closenothing has been to every city in Italy.*

Mercutio crashed back to his feet. *I'll not stay here to be insulted. My horse! My horse! To Padua at once!*

Romeo laughed and threw an arm about his shoulders. *We'll all go,* he promised.

"No," Benvolio murmured, breaking through the ghostly silence of their japery. "We won't."

And just like that, his friends—ghosts, memories, what you will—were gone, and Benvolio walked on alone through the deepening darkness of the Verona streets, his hand tightened on his sword, not sure if he wanted to prevent a fight or start one.

The choice was made for him when a woman's scream shattered the night air. Benvolio ran toward the sound, feet slipping against the cobblestones in his haste. The scream came again, and Benvolio's heart tightened as he realized the sound was coming from the graveyard—the recent home of so many of Verona's young nobles. From the sound of it, someone was trying to give them yet another new neighbor.

Benvolio's breath burnt in his lungs as he churned up the hill to the graveyard gates. Five young men stood clustered there. He recognized several of them. His jaw clenched.

Orlino, Marius, and Truchio were young Montague cousins. They'd idolized Romeo. No great surprise to see them starting trouble now, but he'd have thought they had better taste than to do it in the shadow of the new statues of Romeo and his bride, Juliet.

He drew nearer, and sure enough, steel glinted in the torchlight. His young kinsmen faced off against two other youths, swords raised. Benvolio cursed silently. The pair wore the Capulet crest on their sashes.

"Misbegotten Capulet stale!"

At first Benvolio thought Orlino's vile insult was intended for the statue of Juliet. But his sneer was directed at the ground. Benvolio realized there was a woman sprawled in the dirt between the swordsmen. The black of her mourning dress had melted her into the shadows.

One of the other young men raised his sword. "Say another word, Montague, and I'll make you eat it!" he shouted at Orlino, the threat rather undermined by the way his voice cracked.

Orlino dipped his sword toward the woman on the ground. "I'll make *her* eat it."

The Capulet youth leapt forward with a cry of rage, and Orlino met him without hesitation. Steel rang against steel over the woman's flinching body, and Benvolio stepped forward. That was quite enough.

"Hold!" he roared. "What is the meaning of this?"

The pack of young swordsmen froze as they realized there was a newcomer. "Benvolio!" Truchio said. "These Capulet scoundrels call us liars. We aim to correct them."

"As if you could," one of the young Capulets yelled, his voice shaking with anger. "We know full well you are liars and villains. Who but a whoreson Montague would so befoul our kinswoman's memory?"

Benvolio followed his gaze to the statue of Juliet, Romeo's five-day bride. He drew in a sharp breath. The Capulet had cause for his wrath—someone had scrawled HARLOT across her pretty face in black paint.

There was a shout behind him. While his back was turned, one of the Capulet lads had attacked. Instantly, the air rang with the disharmonious music of sword against sword as all the young men joined the fray. Young Truchio, the smaller of the Montague lads, faltered under the assault of one of the Capulets, who feinted under his arm and nicked him, a spot of blood appearing on his doublet. Orlino leapt to his aid, and the prostrate girl gave a ragged cry as Orlino trod right over her.

"I said *hold!*"

Wrath sang through Benvolio's blood as he roared the command, so potent he was almost glad the fighters ignored him. His own sword was out and raised in an instant. Finally, a channel for the lonely, bottomless fury that had him stalking Verona's streets all night. He cared for neither Capulet nor Montague. These fools all needed to be taught a lesson, and Benvolio was the man to do it.

He laid about him right and left, striking Montague and Capulet boys alike with the flat of his blade. His blood thundered in his veins and he felt a fierce grin spreading across his face. For the first moment since his friends had died, he felt like himself. Mercutio had been their clown, and Romeo their leader, but it was Benvolio who was the true swords-man. Whatever else had happened, his sword still fought true.

Despite his skill and the others' youth, five on one was a challenge. He would have to disarm them quickly. He turned on his kinsmen first. Benvolio slammed his hilt down on Truchio's sword hand, sending his rapier falling from his grip. Before it had hit the ground, Benvolio had sent Mari-us's sword to join it with a flick of his wrist. Orlino, seeing his older cousin's wrath, lowered his sword and drew back. At least one of Benvolio's kinsmen had sense.

The two Capulet lads, seeing their enemies disarmed and not caring by whom, pressed forward in triumph. But Ben-volio was far from finished. He turned to face them.

"Poor Benvolio," one of the Capulets mocked. "So mired in grief for his sweet slain cousin that he cannot tell friend from foe."

"Fear not," said the other. "We'll teach you to remember."

Benvolio huffed a breath, flicking his sweaty hair back. "How kind. But you will find me slow of study." And he was upon them. Unlike his kinsmen, they were ready for him, and they pushed him back steadily till his back was pressed against Romeo's statue.

But they were unused to fighting as a pair. One boy got tangled in his fellow's feet and fell, and before he could right himself Benvolio had kicked his sword away. After that the other was quickly dispatched, and Benvolio stood panting over the groaning, disarmed youths of both houses.

Catching his breath, he pointed his sword toward the statue of Romeo that rose above them, gazing with eternal longing at his Juliet. "My cousin married a Capulet," he told the pack of them. "Thus you are all my kinsmen now. 'Tis the only reason no man"—he snorted and corrected himself—"no *boy* among you felt more than the flat of my blade this night. Go home, all of you. Next time I'll not be so kind, kin or no, and neither will the prince's men should they find you."

Truchio struggled to his feet. "Cousin, they—"

"GO!"

They went. Sullen, sore, but they went, Marius and Truchio down toward the square, the Capulets east to the hills, and Benvolio breathed out a sigh of relief. No one would die this night.

Wait. Where was the lady?

Benvolio whipped around just in time to spot Orlino dragging a struggling female form behind a vault.

Heaven above. Would it never end?

The Montague held Rosaline's arm fast.

Rosaline struggled to free herself from his hold. He was older than the other Montagues, with the size and strength of a man, if not the sense of one. When this Benvolio had appeared, she'd thought she was saved, and she'd tried to slip away during the fighting. But this villain had followed her. One of his hands gripped her arm so hard she was sure he'd leave a bruise.

If she survived, that was.

"Do not do this," she begged, fear stealing her voice. "The prince hath commanded—"

"Hang the prince."

"But you will be exiled, killed—there is peace between our families now, you know there is—"

His hand cracked across her cheek. "I need no lesson in law from a Capulet jade." Rosaline clutched her cheek, willing the tears from her eyes. Her captor looked her over, his young face twisted with hate. He shoved her to the ground.

"We never defiled your thrice-damned Juliet's statue," he said.

Despite the circumstances, Rosaline let out a laugh. "Who but the Montagues would do that to poor Jule?"

The Montague boy's jaw clenched. "Think you so? I'll make your lies true and one better. Aye, I'll carve *harlot* on the face of a Capulet—one who can still weep for her lost beauty." With that, he advanced on her, sword held high. Rosaline's stomach roiled as she realized his intent. She tried to scramble backward, but he lunged for her, grabbing her by the hair. His other hand brought his blade closer, and closer, the tip gleaming in the torchlight as it drew near to Rosaline's face. She shut her eyes tight. The cold steel kissed her cheek and she prepared herself to feel the agony of the blade.

It never came.

Her attacker gave a yell and Rosaline felt his sword drop away. She opened her eyes to find him locked in a struggle with the man who had joined the fight before.

The two swordsmen separated and stood, facing each other, blades raised.

"The Capulets spoke aright, Benvolio," her attacker said. "The loss of thy playfellows has made a weak, womanish fool of thee. Thou shouldst join me in teaching this canker-blossom a lesson."

The other man just lifted his sword higher and growled, "Not another word out of thy craven mouth, Orlino."

Then they were upon each other, and Rosaline gasped, her heart pounding as their swords slashed the air faster than her eye could follow.

The fight was short but brutal. Rosaline could see that the two Montagues knew each other's swordsmanship—they targeted each other's weaknesses with terrifying accuracy. The younger man had the first touch, nicking Benvolio's arm, and Rosaline cried out, certain her defender was defeated, but he ignored the slash on his sleeve and somehow twisted his foot with his opponent's, and suddenly Rosaline's foe was sprawled in the dust, his sword lay six feet away, and her savior had the point of his blade at the man's throat.

"Yield."

"Benvolio, 'twas just a bit of—"

"*Yield.*"

"Very well." He raised his hands sullenly. "Now will you let me rise, cousin?"

The other man stood frozen, as though he had not heard him.

"Cousin? Benvolio? What—"

Benvolio's sword flashed, and then Rosaline's assailant was crying out, hands clutched to his face. He pulled his hands away to stare at the red that coated them. Benvolio had given Orlino a long slash across his right cheek.

"How dare you!" Orlino snarled as he struggled to his feet.

Benvolio stepped back, lowering his sword at last. "I'd dare much worse against any man who raised his sword against a lady, no matter her name. Get thee gone, Orlino, and never touch her again."

Orlino glared at them both. His breath was coming in pained hisses. Blood was streaming down his cheek, coating his neck and staining his doublet, but his injuries did not prevent his face from twisting with anger. Rosaline's sweaty hands clutched her gown. Had she really thought him a boy? No child's face could hold such hate.

"You'll hear more from Orlino anon," he promised. "Both of you." Then he stumbled out into the darkness and was gone.

"Are you well, lady?" The victorious Montague turned and knelt before Rosaline, and finally she saw her savior plain.

He was young—not so young as her assailants, nor as the Capulet cousins they'd brawled with, but younger than she would have thought for such a skilled swordsman. No more than eighteen. But something in how he held himself made him seem much older.

Even had he not named himself a Montague, Rosaline would have known him for one. Pale skin, proud features, dark hair that must have many times been the despair of a nurse's comb—aye, here was one of the handsome, dark, devilish Montagues her mother had warned her of when she was a child. He looked familiar, but she did not think they'd ever met. She'd seen most of the young Montagues from a distance, at feasts and in the market, but Romeo was the only one she had ever spoken to at any length. Montagues and Capulets did not mix.

"I am well," she said, running shaky hands over her muddy gown. It took her a moment to be sure it was true. A bit bruised by Montague and Capulet feet, for she'd walked into this brawl before she knew what had happened, and her own kin were more interested in crossing swords with Montagues than helping her to escape. She would be black and blue tomorrow, but only her pride was seriously hurt.

He extended a hand, and when she flinched, he laughed at her a little. "Come, lady," he said. "They have all gone, leaving only me, who neither threatened you nor trod upon you."

The crooked smile flared and disappeared from his face in an instant, but Rosaline was surprised to find it warmed away some of the icy fear in her breast. "'Tis true. Mine own cousins, well-meaning though they were, could not say the same, as you can see from the boot prints on my gown. Good sir, I thank you." She extended her hand, allowing him to pull her to her feet.

He sketched a bow. "Your servant, lady." As he bent over, she spotted a flash of red under his torn sleeve. Rosaline rushed forward.

"You're hurt!"

"'Tis nothing," he protested, but Rosaline had already gone to soak her clean handkerchief in water from a nearby fountain. She was greatly in this man's debt; she must at least try to repay it. She returned and sat him down on the steps of a convenient tomb so she could wash the dirt from his wound.

"Nothing it may be for one so stalwart as you," she said, "but since we of the weaker sex are known to swoon at the sight of blood, if you are a courteous gentleman you will let me clean it for you."

She stood over him and carefully peeled his sleeve away. He bit back a hiss as she began to dab the blood away from his wound. It wasn't a grave injury—less likely to scar than the cut he'd given his cousin. He looked up at her as she worked. Rosaline could see the ruddy torchlight reflected in his eyes. "A lady of your beauty is right welcome to swoon into my arms whene'er you wish."

Rosaline pressed her lips together and bent her head closer to her task, so that her hair shadowed her face. Gentlemen of the court offered such flirtatious compliments to ladies as a matter of course. If there was a blush staining her cheeks, it was no doubt due to the excitement of the night.

"You seem not like a lady given much to swooning, anyway, from what I've seen," he said.

"Not much, sir. Swooning stains one's gown with earth."

"But not if one is there to catch you, lady."

"'Tis true. But men can't be relied upon to follow me about with outstretched arms, and so I think it best to stay upright." Rosaline wrapped her handkerchief around his arm as a makeshift bandage.

"Your pardon, lady, for what my kinsmen did," he said. "They never should have offered such discourtesy to any lady, Capulet or no—ow!"

Rosaline had tightened his bandage. " 'Capulet or no'?"

He flinched away from her ministrations. "I mean *your* kinsmen ought not to have provoked them."

"Provoked them? Saw you not what *your* kinsmen did to our poor Juliet's statue?" To Rosaline's horror, her voice had started to shake. "Has she not suffered enough, but must be slandered from past the grave as well?"

"They made no slander, lady. For your kin had no right to presume that it was they. No kin of mine would so defile the dead."

"Nay, only one that lives. Your wound is sound, sir. Good e'en." Rosaline tied off his bandage and rose to leave the churlish Montague.

"Lady, wait." He caught her hand, and she turned to find him looking sheepish. "I am sorry."

Rosaline sighed. "A thousand times have I cursed this grudge between our houses," she said. "Yet I no sooner meet a Montague than I have mounted a new battle. 'Tis I who must beg your pardon, sir."

He gave her that crooked smile again and bent over her hand in a florid bow, as though they'd just been introduced at a ball. "We'll start again, then. Benvolio, at your service, lady."

She returned his smile and swept him the prettiest curtsy

ever made by a mud-covered girl in a graveyard. "Good e'en, sir. They call me Rosaline."

He dropped her hand like it had burnt him.

"Rosaline," he repeated. "Rosaline is thy name?" He sat down on the steps of the tomb and barked a laugh, running a hand across his forehead.

"Do I amuse you, sir?"

"Oh yes, lady," he said. "An excellent jest, to find myself bowing and begging for pardon from the very cause of my family's misfortunes."

"Cause of your misfortunes?" she said. "When have I ever given a Montague a moment's care? Except—"

"Aye. Except." Benvolio surged to his feet, all traces of mirth gone from his face. "Except that you, in your pride, your prudishness—*you* brought this plague of death down on both our houses."

Rosaline met him glare for glare, refusing to back down in the face of his fury. But her heart sank. Benvolio. She had been too frightened during the fight to remember why his face was familiar, but she knew him now. He was not just any Montague—the bloody youth clutching his sword before her had been Romeo's best friend. So she knew what was coming. Few in Verona knew of Romeo's brief passion for her, but Benvolio was certainly one of them. "If you refer to my friendship with Romeo—"

"By God! Say not his name." Benvolio grabbed her by the arm. She tried to pull away but his grip was firm as he hauled her toward a fresh grave. "Mercutio," he read from the tombstone. Before she'd had a chance to reply or even catch her breath he'd hauled her away to another recently opened crypt. "Paris." Another. "Tybalt." His grip was as tight as Orlino's had been. When they arrived at the entrance to the cemetery, he spun her around, holding her shoulders from behind. "Look," he said behind her. Rosaline felt her back stiffen. He was a solid wall of fury behind her, his angry breaths hot against her ear. "Look upon thy handiwork."

She didn't want to. She wanted to close her eyes—didn't want to look on the face of her erstwhile suitor, now immortalized in stone. But she would not show such weakness, so she took a deep breath and looked on Romeo's lifeless golden visage.

"He loved thee," said Benvolio, giving her shoulders a little shake. "He spoke of nothing but thy wit, thy beauty, thy kindness"—his fingers dug into her arms— "and thou—thou didst spurn him."

Rosaline finally shook him off. "And after what hath passed, you dare tell me 'twas imprudent?" she said, whirling to face him. "I would not hear Romeo's suit because I wished not to add fuel to the troubles that have consumed our families so long. 'Tis not my fault that he straightaway lighted on an even worse choice of bride, nor that poor Jule succumbed to his advances. Think you Romeo would have fared well had he married a niece of Capulet, rather than a daughter?"

Benvolio's breath hissed through his teeth. "Would he have fared well? No. Would he live? Aye. My friends would live still, and so would Juliet, hadst thou the wit to accept the love of a man a thousand times thy better. Or for that matter, had 'poor Jule' the wit to keep her legs closed."

Rosaline's hand flashed out and she slapped him hard across the face. "Speak so of Juliet again and I swear I'll cut thy throat!"

The chiming of the nine o'clock bell broke the spell of their vicious grief. Rosaline tore her gaze from his furious face and stepped back. "I go," she said. "For repelling your brutish kin, you've my thanks. I shall show my gratitude by troubling you no longer. Good night, sir."

She searched for her black shawl, lost in the earlier scuffle. Finally spying it, she shook the grass away and wrapped it over her hair, then headed for the gate.

Benvolio followed. "'Tis not a safe night for a lady alone. I'll go with you." He did not sound as though he relished the prospect.

Rosaline shoved away his proffered arm with as much rudeness as she could. He may have saved her life, but after calling her an idiot and her cousin a whore, did he really expect her to be grateful for his grudging show of courtesy? "Your kinsmen have taught me well how dangerous this night is. But I'd rather let the villains hack me to bits than go one step with you."

She set out for the cemetery gate. He strode after her, grabbing her arm again. "You brainless girl. I am trying to do you a kindness."

"Montague kindness is of the sort that gets one killed. I've no wish for it. Let me be, Benvolio."

His nostrils flared, his dark eyes furious. For a moment

she thought he might throw her over his shoulder and lend her his protection by force—even now, she was oddly certain that he would not offer her any physical harm himself, no matter how he hated her—but instead he spread his hands and backed away, offering her a mocking bow. "As you wish, my lady Rosaline. And if you meet with more brigands who wish you harm, do give them my compliments."

"I shall, for they will likely be your kin." Without another word, Rosaline turned and left the cemetery, heading up the hill toward her uncle's house. As she hurried through the dark streets, fingernails still biting into her hands in anger, she sent up a silent but vehement prayer that she would never see Benvolio of Montague again.

Benvolio soon walked the streets once more.

The skirmish with the young men, far from clearing his head, had only made him feel worse. The yearning fury that swelled in him when he thought of Romeo and Mercutio was growing in strength, and he felt that if he did not get an outlet for it soon, he might burst.

Especially when he thought of that devil of a girl.

Benvolio's steps quickened. The hilt of his sword bit into his palm. What sort of a lady insulted a man who had just saved her life?

In his mind's eye, he could see her straight, proud back, hands clutching her shawl as she marched away from the graveyard, from him, to be swallowed by the Verona night.

Hell. He shouldn't have let her go.

No gentleman would have let a lady walk alone into the night, no matter how grievously she'd insulted him. Not with the city in the state it was. But she'd been so vexing, so ungrateful.

No fool, though. He thought of the moment he'd first seen her clearly, after he'd chased off her attackers. Loose brown curls tumbled over her shoulder, face flushed with fear and red from Orlino's slap, and yet her eyes had been keen and searching as she decided to trust him enough to let him help her to her feet.

Benvolio scrubbed a hand across his face. Aye, 'twas no wonder his cousin had spent long weeks in her thrall. She was a beauty, there was no doubting it. All the easier to flay a man with her hell-forged tongue and icy scorn.

Benvolio wondered suddenly what had won Romeo's heart away from this Lady Rosaline. He'd never met Juliet—his only memory of her was watching her whirl across the dance floor from afar, the night she had met Romeo. She'd been young, not much more than a child. With her long dark hair, she'd had much the look of her cousin, but Benvolio could not imagine that laughing, innocent face ever holding the pain he'd seen in Rosaline's.

But of course, it must have. For had they not all felt that anguish these past weeks? He did not imagine there had been much mirth left in fair Juliet by the time she buried her husband's dagger in her own heart.

Two ladies of House Capulet had Romeo loved. Gay Juliet, reserved Rosaline. The latter a scandalous enough choice of bride for Montague's heir, but the former so unthinkable as to be fatal. Benvolio and Mercutio had tried so many times to sway Romeo from his Rosaline-induced melancholy by swearing to him that one pretty wench was much like another. How wrong they were.

Somewhere in the darkness a bell tolled the quarter hour, and Benvolio came to a halt. Oh hell. In all the trouble, he'd forgotten that his wanderings were not entirely aimless tonight. His uncle Montague had asked to meet him at a nearby church.

Benvolio turned and retraced his steps back up the hill. He knew not why his uncle had instructed him to go to the church instead of the Montagues' house, but if he took a shortcut, he could be there inside of five minutes.

His uncle was already waiting outside when Benvolio arrived. Lord Montague was a tall man, like Benvolio himself. His close-cropped hair had been a steely gray as long as Benvolio could remember, but it was almost white now. Unlike his wife, Romeo's father had survived the death of their son, but he had become an old man almost overnight.

"Ah," Lord Montague said. "Benvolio." He started, as though just then noticing him. "My boy." His normally sharp eyes betrayed a certain dullness—perhaps grief had so shrouded his sight that even the familiar face of his nephew was hard to recognize.

Benvolio bowed. "Uncle."

Lord Montague frowned, taking in his disheveled state, then inclined his head toward the door of the chapel. Benvolio followed him inside.

Lord Montague took a seat in a pew in the back. Benvolio sat down beside him. He knew not what to expect when his uncle had summoned him. This small chapel in an unfamiliar part of town, far from the square where the Montagues made their homes, did nothing to abate his confusion.

They sat in the dark, empty chapel for some time before his uncle broke the silence.

"Thou art grown so tall," he said.

"My lord?"

His uncle sighed. "I remember the three of you, hopping around the courtyard with wooden swords." He held out his hand, as though measuring the height of an invisible small boy. "And now thou art the last of them."

A chill washed over Benvolio's skin. His uncle was a kind man, but proud and reserved. He had never spoken so to Benvolio in his life. "Uncle, why have you summoned me?"

A slight smile flickered on Montague's face. "Because," he said, "I was sure that if I told thee where we were really going, thou wouldst not have come."

"Where—"

"Mark me well." Lord Montague turned and gripped him by the shoulders. "The Montagues have never known such a dark hour, Benvolio. My wife is dead. My only child—" For a moment his mask of composure cracked, and he looked as though he might break down in tears. But he recovered, gripping Benvolio harder, heedless of his wound. "But thou, thou liv'st." He shook him slightly. "Thou *liv'st*. And we Montagues have need of thee now. Wilt thou help us?"

Benvolio clasped his uncle's hand. "Anything."

The gates of Capulet had ne'er before filled Rosaline with such intense relief.

She'd always thought her uncle's house ugly, an overdone monstrosity perched on top of the hill for all those not fortunate enough to be Capulets to admire it. She would walk streets out of her way sometimes so as not to pass by it.

But now she walked toward its many-torched walls with all haste. Fear winged her feet and she all but ran for the house, sure that now when she was nearly safe was the moment the Montague brutes would spring upon her again. Down the hill to her left stood the house she and Livia had lived in as children, dark as usual—its foreign tenant must have had less business in Verona than he had expected, for he never seemed to use it. Normally it gave her a pang to see her home out of her reach, but now she welcomed the sight, as it meant she had nearly reached her destination. It had been the height of foolishness to insist on making this walk alone, as her fluttering heart seemed ever more determined to remind her. She ought to have endured Benvolio's detestable company as far as her uncle's door. 'Twas not as though he would have followed her inside.

But Rosaline was lucky, and she arrived at the gate, panting and no doubt in utter disarray, but safe. She nodded to the sentry and said, "My uncle expects me."

The man motioned her inside. Rosaline's hands clutched her shawl as she passed the threshold. The last time she'd been here was two weeks ago, on the eighteenth of July. She'd come for Juliet's wedding to Count Paris. It had been Juliet's funeral instead.

The servant took his torch and hurried into the house, leaving Rosaline alone in the darkened courtyard. She shivered, though the night was still warm, and pulled her shawl closer about her.

Juliet's was not the first corpse she'd seen in the Capulet courtyard.

"Open the gates! Niccolo is wounded!"

"A duel with the Montagues—"

"Bind his wound—so much blood—"

"Look to the child!"

Rosaline had been eleven years old the day she watched her father bleed to death on these very cobblestones. Ever since, the elegant yard seemed to smell of the tang of blood.

A light far above caught her eye. Looking up, she saw a glow at one of the upper windows. Odd. That wing of the house was not in use—her uncle Capulet had a smaller family than his ancestors, and the unused bedrooms were rarely opened. Juliet's nurse used to shoo them away from the locked door when they wanted to play there.

As she looked up, the light winked out, as though aware of being watched.

"Well, come in, niece, stand not there in the dark."

Rosaline turned to find her uncle silhouetted in the doorway, his bulk blocking most of the light from within. He turned, motioning her inside with a jerk of his head.

Rosaline followed him. Past silent servants bowing, over

the impossibly rich red carpet in the hall, up the marble staircase toward her uncle's private study. If he noted the mud on her gown, he gave no sign. At least her cheek felt cooler. Her face would bear no bruise from Orlino's slap, she thought. She wondered if she'd left Benvolio's cheek as unmarred. Her uncle waved a hand toward a chair outside the door. "I've other visitors to entertain. Wait thou here."

With that, he disappeared through the oak door to his study. Rosaline fumed. He had demanded her presence, and now he would make her wait? She should have expected no better, she supposed. Her uncle probably thought she should be flattered he'd deigned to speak to her at all.

Rosaline was about to settle into the proffered chair when she heard a familiar wheeze approaching up the servants' stair.

"Oh bless me, bless me, but these stairs are become as steep as mountains. Ah me! My poor knees."

A slight smile pierced Rosaline's annoyance. Juliet's old nurse never missed a chance to complain. It was good to know she, at least, was unchanged.

"Nurse?"

Rosaline went to the top of the stair just as the nurse heaved herself into view carrying a large basket. When she spotted Rosaline she froze, her burden nearly slipping from her fingers. Rosaline hurried to help her. "How now, good nurse?"

The nurse clutched her chest with one hand, gripping her basket tight to her bosom with the other. "Ah! 'Tis young Rosaline. I' faith, lamb, you did affright me. To see you standing there, I thought you were my mistress come back again. What brings you here so late?"

Rosaline winced. She and Juliet had looked much alike. "I am sorry to startle you. Mine uncle summoned me. Come, sit." She tried to pull her toward the chair, but the nurse shook her head.

"Nay, nay, I must to my lady."

Rosaline pushed her shoulders down gently. "I am sure thy care is crucial, but my good lady aunt can wait a moment. Thou art as pale as ashes."

The nurse acceded with a sigh, sinking into the chair. Rosaline gripped her hand. The nurse's face had become a mass of wrinkles. In the years since Rosaline had been Juliet's playmate, her cousin's caretaker had grown old.

"To think that you should resemble her so much," the nurse said. "You have heard, I suppose, that my mistress Juliet is dead?"

"All Verona knows she is," Rosaline said with a squeeze of her hand. "I was at her funeral."

"Ah, but then she yet lived, mark you." The nurse frowned in grief-muddled confusion. "We lay her in the tomb, and in the night she woke and slew herself anew, while I slept. I knew not of her second death until the next day."

Rosaline swallowed an angry reply. Of course the Capulets had little thought to inform a mere servant of Juliet's strange fate. No matter that the nurse had been their daughter's loving companion her entire life.

"My sweet ladybird!" the nurse continued, her voice growing hoarse. "To think a dagger split its pretty breast.

And in the tomb! Surrounded by dusty bones— Ah! Could I but have held her in my arms, let her blood spill 'gainst my breast instead of on the cold stones! Oh, my poor lamb!" She shook her head. "'Twas that Romeo, mark. I had thought him an honest gentleman. Had I but— Ah well." She began patting herself, and from somewhere amongst her voluminous folds she produced a handkerchief, which she used with a great honk. "Enough moans. Servants may mourn, but they must do so on their feet. I must to my lady."

"I'll go with thee." Rosaline took the nurse's arm to support her. If her uncle intended to keep her waiting, she might as well accompany the nurse. Clearly no one else in the household gave the poor old woman a moment's consideration.

"Nay, madam," the nurse said. "My lady is abed."

"I know. My guardian attends her. Is she awake?"

"Aye," the nurse admitted with reluctance.

"Then perchance a visit shall be some succor. Pray ask if she will receive me."

The nurse pressed her lips together, looking about to refuse. "Aye," she muttered.

Rosaline followed the nurse down the long hallway to the blue doors that led to Lady Capulet's bedroom.

Rosaline waited a long time before the nurse reemerged, her face beaming. "Come in. My lady will see you."

Her aunt's room felt as stale as a crypt. Despite the summer heat, heavy drapes were drawn over the windows. At the far end was her aunt Lady Capulet's large canopied bed, the tall, silver-haired Duchess Francesca of Vitruvio bent over it.

As Rosaline drew near, her guardian straightened and looked her up and down.

"Ah, niece," the Duchess said. "What, didst thou crawl here through a field of brambles?"

"My ladies." Rosaline sank into a curtsy, allowing her hair to fall to hide her burning face. She'd done her best to straighten her mussed gown, but there was a tear at the shoulder and a smeared, muddy boot print on the hem. But she had little interest in recounting the night's events to House Capulet. They'd know soon enough, if her hothead cousins could not keep their mouths shut.

"Nurse, get her a cloth and pin her gown. Filthy as an urchin may'st thou be, Rosaline, but at least thou mak'st a pretty curtsy, fit for any court. Though even that is wasted on my sluggish daughter here." The duchess gave the figure in the bed a sharp nudge.

After the nurse had fluttered around her, setting her gown to rights, Rosaline drew beside the canopy. Her aunt showed no sign of recognizing her presence. Rosaline smothered a gasp at the sight of her. Lady Capulet had been one of the most admired ladies of Verona for as long as Rosaline could remember. Small in size but great in beauty, she commanded every ball and festival, her sharp gaze raking the room as lesser Capulet ladies trailed in her wake. No woman could hope to ascend to the upper ranks of Verona's society without her patronage.

Now the delicacy of her features remained, but her power seemed to have fled. Her skin was waxy and pale, her once-fearsome gaze was dull and unfocused, and she was as docile as a child as the nurse and her mother sat her up against the pillows. "See, Lavinia?" the duchess said loudly. "Thy niece is come to visit thee. Wilt thou not rise to greet her?"

Lady Capulet did not seem to hear. Her gaze was fixed in a dark corner of the room, her fingers dancing fretfully along the hem of the coverlet. Duchess Francesca gave a great sigh. "'Tis ever so since her Juliet bled away in the tomb," she said to Rosaline. "Grief is a foe, but she welcomes it like the dearest of friends, and will keep company with none other."

"She has had a terrible shock," Rosaline said. "Certainly she shall recover."

"Shall she indeed?" the duchess demanded. "Lady Montague did not. She died when she learned her son had slain himself in the arms of a Capulet." She gave her daughter a little shake. "The Capulets can ill afford such feebleness. Daughter, thy family has already lost their heir—must they lose their mistress too?"

There was no response. The nurse, with an apprehensive glance at Duchess Francesca, pushed closer to Lady Capulet, cooing soothing murmurs in her mistress's ear as she readjusted the blankets around her.

The duchess shook her head, turning away from the bed. "What's Lord Capulet's will with thee, Rosaline? He would not tell me."

"I know not. I am but just arrived, and my uncle has other business."

"Let us hope he's kept more wit than his wife. 'Tis a

scandal, to see the Capulets brought so low. And our prince complicit in it! Knowest thou, child, he means not to bring the Montagues to justice?"

Rosaline frowned. "Justice? What wrong have the Montagues done that's not already punished?"

Her great-aunt snorted. "Seduction. Abduction. Murder. For a man to steal a maid from her parents' home, to seduce her, ravish her, lead her to her death—the prince is far too forgiving of House Montague's crimes."

"Even had Romeo done those things, he is dead now."

"Perhaps, but his house prospers on. The prince cares not for justice, nor to bring peace to souls afflicted by this strife like my poor daughter."

"Peace?" Lady Capulet's voice issued behind them. Rosaline turned to find her aunt's position unchanged. Her gaze still fixed a thousand leagues away, she seemed unaware of their presence as she continued to speak. "Think you, Mother, that the fall of House Montague would be enough to salve the wounds of Juliet's death? 'Twas our own Tybalt's sword that slew the prince's kinsman Mercutio. Will you demand the prince pull House Capulet stone from stone too? Would that then be enough to buy back a moment of my sweet child's life?"

"Hush, fool. Speak not such nonsense 'gainst your own." Duchess Francesca shook her hard. Rosaline cried out, seizing her great-aunt's hand.

"Let me go, girl. Thou forget'st thyself."

"She's grieving! Think you a beating will cure her of it?"

But the blow had failed to dislodge Lady Capulet's dreamy

smile. "The dead cannot return," snapped the duchess, "but they can be avenged. Grief is no excuse for feebleness."

At last, Lady Capulet's gaze found them. She looked surprised to see Rosaline. "Thou, child," she said. "My husband and his cousins slew the Montague who slit thy father's throat. Pray, was't enough blood for thee?"

Rosaline could not answer.

"No," Lady Capulet murmured. "No, Capulet blood is dearer still than that."

The door banged open and Lord Capulet was in the doorway. "Ah, thou art here," he said to Rosaline. "I told you to wait."

She gave him a polite smile. "You were occupied, Uncle. I came to pay my respects to my aunt."

"I am ready for thee. Come hither." He ushered her toward the door, then hesitated, jerking back over the threshold. "My lady," he said in the vague direction of his wife's bed. "How fare you?"

She smiled faintly. "Well, sir."

"Good." He took Rosaline by the elbow. "Come, child."

Her uncle led Rosaline back to his study, indicating she should sit in the chair opposite his desk. She had only been in here a handful of times. When she was a child—the last time she was a regular guest in this house—she, Juliet, and Livia used to sneak in here, though it was strictly forbidden. She could remember hiding under the large oak desk, her hand pressed over Juliet's mouth to stifle her giggles.

Her uncle settled himself behind that desk now, hands clasped over his prodigious stomach. He peered at her, but he made no move to speak. His forehead furrowed. "Rosaline," he said. "Rosaline of House Capulet."

Rosaline fought to keep her features even. "Of House Tirimo, my lord." Verona might be inclined to forget her dead father's name, but she was not.

Her uncle, as she expected, waved this off. "Thy Tirimo sire wedded my sister. That makes thee Capulet enough. Besides, he proved himself one of us in the end, eh?"

Rosaline laced her fingers together. "I suppose there is no more Capulettish trait than falling to a Montague blade."

"Curb thy tongue, girl." He grasped for a bowl on his desk and thrust it toward her. "Here, have a sweet."

"No, thank you."

He shook the bowl at her again. "Go on. You children loved these."

"Aye, when we were still in the care of a nurse."

Her uncle peered at her, as though startled she was no longer a small girl running about underfoot. He cleared his throat. "I suppose we've not seen much of thee these last years, thee and—ah—"

"Livia."

"Livia. Of course."

Had her uncle ever known his niece's name? Or had he forgotten it in the six years since they had been regular guests here? Father had died when Rosaline was eleven; Mother had followed two years later, after a long time of being sickly. Even before she went, two fatherless girls with no great prospects had not been thought fit companions for the young flower of the proud, ambitious Capulets. Rosaline and Livia had been invited to the house for feasts and holidays, but their friendship with Juliet had come to an abrupt end. Rosaline considered reminding her uncle of this, but the man looked so tired she found she had not the heart.

He broke the silence. "Thou wast ever a sweet child . . . Juliet—" He cleared his throat. "Juliet missed thee."

Rosaline nodded slowly. "Sir," she said. "Tell me why I was summoned."

"Rosaline," he said. "From whatever house thou tak'st thy name, thou art a Capulet and thou wilt obey."

"What mean you, Uncle?"

He rose and walked over to her, taking her chin between finger and thumb and turning her face this way and that as though she were a calf he was thinking of buying. "Quite pretty," he said, as though to himself. "True Capulet looks, so the picture will be just right. And old enough that thou shouldst be married by now, anyway. Yes, thou art just what he asked for."

Rosaline grew cold. "Married, sir?"

"Aye, I've made a match for thee. Well, not I alone. Boy!" Capulet leaned out the door and roared to his valet. "Bring in our other guests."

The next moment Rosaline leapt from her seat, because in walked a man she recognized as Lord Montague. And with him was Benvolio.

Her cry of "What?" broke the air at the same moment as Benvolio's "Uncle! *Her?*"

She whirled on him, gaping. "You knew of this?"

Lord Montague put a restraining hand on Benvolio's

shoulder. "Now, boy, you consented to wed a Capulet maid, not half an hour ago."

"Aye, I consented to marry a maid, not a harpy!"

"Niece," Lord Capulet said drily, "I see you and your betrothed have already met."

"I am betrothed to no man," she snapped. "And certainly not to *him*."

Benvolio crossed his arms. "On this we may agree, lady."

Lord Capulet raised his hands to quiet them both. "You *will* marry!" he thundered. "Insolent children, you will do as you are told. For the sake of your families."

Benvolio snorted. "The last thing my family needs is for me to bring home a snake."

Lord Capulet shook a finger in Rosaline's direction. "For your honor—"

Rosaline glared at him. "Uncle, if you but knew how little I cared for Capulet honor—!"

"How about for Verona?"

A smooth voice cut through the strife. Softer it was than their shouts, and yet it silenced them instantly. Rosaline swallowed when she saw the newcomer.

"Your Grace," she said.

Her face burnt as she sank into a deep curtsy. Prince Escalus stood in the doorway of the study.

His arms were crossed as he looked round the room, surveying the tableau of squabbling subjects before him. Verona's ruler was a young man of twenty, only four years on the throne, but the cool, commanding glance he directed toward the two middle-aged vassals bowing to him carried no hint of hesitation or deference.

"Rise," he said to Rosaline with a nod. His lips twitched slightly as he looked at her, as though he might smile at her fury. *My lady Thorn,* he used to call her, because, he said, she was much too prickly for her sweet, flowery name, but if he remembered how he'd once teased a small Rosaline to distraction with the nickname when he was a boy, he gave no sign.

Rosaline stood, meeting her sovereign's gaze with a deep breath. "Your pardon for my conduct, but if you only knew what they were planning, Your Grace—when I tell you of this sodden-witted plan of betrothal—"

"I know it well. 'Twas my idea."

Rosaline's voice lost its stridency. "Yours?" she whispered.

The smile he gave her was not unkind. "Indeed," he said. "One of my better ones too." He looked around at them, hands clasped in front of him. "You Montagues and Capulets are a plague on this city," he said. "I've lost too many subjects and too many friends to your senseless hatred. I know"—he held up a hand when Lords Montague and Capulet both moved as though to protest—"you swore on your children's graves that your hatred died with them, but 'tis not the first time such vows were made. 'Twill take more than pretty statues to keep them." The prince gave them a hard stare, and Rosaline and Benvolio exchanged a glance. It seemed the prince knew about how Juliet's statue had been defiled, but their uncles appeared oblivious. She decided not to speak of it. She was not at all sure Lords Montague and Capulet would be much better at keeping their tempers than their nephews. Better to let them find out on their own, separately.

The prince turned to Rosaline once more. A little of the regal coolness left his face as he looked at her. For a moment, she was able to see the tall blond boy who had once run and chased her through the palace garden. During her days of playing in the palace she'd thought Isabella's elder brother the handsomest, bravest knight in all of Italy, for all that he'd been only three years older than she. Before he was sent away to foster in Venice and learn the ways of knighthood, he'd had a small, adoring Rosaline-shaped shadow that followed him everywhere. He'd treated her with the same exasperated affection he held for Isabella.

Her own feelings toward him had never been sisterly, though. Now, as he reached for her hand, her heart stuttered out an odd rhythm at the feeling of his warm fingers around hers.

"Dearest Rosaline," he said, looking straight into her eyes. She tried to breathe. His eyes were so blue, so full of honest affection. "My earliest playfellow. There is no dearer soul in all Verona. That is why I chose you to be Benvolio's wife, you see."

Rosaline stood frozen, unable to do anything but stare. How could it be he who had chosen this fate for her?

"Your families must not further destroy each other," the prince was saying. "'Tis clear you cannot exist as two, so you must become one." He turned to the Montagues. "Benvolio is now the highest-ranked unmarried gentleman who bears the name of Montague; Rosaline the closest kinswoman to Juliet yet a maid." Prince Escalus reached for Benvolio's hand and pressed it together with Rosaline's, sealing them together with his own. "You will marry, and the two families will be knit together. And the city will see that a marriage of Montague and Capulet need not end with a half-dozen corpses."

The prince's words were light, almost jesting, but there was strength in his grip on their hands. "I do not normally interest myself in whom my subjects marry, but in this case I truly believe my city's survival depends on it. Be ruled by your families and your sovereign in this."

Rosaline's gaze caught Benvolio's. His face was set in an inscrutable scowl as he stared at her. He opened his mouth as though to protest, then closed it again. A muscle twitched in his jaw. Rosaline's heart sank. If even a man who loathed her would not speak out against their marriage, who would?

"There is another reason I thought of this match." The prince's voice softened slightly. "So many are dead, but you—you, Benvolio, you, Rosaline—you *live*. You survived. This whirlwind of death that has decimated your families and even taken Paris and Mercutio, mine own cousins—it has passed you by, left you unscathed."

Benvolio's dark eyes caught hers again. The depth of pain she saw there made her own throat ache. "Hardly unscathed, my lord," she said softly.

The prince's hands tightened over theirs. "No. None of us

is. But still, you are here, and they are not. For the others, strife and death; for you two, peace and life. Do you know why that is?"

They said nothing.

"Nor do I," said the prince. "But whatever fate or chance or wisdom 'twas that saved you, Verona hath need of it now."

Rosaline broke his pretty words with an inelegant snort. "Peace?" she said. "Peace?" Ripping her hand free, she pointed to the red mark on Benvolio's face. "Would you like to know how the peaceful Benvolio got that? From mine own peaceful hand."

The prince's eyebrows shot up. He turned a questioning look to Benvolio, who nodded. His fingers traced lightly over the welt she'd raised on his cheek. Rosaline had not known she could hit that hard. "Aye," he said. "Not an hour since."

Rosaline laid her hand on Benvolio's cheek, showing how the mark fit the shape of her fingers. He winced and drew away from her touch. "This is what five minutes' acquaintance with this rascal brought about," she said. "Imagine what a lifetime of marriage would wreak. We'd bring no peace to Verona, Your Grace."

Benvolio turned and stood shoulder to shoulder with her, facing down the prince. "She speaks aright, my lord. You would sentence us to a lifetime of misery."

The prince said nothing, merely stared his young vassal down, arms crossed, eyebrows slightly raised.

A strained smile crossed Benvolio's face. "But of course," he said, "my misery is ever at Your Grace's command."

Rosaline stared at him. How could he accede to this madness? He hated her far more than she loathed him. The vicious words he'd spat at her in the graveyard had proven that.

Well, if she had lost her only ally, she'd simply have to prevent this madness herself. Stepping forward, she fell to her knees at the prince's feet, taking his hand in hers. "My prince," she said. "I beg you. As your loyal subject and"—she swallowed, and made herself look into his eyes—"as one thou may'st once have considered a friend. Escalus, please do not ask this of me."

Behind her she heard old Montague draw a sharp breath. Her uncle lurched as though to seize her, but checked it. Rosaline sat frozen. Her familiarity was inexcusable, she knew. To call the prince by his name! To call him *thou,* as though he were her equal, her intimate friend! Quite possibly she was the first to address him so since he had taken the throne. But she was sure that if she could only reach him—if he could only break through that cool, absent mask of majesty and *see* her—

He pulled his hand away. She thought she saw a flare of something in his eyes, but he turned away, leaning against her uncle's desk with his back to them.

"You forget yourself, lady," he said, turning back around, that mask of regal uncaring ease once more on his face. "And I was not *asking.*"

Rosaline let her hands drift back to her lap. She stared at the faces above her. Her uncle, as red-faced as if he'd drunk a bottle of wine. Montague, drawn and cold. Benvolio, miserable but resigned. Between them, these men had sealed her fate.

Or so they thought.

Smoothing her skirts, Rosaline rose to her feet. "I was not asking either. My lords, I *will not* marry Benvolio."

Her uncle harrumphed. "Do not be mad, girl. You've no choice."

"Oh? Powerful men you may be, but even you cannot force a lady into marriage vows she will not speak."

The prince frowned. "No," he said. "But I can forbid you from marrying another. Refuse Benvolio, Rosaline, and you will die a maid."

Rosaline actually laughed. The men surrounding her were certain they had her trapped into doing as they wished; little did they know she'd already slipped the net. "Oh, my lord, 'tis my dearest wish. Long ere Romeo heard the name Juliet, 'twas my intention to one day remove from Verona and take holy orders somewhere Montagues and Capulets are unknown." She moved for the door. "And it seems I have tarried long enough. Perhaps my lords will find another lady willing to bear sons to be fodder for Montague and Capulet swords, but you'll find her not in House Tirimo. Good night, sirs."

And with that, Rosaline walked past the astonished men, down the richly carpeted stairs, and through the gates of House Capulet into the cool air of the Verona night.

The breeze was soothing on her heated cheeks. House Capulet's sentries blinked at her, and Rosaline could not help but laugh again, remembering the way her uncle's jaw had hung open. Probably he'd yet to shut it. How often had she imagined telling her Capulet kin just how little she cared for their brawling, selfish ways? She never thought she'd have a chance to say it to their faces. To thwart the plans of both Montague and Capulet at once—ah, furious as she was, it was a heady thrill.

Of course, having Escalus there to see her screeching like a harpy had never been part of her daydreams.

His Grace, she reminded herself, *not Escalus.* She pressed her hands to her cheeks, which burnt anew. He'd not spoken so much to her in years. And when he did seek her out, it was for *this.* To trade her off like chattel.

She'd spoken true: Ever since her parents had died, she'd been determined to become a nun rather than allow herself to be married off to some minor noble or other who would like as not die at the end of a sword. No, the life of a nun might not be exciting, but at least she would not watch her kin slaughter and be slaughtered. She would take orders as soon as Livia found a husband. She'd told no one of her plans, not even Livia. It was her greatest secret.

No, not her greatest secret. She rarely admitted it even to herself, but with her heart still pounding in her chest and the heat of his palm burning on the back of her hand, it was impossible to deny. There was, in fact, one man who could stop her flight to a convent with a word. Escalus.

"Rosaline!"

Speak of the devil. Her sovereign's voice rang out behind her. Even now, there was little urgency in his tone, only annoyance; the prince, it seemed, was little used to being refused, and did not quite believe it.

"Rosaline, stop, I say!"

Rosaline halted and turned around. There stood her prince in a pool of torchlight, looking cross. She sank once more into a mocking curtsy. "Even as Your Grace commands. What's your will?"

"Thou knowest my will."

Now it was he who *thou*'d her. Did he do it as she had, to remind her of their old friendship? Or was he addressing her as he would a servant? "I am Your Grace's loyal subject to command," she said. "In all things but this."

"By heaven, Rosaline, Benvolio is an excellent gentleman."

"He is none."

"I say he is. Wilt thou not take my word?" His smile, when it came, was as dimpled and sweet as ever. How was that possible? "As thou didst say, we were friends once."

"Sweet little Rosaline, why dost thou weep?"

"Thou knowest right well why, thou churl," she said with a sniff. "'Tis right a maid should weep when she's heartsick."

Escalus began to laugh. "I' faith, who has left thy tiny heart so bruised?"

"Is't true, my lord, you go at dawn to Venice?" She turned her little tearstained face to his.

Escalus looked startled. "Aye, of course." His adolescent chest was puffed with pride. "I serve the Duke of Venice as his squire." Rosaline burst once more into tears. Escalus patted her shaking back. "Cry not."

"I shall," she vowed. "Yea, I shall weep and weep, and never cease till thou return'st to wed me."

Escalus laughed, and ruffled up her curls. "Pray dry thy tears. I swear I shall return."

Return he had, several years later, when his father fell ill. But her own father had died in the meantime, and her mother died shortly after his return. The little girl of seven he'd left behind had been replaced by a poor, grim young maid barely acknowledged by her own family, not nearly grand enough to be friends with the prince. She'd seen little of him.

All traces of that merry, adoring child were long gone, except her love for him.

She stayed sunk in a deep curtsy, eyes modestly lowered— the picture of the polite obedience she was refusing him. With an impatient sound, Escalus's hands gripped her shoulders, pulling her gently upright. "Stand up, for God's sake."

Rosaline tried to hide the way her breath hitched at his touch. He was standing just a handspan away from her, peering quizzically into her eyes as if he could divine the secret to her defiance there. "Aye, we were friends once," she said, stepping back out of his grip. "But thou hast spoken not a hundred words to me since thou didst return to Verona, Escalus. Canst truly say thou account'st me amongst thy dearest friends? If not, why should I count thee so? Pray do not so insult me."

Escalus's frown deepened. "You are too familiar, lady. You forget yourself."

"Familiar, am I?" There was a harsh, jeering tone in her voice, but she could not seem to stop herself. "One moment thou dost plead thy will on the strength of our friendship, the next thou dost chide me as an upstart peasant. Punish me, then, your lordship, for my temerity. Deprive me of my fortune—I have none. Forbid me to wed. I shall thank you. Exile me—oh, dear sweet *friend,* you could do me no greater boon."

"You're so angry," Escalus said, but quietly.

She swiped a furious hand across her eyes. "No less are you."

Escalus looked a bit surprised at that. But yes, she still knew him well enough to see the fury beneath that polished surface of his. "Aye. This feud has treated neither of us kindly." He took out his handkerchief and offered it to her. She ignored it. "'Tis why I would move to bring it to an end."

"A noble aim, but your methods are wanting. Marry me with Benvolio and our cousins shall slaughter each other over the wedding feast."

"You're wrong."

She smiled mirthlessly. "We shall never know. I have given this feud my blood. It shall not have my body too. I know Your Grace cares little for my happiness, but I promise you 'twill be so."

He looked as though she'd struck him. "Think you truly I care not for your happiness?"

"I know you do not." She swallowed hard. "'Tis no matter. A sovereign's not obliged to befriend orphans of modest means, too lowly for notice even by their own kin. Livia and I have no need of your patronage, nor that of anyone else in this accursed city."

A flash of sadness passed across Escalus's face. "Think you that is why I stayed away? Rosaline, I—mine own father was newly dead, my sister in a foreign city, myself just crowned. My old intimacies could not continue once I took the throne. I thought only of Verona."

"So do you still," Rosaline said. "An excellent trait in a sovereign."

"They all abandoned thee?"

"Had the Capulets had their way, Livia and I would have gone straight to a convent after our father's death. 'Tis but luck that renting our house gives us a little income. That is the only reason the duchess lets us keep house in a corner of her estate until we may marry."

"Your house is in Verona," he pointed out. "Perhaps you've more need of this 'accursed city' than you think."

"Aye, but we shall live in it no more." She hated the look of pity on his face. Had this evening not been bad enough, but he must pry into her and Livia's years of humiliation? She closed her arms around the pain in her chest. "Set your heart at rest. 'Tis none of your concern."

He reached out two fingers, gently tipping her chin into the light. Rosaline took a startled, broken breath as he gently wiped the tears from her face with his handkerchief, just as he had when she was small. Her eyes fluttered shut at his touch. "You would regain your station, and more," he pointed out, "were you mistress of both the Montagues and Capulets."

She laughed. "Poor persuasion, after all that you have ranged against my defenses this night. Admit defeat, Escalus.

63

My chastity shall remain untouched." She pulled away, offering him a curtsy once more.

He cocked his head, examining her with narrowed eyes, then nodded, giving her leave to depart. "As time shall try, Rosaline," he said softly. "I am not so easily thwarted."

"As you say. As time shall try."

Part 2

I had rather hear my dog bark at a crow
than a man swear he loves me.

—*Much Ado About Nothing*

$\mathcal{P}$RINCE ESCALUS WAS NOT sure what to do.

He leaned out the window, feeling the morning breeze on his face. All of Verona was spread out beneath him, and beyond her walls the river, neat green fields, and roads ribboning off past the horizon. The palace of Verona was at the very height of the city, atop the summit of the highest hill. *Verona's welcome,* it was sometimes called, for if one came up the river, the towers of the palace were the very first part of the city a weary traveler would spy.

Escalus's perspective on the palace was an unusual one. Immune to its beauty, he found its thick gray walls stifling. Even more so now that he dwelt within them alone. His mother had died when he was fourteen, three years after he'd gone to Venice to be the duke's squire; he had been too far away to return for the funeral. The next time he had come back was to bid farewell to his father, who was wasting away from a fever. Three days after he arrived, the old prince had died, and Escalus took the throne shortly after his sixteenth birthday. The crown was heavier than he'd expected.

Which was why he was now leaning out the window and

staring down at the river, indulging in a game he had been refining since he was small: Suppose Prince Escalus Forsook His Crown to Become a River Pirate.

A game all the more charming for its juvenility. No more squabbling families. No more demanding ambassadors from neighboring tyrants. No more hurt in the eyes of his childhood playfellow, just because he asked for her aid in keeping the city from flying apart at the seams. Just himself, his trusty crew, and the sparkling blue water . . .

"Your Grace."

With an inner sigh, Escalus turned to find his chancellor, Penlet, waiting patiently for his attention. Penlet was middle-aged, and had been for as long as Escalus could remember. His drab black robe, his colorless hair, his mouth always set in a frown—all these looked the same as they had when Escalus was still in the nursery. The man seemed always to have the slightest of colds—not enough to keep him from his tireless work, but enough to provide a discreet cough to draw his liege's attention back to the business at hand. Escalus trusted him, relied on him utterly, and sometimes loathed him as the plow horse does the whip.

Escalus settled himself behind his desk. "Yes, Penlet," he said. "What news?"

"My lord," Penlet said, after covering his mouth for one of those genteel little coughs. "'Tis something concerning the houses Capulet and Montague."

Escalus resisted the urge to turn back to the window and ignore him. "Yes, what now? Has Capulet finally rousted Rosaline to the altar? I've waited three days for him to persuade her. How long can it take a lord to bend a maiden to his will?"

Penlet shook his head. "She claims she is sick, and will see no one, not even her uncle."

If Rosaline was sick, he was the Emperor of Russia. "What then? Have the watch discovered who defiled Juliet's statue?"

"No, Your Grace. Lord Montague has had it cleaned and returned to its former beauty. The Montagues swear it was not they who defiled it, and the watch can find no proof it was."

Of course not. The watch was incapable of finding anything not hidden at the bottom of a barrel of ale. Escalus pressed his fist between his eyes.

Penlet gave another little cough. "There is more, my lord."

"Yes? What else?"

"'Twas in the market square this morning," said Penlet. "When the merchants arrived at dawn to open their stalls, they found this hanging from a tree in the center of the square."

He rang a bell, and a footman came in, bearing an oddly shaped bundle of cloth and rope. At Penlet's nod, he held it up.

It was a cloth effigy in the shape of a man with a noose round its neck. Scrawled across its chest were the words DEATH TO HOUSE MONTAGUE.

"Fie and fie again!" Escalus burst out. "Who did this, Penlet?"

His chancellor swallowed. "Not a soul saw it happen."

"No, of course not. But all the merchants saw it hanging there this morn. Which means the whole town knows." Escalus slammed a fist against his desk. Penlet jumped and suppressed a small squeak.

Damn them all. If this kind of provocation continues, it shall not be long before the two houses are in open war. God only knows what else they'd bring down with them. "Send runners to Montague and Capulet," he told Penlet. "Tell them to keep their swords sheathed. We'll learn the truth of this. And tell old Capulet that if he knows who did this, he'd better tell me now or 'twill go badly for him."

Penlet nodded and bowed, backing out of the room.

"Oh, and Penlet," Escalus called, "tell Capulet I want that niece of his married before the month is out."

Rosaline had shut and barred the doors.

Usually at this time of year the cottage doors were opened to let cool breezes chase the heat from the house. But for the past three days, they had been closed and locked at Rosaline's order. Any visitor wishing to speak to the sisters would have to knock on the door and wait to be admitted. Which none were.

"I' faith," said Livia, putting aside her sewing as the boom of the door knocker sounded through the house. "That's the third one today. 'Tis certain we never had so many visitors. Thou shouldst flout the prince's will more often, Rosaline."

Rosaline finished an embroidered rose with such violence

that the needle stuck into her hand. "Such company we can well do without. Go and send them away, prithee."

Livia nodded, carefully folding the tablecloth she was mending. "Who think'st thou it is this time? Uncle again, or one of his servants, or the prince's men?"

Rosaline laughed, hissing a bit as she unstitched herself. Her uncle and the prince had taken it in turns to try to wheedle, cajole, and command her to wed. Luckily, the duchess, the only person with any real power to threaten the Tirimo ladies, had declined to involve herself. Which, given her hatred of the Montagues, was not surprising. "I care not. Only tell them—"

"I know." Livia threw a hand across her forehead in an imitation swoon. "Oh, my lord, my dear sister is deathly ill. And though she longs—nay, pines—to see the face of her very favorite Capulet uncle who has not spoken three words to her in years, the doctor has strictly forbidden her to see anyone who wishes to induce her to marry, as hearing the name 'Benvolio' makes her break out in pox."

Rosaline laughed and gave her sister a shove toward the door. "Leave the dramatics to the stage players. Just tell him I am sick and can receive no visitors." This was the reason she gave for becoming a hermit these last few days, and no one would publicly contradict it. Only a few Montagues and Capulets knew the truth about the betrothal the prince was trying to force on her—her uncle and the prince had not announced it publicly. In this, at least, they were wise. If Verona society knew a Capulet maid had spurned a Montague suitor, House Montague's humiliation would know no bounds.

"That's dull," Livia's voice floated back from the corridor.

Shortly Rosaline heard the scrape of wood from the front hall as Livia hauled the front doors open. Her sister's voice rose and fell in polite tones, though from her bedroom Rosaline could not make out the words. Then another voice answered. A woman's, but not the genteel, courtly accent of a Capulet lady. This voice was loud, and common. Rosaline frowned. It almost sounded like—

Rosaline threw her sewing behind a chair, pulled her hair out of its pins, and had just enough time to toss the covers aside and jump into bed before the door flew open and Juliet's nurse burst in.

"Good morrow, Rosaline dear," she said. "I heard you were sick."

Livia, trailing in after her, shot Rosaline an apologetic glance over the nurse's shoulder. "Dear nurse, I told thee, the doctor has said Rosaline is to receive no one—"

"And quite right he is too." The nurse plumped her prodigious bulk down on Rosaline's bedside and began searching around inside a large sack that smelled strongly of cabbage. "Ah, my dears, I pray you never know the torture of my corns. A stream of bothersome visitors? 'Twill do naught for your health. 'Tis just what I always told your mother when you two were small. I'd say, dear lady, you go and attend the princess, leave the pretty wretches with the old nurse when they've caught fever. I'll soon make a physic so hot 'twill burn the fever out of them."

Rosaline could see Livia trying not to laugh. Indeed, the nurse's homemade medicines had been the terror of their young lives. As children they'd rarely been at home; they were either with their mother at the palace or playing with Juliet at House Capulet. They'd spent so much time with their cousin as children that the nurse had come to consider them nearly as much her charges as her beloved Juliet, and she was especially fierce when any of them fell sick. Her medicines tasted so vile they required immediate recuperation.

"Your color's good," she said, taking Rosaline's chin in a critical hand and turning it side to side. "Of course, so they say ladies in a consumption look just before they die."

Rosaline sighed. "I am not in a consumption, nurse."

"No? Good. We'll soon have you right, then. I cured every fever and cough dear Jule had from the day I weaned her. Dost thou mind when I weaned her? I laid the bitter wormwood on my dug"—the nurse gave her breast an affectionate squeeze—"and she did scream! Thou wast then a little puling thing of six, Rosaline."

Rosaline's eyes narrowed. The nurse's lethargy of the night at House Capulet had given way to a frantic energy. What had caused so great a change in mood? Her contemplation was interrupted by the glug of the medicine bottle as the nurse poured out a dose. "Truly, there is no need—" Rosaline's words dissolved into sputtering as a spoonful of horror was shoved into her mouth. She sat up, the burning from the brew racking her with coughs.

"There, you see? You've more spirit already." The nurse brandished a jar of murky liquid. "Just you drink a dram of this every hour and you'll soon be on your feet."

"Worry not," Livia said with a wicked gleam in her eye. "I'll see she takes it." Rosaline shot her a glare.

"Good," said the nurse. "I'd stay here and attend to her myself, but my lady has much need of me."

"How does my lady aunt?" said Rosaline, in a desperate attempt to distract the nurse from the second spoonful she was pointing Rosaline's way.

A strange look crossed the nurse's face. "She is well," she said, then pressed her lips together.

"Is she? I thought that she was still abed since Juliet's death."

"Aye," the nurse said uneasily. "She's very well, for one that has not left her bed for grief. 'Twas that I meant."

Rosaline blinked and said, "Ah." It had never been profitable to try to follow the paths blazed by the nurse's brain.

"Well," the nurse said. "I must away. See you take your medicine, ladybird. My lord is very anxious you should get well, that you may wed that handsome fellow." She frowned as she stood, brushing off her skirts and absently licking a stray drop of medicine from her hand. "Not that I hold with the marrying of Montagues, mind. If I'd only kept my Jule from their clutches . . ." She crossed herself. "Well. She's with God now, and the Montagues will surely get their punishment in the hereafter, so I suppose you may as well marry one in the meantime. 'Twould certainly be better than wasting your beauty in a nunnery." Next to the bed, Livia went very still.

"No waste will it be," Rosaline croaked. She found her poor scorched throat needed no encouragement now to make her sound as if she were at death's door. "What waste is there in dedicating my life to God and helping the poor?"

"Hmph. Nunneries are for ugly girls. Good day, my dears."

When she had gone, Rosaline gave a sigh of relief and got out of bed. "Thank heaven. I thought she would cover me with leeches next."

"Mmm." Livia had shut the door behind the nurse; she lingered with her hand on the doorknob. Finally she turned back to her sister. "Rosaline . . ."

Rosaline was taking up her sewing again. Throwing it down like that had tangled the thread terribly. She tensed, having some idea of what was coming. Why had the nurse mentioned the nunnery in front of Livia? This was not how she wanted her sister to learn of her plans. "Yes, dearest?"

"Is it true, what she said?" Livia curled up in her chair. "About taking holy orders? Uncle Capulet mentioned it on one of his visits, but I thought 'twas but a way thou didst seek to escape this match."

Rosaline winced. She'd been lucky to avoid this conversation for so long; it wasn't one she looked forward to. "Well . . . no. I truly do wish to go into a convent."

Livia picked at a loose thread in the hem of her gown. Rosaline waited for expressions of horror that Rosaline could be thinking of adopting a way of life that included neither dancing nor young men nor the latest hairstyles, but Livia said nothing.

"I know it may seem strange," Rosaline said. "But 'twill take me away from all things Montague and Capulet forever, and I have no dearer wish than that."

Livia did not look up. Finally she said, "When meant you to tell me?"

"I'd hoped to see thee betrothed first," Rosaline said. "There seemed no need to mention it before— Oh God's teeth, not again!"

The boom of the door knocker was sounding through the house once more. Livia went to the window, where she could lean out and see who was at their gate. "It's one of Uncle's servants." She called down to him, "What is your will?"

"I've a message from my master," the man yelled up. "His niece Rosaline is to unbar her doors and come to his house forthwith. I'll not budge from your threshold till she does."

Rosaline peeked over Livia's shoulder. Sure enough, the man had sat down and made himself comfortable outside their door. "Lord. I'll go down and chase him off—"

"No need," Livia said. She turned away from the window. "I'll go to Uncle's house in your stead. Perhaps if I speak to him, he will leave us alone."

"Thanks," said Rosaline. Livia's dress was askew from sitting in various unladylike positions all afternoon. Rosaline reached out to straighten it. "But really, Livia, thou need'st not involve thyself—"

"Nonsense," Livia said, tugging her dress away from Rosaline's helping hands. "After all, you are soon to take holy orders. Your thoughts should be with God." She smoothed the wrinkles from her skirt, lifting her hem to examine the loose thread she had been worrying at before. "Your family should not be such a distraction." She broke the thread off with a snap.

Escalus thought that Capulet might die.

The man's face was as red as Mars and sweat was pouring off him in rivers. His horse, unused to such a nervous rider—or perhaps not used to one that weighed the same as at least two normal men—danced sideways, and Capulet's bulk jiggled in time.

"Are you well, sir?" Escalus asked.

Capulet nodded as he waved off the prince's concern with one hand and mopped his streaming face with the other. "Oh yes, sire. 'Tis very—" He had to pause for a racking cough. "Very invigorating."

Escalus hid a smile. It was considered a great honor to accompany the prince on his daily ride outside the palace walls. Capulet would never have dreamed of turning down the invitation, nor would he dream of complaining now. He had no choice but to endure his discomfort as long as the prince wished.

Which was exactly why the prince had invited the man in the first place. He was not well pleased with the head of the Capulets.

"I am glad you are enjoying yourself," he said. "Trot on, Venitio." He heard a deep sigh behind him as Capulet urged his horse to follow. "Now," Escalus said, "I believe you were telling me you have no idea who hung that Montague dummy in the town square."

Capulet shook his head. "My lord," he said, "upon my life,

'twas no man of my family. Or if it was, I have been unable to discover it. And I've tried."

"Mmm. Capulets are not known for their willingness to bring their guilty before me for justice."

"'Tis this sort of villainy that slew my child," Capulet said. "If this poison lives on in my house, I would cast it before Your Grace the instant I found it."

"Good," said the prince. "I assume that means you are still making all efforts to see your niece married to Benvolio."

His companion groaned. "As Your Grace well knows, she will not leave her house! What am I to do, marry them through the window?"

The prince frowned. "Her door is yet barred?"

"Aye. She claims she is sick. And old lady Vitruvio is no help." Capulet's face managed to go even redder at the thought of his mother-in-law. "She says if we mean to make her ward a match without consulting her, then surely we do not need her aid to accomplish it." He dropped his handkerchief, and his horse promptly trod it into the dirt. He cast a longing glance at the road back toward Verona's gates. "This very day did I once more command her to come to my house. I ought to go back, in case she has obeyed at last."

Not likely, but the prince had tortured his vassal long enough. "Go on back," said Escalus. "I do not wish our pleasure to keep you from your duties."

"Thank you, my lord." Capulet's voice held the first real gratitude Escalus had heard all afternoon. He turned his horse back to the city.

Escalus thought about following. It was time he returned—Penlet was surely making little coughs of distress at his absence. But on impulse, he turned Venitio in the opposite direction, spurring him into a run away from Verona's walls.

A good hard ride usually cleared his head. Vineyards and houses and streams flew by as his horse's hooves thundered under him. But run though he might, the cares of his city followed him.

What was he to do about Rosaline?

He could go into her house and drag her out, of course. But dragging a screaming girl to the altar was hardly likely to cool tempers on either side.

And, he was reminded by the part of himself that was still allowed to care for things other than the city's best interests, it would make him a right bastard.

There was her sister. Livia was just as much a Capulet as Rosaline. But Escalus had meant what he told Rosaline: He had chosen her to marry into the Montagues because he knew she was up to the task. Even when they were children, she was by far the cleverest of them. Since then he'd seen little of her, but he'd found himself listening closely whenever she was mentioned. When Verona society spoke of the eldest lady of Tirimo, after her misfortunes and her beauty, it was her wit they mentioned. Besides, the steady hand with which she'd kept herself and Livia free of entanglements in the feud spoke for itself. His valet's niece served the Duchess of Vitruvio, and the servants gossiped that before Romeo had fallen under Juliet's thrall, he had nursed a brief passion for Rosaline. But unlike her cousin, she had refused him.

Young Rosaline hid more wisdom behind those assessing eyes than most graybeards. Livia was clever too, but all Verona knew she had absolutely no rein on her tongue. Juliet had caused a bloodbath; Livia would start a war.

Which left him right where he'd been for the last fortnight. With a Montague groom and no Capulet bride to wed him.

It was then that he remembered Isabella's injunction: *"You must hold a feast for me."*

Livia did not try to hide her scowl.

How could Uncle Capulet be so rude? She'd come all this way to see him at his request, and then he wasn't even here!

Of course, she was not the lady he'd asked to see. But he didn't know that. Because he wasn't here.

"The master should be back from his ride soon, lady," a nervous little chambermaid assured her.

"Hmph," said Livia. "I'm not angry at you, you know. 'Tis not your fault you have a discourteous lump for a master."

The chambermaid, perhaps determining that there was no safe response to this, merely bobbed a curtsy and departed. Livia turned her scowl toward the window to watch the setting sun.

How could Rosaline be going into a convent? They'd been taught by nuns when they were small. The nuns had beat them with switches and their food had tasted like stewed bricks. How could her sister choose to live like that forever?

They were supposed to marry impossibly handsome, disgustingly rich young men who swore they would die if the beauteous ladies of Tirimo refused their hands.

Of course, Rosaline had already refused at least one such young man. And then he had in fact died.

Livia shuddered. In truth, she could understand Rosaline's wish to escape what had happened with Romeo. But surely the solution was to get married herself, not to run away from everything.

And that, Livia realized, was the real reason Rosaline's plan made an ache grow in her chest. Livia had always had her sister at her side. Since their parents had died and they'd gone to live with their aggressively indifferent great-aunt, Rosaline was all she had. But that was enough. They were young, they were beautiful, and they had Rosaline's strong will and fierce wit to make everything come out right. When she'd given any thought to their future, she had assumed that they would make good marriages to fine Verona men and these degrading years of poverty would be naught but an ugly memory. Little had she known that Rosaline had been plotting all along to escape her.

Perhaps she should have known. Now that she thought of it, she could see how precarious their future truly was. She could not rely on her sister for everything. Livia would die before she followed Rosaline to a nunnery, though, which meant it was time to consider her own path.

A noise startled her. She turned her sunset-dazzled eyes back inside the house. It took her a few blinks to make out the figure hurrying up the back stairs at the end of the corridor, but even in the shadows it was impossible to mistake the nurse's girth. Bored, Livia decided to follow. Perhaps the nurse had a potion that would cause Rosaline to fall madly in love with the first man she saw. She could never be a nun then. Of course, the nurse's medicines only sometimes worked, but at least it would taste bad, which was the least Rosaline deserved.

Livia was about to call out to her when the nurse paused at the top of the stair. Looking around, she went into a cupboard, from whence she took a lantern. After lighting it, she looked around again and, not seeing Livia in the shadows, she carefully opened a heavy door and slipped inside.

Livia frowned. She had never once seen that door opened before. It led to a wing of the house that had been unused for a generation. What was the nurse doing in there now? Surely the Capulets had not had reason to reopen that wing—sadly, the house had fewer occupants now, not more. Livia was dying to know, and never having been one to deny herself what she wanted, she slipped through the door and followed.

Livia kept her eyes on the nurse's light bobbing ahead of her as she followed on silent feet. Though the sun had not yet set, it was pitch-black in the long corridor. The windows of all the rooms must be covered, leaving the nurse's lantern the only source of light.

No—not the only source.

For Livia could see now that the nurse's goal was a room at the very end of the corridor. Faint light crept from beneath its door. As she drew closer, she could hear voices within. One, a man's, was crying out in pain; the other voice, a woman's, was quieter.

"There, there, lie still—"

"It hurts—oh God, lady, it hurts!"

The door flew open as the nurse hurried into the room. Back in the shadows of the corridor, Livia stared at the scene before her.

Most of the room was what she had expected of this wing—a long-abandoned bedchamber, windows swathed in dark curtains, a few pieces of furniture covered with sheets. A corner, however, had been cleared of dust and transformed into a makeshift sickroom. A shelf stood full of poultices, bandages, and some of what Livia recognized as the nurse's medicines. She watched as the nurse moved aside, revealing a cot. And on the cot was a man.

Livia caught her breath as she looked at him. The man was shirtless, tangled in the sheets, his chest covered in sweat. His long light hair was splayed against the pillow. A large, bloody bandage was tied round his stomach. As she watched, he cried out again, his back arching in pain as the nurse tried to check his bandage.

He was, quite simply, the handsomest man she'd ever seen in her life.

"There, there, dear," the nurse said, trying with a combination of anxious fluttering and brute strength to settle the man back against the pillows. "You mustn't sit up—your wound—"

"Romeo," the man was muttering as he desperately fought the nurse's hold. "Romeo."

"Shh, he's gone, duck, he can't hurt you."

"No—no!" The man thrashed harder. "Juliet! Juliet! My love, where are you? *Juliet!*"

The nurse made futile shushing noises, then called, "My lady," in an urgent voice.

Another figure hurried toward the bed. Livia frowned, creeping closer. The figure was shrouded head to toe in black, so 'twas difficult in the flickering lamplight to see who it was, but—surely 'twas not—

"Shh," said Lady Capulet, pushing back the scarf covering her hair as she stepped into the circle of candlelight.

Upon spying her, the man sank back into the pillows. "Juliet," he croaked, eyes glued to Lady Capulet's form. "My angel."

Lady Capulet hummed and brushed his sweaty hair back from his forehead. "Rest now, gentle Paris."

He turned his head into her soothing touch, at last allowing his eyes to close, though the rapid rise and fall of his chest grew no slower. And the nurse and Lady Capulet relaxed slightly.

Which was when they noticed Livia, standing in the doorway in shock.

As her aunt surged from the bedside and hurried toward her, hand already stretching toward the door to slam it in Livia's face, Livia came to a decision in rather a hurry.

She knew not how Count Paris, mourned as dead by all Verona, came to be alive and hidden away in her uncle's house. Nor did she know why Lady Capulet, said to be bed-ridden with grief over Juliet's death, was instead whole and well and impersonating Juliet for the man's delirium.

But what she did know was that if she allowed that door to close, she might never see the man in the bed again.

So instead of demanding answers, she said, "I can help," and ducked under her aunt's arm into the room.

The nurse was wringing her hands. "Livia, Livia, you must not be here—"

"Come," said Livia, hurrying to the bed. "His bandages want changing, do they not? Another pair of hands is what you need."

Before they could object, she was kneeling on the bed, reaching for the knots on his bandages. Though her fingers were gentle, Paris began to groan; after exchanging a glance, the nurse and Lady Capulet hurried forward. While Lady Capulet held his face in her hands, murmuring soothing, motherly nothings, the nurse and Livia swiftly removed the sodden bandages and replaced them with soft, clean ones. Afterward, the nurse gave him a few drops of medicine and, finally, the pain-racked tension that knotted his body seemed to unwind a bit. He twisted his face against Lady Capulet's hand, fixed half-lidded eyes on her face, and after breathing one final "Juliet," fell at last to sleep.

Livia tore her gaze from the way his face relaxed in slumber to find her aunt glaring at her. "Niece," she hissed. "What are you doing here?"

Livia shrugged. "I followed the nurse. Aunt, what are *you* doing here?"

"That's none of your concern, child."

"And I suppose you'll say the same when I ask what *he's* doing here."

Her aunt pressed her lips together in a tight line and looked away. Livia followed her eyes to Paris's face. Even in sleep, his breath hitched fitfully in pain.

"He's dying," said Livia.

Her aunt turned back to her, eyes wide with outrage in her pale face. "Thou foolish girl. Thou knowest not whereof thou speak'st."

Livia shrugged. "Perhaps not. He's still dying. Even a fool could see that. If you are to have any hope of saving him, you'll need help." She drew a deep breath. "I've a steady pair of hands. I know how to tend the sick. I nursed my mother through her months of illness. Let me help him."

Her aunt was watching her. Livia was struck, suddenly, with how much she did look like Juliet. It was no wonder the feverish Paris confused them. Lady Capulet had borne Juliet very young, and was not yet thirty years old herself. They could have been sisters instead of mother and daughter. But Juliet's face had never worn such a look as her mother's wore now. It was as though she'd turned to stone. Livia swallowed. Perhaps it was best if she left after all.

But it seemed she had made her case. "Very well, niece," Lady Capulet said. "If thou'lt do my bidding, thou may'st remain. But only if thou swearest on thy life not to breathe a word of this to any soul."

Livia hesitated. "Even my sister?"

"Even thy sister."

She'd never had a secret from Rosaline in her life.

Rosaline, who had planned for God knew how long to leave Livia behind. Rosaline had no problem keeping secrets from Livia.

"I swear," said Livia.

"I thank you, mistress, but we need no beets."

Rosaline was growing desperate. Though the cottage she and Livia shared was tucked at the rear of her aunt's estate, the persistent vegetable seller encamped on her doorstep had rather a carrying voice, and Rosaline worried she would wake her aunt's household. Where the devil was Livia? Though the sun was scarcely up, her sister, hardly an early riser by habit, was nowhere to be found. Two nights ago she had come home late from House Capulet, and when Rosaline asked her how things went with their uncle, she had mumbled something about how he was too busy to see her, and gone off to bed. The following morning she vanished once more on some vague errand and was gone all day. And when Rosaline woke this morning, Livia was gone yet again. There was a nearly illegible note on the kitchen table in Livia's hasty scrawl that explained that she'd gone to nurse their aunt Capulet, to give the duchess a respite. This seemed slightly improbable, since Livia had never before shown any interest in the comfort of either their aunt Capulet or great-aunt the duchess. Rosaline supposed she was being punished for her plan to take holy orders. She hoped Livia stopped sulking soon. She missed her.

"Come, mistress," the old woman called from deep inside her cloak. "If you'll none of my fine beets, then some fat lovely turnips for your house, sweet mistress?" She waved the aforementioned vegetable up toward Rosaline.

Oh for the love of heaven. "Very well," Rosaline sighed. "We'll buy some turnips, then."

The woman and her turnips bobbed her a curtsy. "And wise you are to do it, lady," she said. "'Twould be foolishness itself to refuse turnips pressed upon you by royal decree."

Rosaline blinked. "By royal . . . ?"

The cloak looked left, then right. The city was still awakening; no one else was to be seen on Rosaline's street. Just for a moment, the woman pushed back her hood. Rosaline's eyes went wide. Instead of an old peasant woman, the turnip seller revealed herself to be a grinning young lady, her head wrapped in golden braids.

"Isabella?"

"The same. *Now* will you have some turnips?"

Rosaline slammed the shutters closed, then leaned against them, a hand to her mouth. Since her marriage to the Prince of Arragon, Isabella was at least as grand in stature as her brother; what was she doing here alone, and in that absurd garb?

Rosaline's shoulders began to shake with laughter. She grinned into her hand. Then again, why should she have expected Isabella to suddenly stop doing exactly as she liked once she was married to a prince of her own?

Regardless, she could hardly leave the Princess of Arragon outside with a turnip cart. Her quarantine would have to be breached.

She found herself flying eagerly toward the door. If Escalus was using his sister to get to her, at least she would be able to see her friend. When she opened the door a crack, Isabella pushed it wide, bringing both herself and her turnip cart into Rosaline's front hall.

"You'll not need to buy vegetables for some time," she said. "They really are very nice turnips. Have the cart as well."

Rosaline shook her head in disbelief. "What in the world are you doing here?" Belatedly remembering her manners, she added, "Your Grace." She sank into a curtsy. "Things have . . . changed since you left Verona, you know. My family does not move in royal circles. You ought not to be seen here." Isabella had gone away to be fostered in Sicilia around the time Rosaline's father died; still, someone in the castle would have told her of the change in Tirimo fortunes.

"True, you're quite poor." Isabella tugged at her cloak cheerfully. "'Tis why I came as a turnip seller, you see. No one much cares whom they speak with." She eyed Rosaline. "And what else was I to do, pray? They told me my oldest friend was too sick to leave her house and come and see me. Though thou look'st well enough to me. Is there some new plague sweeping Verona that alloweth the afflicted the strength to lean out the window haggling for vegetables?"

Rosaline could not meet her old friend's gaze. It had been no hardship to ignore her uncle's many summons, but refusing Isabella's invitations had hurt much more. "I'm feeling better," she offered weakly.

"Hmm."

Rosaline sighed. "Please, Your Grace, come in and sit down, and I shall bring you something to eat. A turnip, perhaps? I find we have quite a few at the moment."

They retired to the drawing room, the only part of the house that was remotely suitable for guests. Rosaline had furnished their rooms out of her small income, and though everything was clean and respectable, it was nothing to the finery they'd once had. Normally she did not mind living simply, but she had never expected to entertain royalty here. Rosaline hoped Isabella would not note the holes in the upholstery, nor how faded the curtains were.

"Your curtains are awfully ugly," Isabella said. "Shall I send you some from the palace? Escalus would never miss them; he never goes anywhere but his chamber and his study."

Rosaline laughed. Indeed, Isabella was as she ever was— perfectly honest, but so free of malice that it was impossible to take offense. Rosaline ought to be quite awed by her friend now, but Isabella was so much the same that it was all too easy to slip into their childhood familiarity. "I thank thee, but we shall manage. Royal turnips are enough unlooked-for honor for our humble house."

"Aye, I warrant thou wouldst know why the turnips and I are here." Isabella waved a note under her nose. Rosaline recognized her own writing. Isabella read, " 'The ladies of House Tirimo are honored by the invitation by His Grace. Rosaline regrets that she is unable to attend the feast in honor of Princess Isabella on August the ninth, but Livia shall appear with pleasure.' "

Rosaline winced. Isabella's sharp eyes were trained on her face. "Have I given some offense, Rosaline? Why refuse my invitation? I can see thou art as healthy as I am."

Rosaline turned her face away. "Your brother told you not?"

"Thou knowest well how pompous he can be. If Escalus knew I was here, think'st thou he'd have allowed me to set foot outside without my proper retinue? Nay, and what has he to do with thy self-imposed solitude?"

"I pray you, do not press me on this subject. 'Tis a matter I prefer to speak not of."

"Very well, but prithee, reconsider." Isabella shifted and stretched. "The feast is tonight. And since I leave for Padua at dawn on the morrow, I had to come and see thee today to beg thee to come."

"Padua? Wherefore? And why leave so soon?"

"My husband Don Pedro was to join me here, but the obstinate fellow sends word he plans to remain in Padua some weeks—his friend Sir Benedick wishes to make him godfather to his child." Isabella sighed. "And hence I must leave my girlhood home for Padua and my royal husband's friends, who are ever spying on one another in the bushes."

Isabella's tone was as light and mocking as ever, but her eyes softened when she spoke of Don Pedro. They were wed less than two years—Verona gossip had only the bare bones of the tale, for their princess's courtship had taken place in a distant city. Don Pedro had met and wooed Isabella in Sicilia, where she was living with the king and his family. Winning her heart had taken two weeks. Waiting for Escalus to visit Sicilia and give his permission had taken another three months. When Escalus sent his leave, Don Pedro wed her and carried her off to his lands. It was strange to see her old friend that way. Isabella was a married woman. Rosaline had never quite realized that before. Isabella had a husband, and a new life far from Verona.

Before she could think it through, Rosaline blurted, "Take me with you."

"What?"

Rosaline's heart was beating hard. She had been praying for an escape from this trap. At last she spied a way out. If she and Livia fled the city with the Princess of Arragon, surely Prince Escalus would let them go rather than demand their return and perhaps give offense to an allied sovereign. "I could be your lady-in-waiting, as my mother was to yours. Livia too. Forgive my forwardness, Your Majesty, but we would serve you well."

"Of course I should love to have you both," Isabella said. "But your home is here. Your family."

"We shall survive the loss," Rosaline said firmly.

Isabella frowned. "I know you two have come down in the world, but you've still your Capulet connections, and you are both great beauties besides. And 'tis certain my brother will help you, if you've need of it."

Rosaline laughed. "Oh yes, 'tis quite certain. Still, I would go with you."

Isabella gripped her hand. "Rosaline, what trouble dost thou face, that thou wouldst so quickly leave all that thou knowest?"

She opened her mouth to admit the truth, but even Isabella's sauciness would not allow her to directly cross her brother. Rosaline closed her mouth again and shook her head.

"Very well," Isabella said slowly. "If thou art certain this mysterious strife will not follow thee to my new kingdom, meet me at the city's east gates at dawn tomorrow."

Rosaline released a shaky breath. "Oh, thank you! Your Majesty, a thousand thanks."

"Of course." Isabella stood. "And now I must return to the palace, before my brother wonders where I have gone. I am sorry for the shortness of my visit."

"Do not trouble yourself," Rosaline said. "I shall need the morning, anyway, to find a gown for your feast tonight."

"Oh, aye? I thought thou wouldst not come."

Rosaline smiled. "I suddenly feel like dancing."

In Paris's room, the torches were burnt down.

Livia coughed as she let their smoky glow guide her toward Paris's bed. She'd spent the entire evening here after discovering him, and much of the following day, but no amount of time by his side could ever be enough. She'd awoken before dawn today, and lay awake until it was a decent hour to leave the house, staring at the ceiling but seeing his flushed cheeks and long fingers twisting in hers, entreating. He was still delirious—what if he woke and recovered enough to leave before he'd met her properly? Worse, what if he died? If she could, she would have spent every hour by his side, but of course she could not do that without telling Rosaline the truth. Finally, she was able to rise and run to House Capulet. Unfortunately, her Paris was asleep. She took comfort in seeing that his wound was much better, though. She believed he would live.

His shallow, wheezing breath echoed through the small chamber. "Aunt," Livia whispered. "Can we not extinguish these torches? I am sure the smoke does him no good."

"We have tried," her aunt replied. "The torches must remain."

"But why?"

Her aunt gave her a sad smile. "I shall show thee. Go and sit with him."

Puzzled, Livia went and sat on the side of Paris's bed. He was still in a fitful but deep slumber. Her aunt walked to the corner of the room and took one of the torches from its bracket, plunging it into a bucket of water. There was another torch in the room, but instantly the shadows deepened.

"No—no!"

Livia gasped at Paris's hoarse cry. He shot upward, his skin tense and hot when she laid a hand on his shoulder.

"There, there, good sir—"

"Light," he begged her, eyes boring into hers as he seized her arm. "Please, *please,* light."

"'Tis but a burnt-out torch, there is still light—"

His nails dug into her skin. "I am County Paris of Petrimio, brother to Sir Claudio, nephew to old Count Anselmo, kin to His Grace the Prince, husband to she who slumbers in this tomb, fair Juliet—"

"I know, I know who you are, shh—"

"Let not the torches burn out! Tell them where I lie bleeding! Leave me not in the dark!"

His voice had risen to a near scream, and Livia herself was almost crying as she tried in vain to soothe him. Oh, her poor sweet Paris.

Behind her, light bloomed. Lady Capulet had lit a fresh torch. "There, you see?" Livia whispered. "You're here. You're safe."

Paris's eyes flitted about the room in confusion. His hands loosened their grip on her and she laid a soothing palm along his cheek, brushing back his hair.

He looked at her in confusion. "I—I—" He half reached toward her face. "Lady, who are you?"

Before she could answer, his breathing began to ease, and his eyes slipped shut. Livia gently laid his outstretched hand on his chest as he fell once more to sleep. Livia's aunt put a hand on her shoulder. "He'll sleep now," she said. "Come, let him rest."

The corridor was cool after the stuffy sickroom. Lady Capulet walked to one of the windows and drew the curtains a little. The sun was rising over Verona's walls, beginning to tint the gray predawn stone a rosy hue. Livia watched her aunt in profile as she drew in a deep breath of cool fresh air, the breeze combing her dark hair back from her face. With her hair loose, in the simple gown she'd donned for the sickroom, Lady Capulet looked very like her daughter. Livia had the odd sensation that she *was* looking at Juliet—the Juliet who could have been, had she lived to adulthood. No wonder Paris so often confused them.

"'Tis ever so," her aunt said, breaking the silence. "He must have light, even as he sleeps, or he thinks he's once more lying before Juliet's tomb, dying unregarded."

Livia shivered. "Why did no one help him?"

"He was so grievously wounded they thought he'd been slain." Lady Capulet passed a weary hand over her brow. "I was the last to leave Juliet's tomb, and 'twas then I heard his moans." She gave Livia a tired smile, squeezing her shoulder. "In any case, thou knowest now why the torches must stay lit. I must to bed—he'll wake soon and need me."

But Livia was not about to let this talkative mood of her aunt's pass without taking advantage. "But the torches need not stay lit if we open the curtains. Aunt, why do you shroud his recovery in such secrecy? All Verona would rejoice to find he lived."

Lady Capulet laughed. "Would they? Oh, child, how little thou knowest this feud of ours. Think'st thou they would let him live in peace?"

"Who?"

She shrugged. "Montagues? Capulets? Whoever chose to

make an enemy of him. He's a part of it now. I cannot take the chance. Poor soul, our families have done enough to him."

"But Paris is neither Montague nor Capulet."

"Nor was Mercutio," she pointed out. "Nor was thy father."

"You can't keep him here forever. When he recovers, the city will have to know."

"If he likes," Lady Capulet said, smiling.

"And if he does not?"

Her aunt turned to look at her. Her eyes searched Livia's face. "You will not tell a soul?" she whispered. "Swear, niece. All is lost if you tell."

"What is it?"

Her aunt's gaze strayed back to the window. "When I wed Lord Capulet," she said, "my father showered us with gifts. But one he gave to me only. A small and distant estate." A fond smile touched her lips. "So small and so distant that my lord has quite forgotten it exists, but for all that it's rich and beauteous." Her hand gripped Livia's. "When Paris is recovered, I intend to go there, and remove from Verona forever."

Livia felt as though her eyes might pop out of her head. Fleeing her husband and her home, refusing to return? Women sometimes did such things—adulteresses, outcasts, those who'd fallen so far in Verona's esteem they might as well abandon it—but not the matriarch of the Capulets. It would be the greatest scandal the city had seen. Ah, but then it dawned on her. Lady Capulet had already removed herself from the public eye. All Verona knew she'd been bedridden with grief for weeks—none would be surprised, even her neglectful husband, if she left the city to recover in her childhood home. And none would be surprised when word returned that she had died there. Who would ever come to see if it was true?

"You mean to die yourself."

"Thy wits are quick, dear niece." Lady Capulet gave her a sad smile. "And Sir Paris's lands are many, near and far. If he wishes, he shall vanish too, without Verona ever knowing that he yet lives. I owe him such, after his love for my daughter brought him to such disaster."

Livia felt a great wave of pity for her aunt. What must it be like, to go from being one of the greatest ladies of Verona society to someone who'd lost so much she could depart nearly unnoticed? But surely, this was too much. "Aunt, the feud is over," Livia said gently. "The prince, my uncle, and Lord Montague have all sworn it. I do not think noble Paris will want to abandon his home. Surely the prince would protect his kinsman from any further peril."

Her aunt gave her that tired, sad smile. "There is more evil that walks this city than you see."

"I've done as you have asked. She'll come tonight."

Escalus smiled. "Good. A thousand thanks for persuading her, Isabella."

His sister threw him an irritated glance as she shook out the rough peasant cloak she'd reappeared in. Clods of dried mud from the hem littered the floor of his study. Penlet would not be best pleased with him. Which, he suspected, was why she'd done it. Isabella was not best pleased herself. "She required little persuasion, once I granted her a small boon."

"What boon was that?"

"None of your affair. She asked me not to tell you." Isabella stared at him, hands on hips. "Just as you ordered me not to tell *her* that you'd sent me there. What is afoot, Escalus? Rosaline is frightened, properly frightened, and it seems to have something to do with you."

"I answer not to you, foreign princess. My subjects are mine own affair."

"Oh, that way goes the game, does it? Thou hast grown hard, brother. Rosaline adores thee, thou knowest. I used to hope—" She shook her head.

"Hope what?"

His sister shook her head again. "'Tis nothing."

"Nay, speak. You've my leave to speak your mind."

"Oh, have I?" She gave him a mocking curtsy. "Your lordship is all kindness to this poor foreign princess."

"Isabella, please. I've much to do, so if you've something to say about the Capulet maid, pray do so."

The look she gave him reminded him of their mother when he'd failed once again to use the correct fork at dinner. "Escalus! Have you truly never noticed how much that 'Capulet maid' occupies your thoughts?"

"What? I've scarce spoken to her since we were children."

"And yet every letter you have ever sent me since mentions

her name. *'I hear your young friend Rosaline has gone to live with the Duchess of Vitruvio.' 'They tell me your young friend Rosaline has several suitors, though she is betrothed to none.' 'Your young friend Rosaline was at the feast last night, and she looked very well.'*"

She was making him uneasy. He felt exposed, as though she'd caught him in a lie. "I never even spoke to her at that feast."

"Which makes it all the more remarkable that your eyes, it seems, never left her."

"You speak nonsense," he said, and even to himself he sounded stiff, pompous, their father come to life again. "I wished merely to give you some news of those you'd left behind. Such I deemed my duty."

"Duty? Is that all?"

"Of course. She's but a lowly member of her family. I could have no other reason to notice her. She had no way to be of service to the Crown."

"Then why do you notice her now? What service is she to do?"

He said nothing.

"Oh, Escalus." Isabella sighed. "Just promise me thou wilt not hurt her."

Escalus steepled his hands in front of his face, looking daggers at his sister over his fingertips.

She held up her hands. "I am sorry. Of course you'd never harm our oldest friend."

Escalus swallowed. "Go and dress for the ball."

Isabella nodded and took her leave before she could force him to make a promise he already knew he would not keep.

The palace walls pressed in on Rosaline.

Her heart raced as she waited outside the great hall. Her palms were sweating. She resisted the urge to wipe them on her red silk dress. It was far too plain for this season's fashion; no need to stain it too.

Behind her, she could hear whispers and giggles from the other ladies in the receiving line. She was sure their titterings were aimed at her—Verona society did not know the truth behind her would-be betrothal, but their nose for gossip was keen enough to be sure *something* was behind the eldest Tirimo's becoming a recluse. She stood straight and tall, Livia at her side, refusing to turn around and look. Instead she stared straight ahead at the immense oak doors that would bring her into the prince's feast.

She had spent the morning packing. Not everything—she did not want to cause enough of a commotion to draw the attention of her great-aunt's household—but just enough for her and Livia to make a new start. She would wait to tell Livia of her plan until after the ball, since her sister could not keep a secret. Luckily, Livia had been gone most of the day. Apparently, she really had gone to House Capulet to tend to their aunt. Why Livia would do such a thing Rosaline was not sure, but since it kept her out from underfoot, Rosaline chose not to question it. And now all was in readiness. This would be their last glimpse of Verona society. The prince would not dare to make marriage demands of her before all Verona. And if Isabella had kept her word and not mentioned Rosaline's plans to her brother, these candlelit hours would be the last she'd ever see of him. She was already free.

So why did the back of her neck still prickle with unease?

Beside her, Livia preened, oblivious to her distress. The duchess was waiting just in front of them, and turned to give them a glance.

"Hmph," she said, before sweeping through the doors, which Rosaline took to be a grudging approval that her nieces' appearance would not disgrace her. For the thousandth time Rosaline reluctantly blessed the absent tenant who so generously rented their house. His steward had just sent a pouch of gold for another year, so in a rare fit of extravagance, Rosaline had had a new dress made for Livia, and her sister was in heaven. The delicate blue and cream concoction was the latest fashion, from the embroidered collar to the beaded hem, and Livia looked like an angel in it. An effect that was rather spoiled once she opened her mouth.

"Look at Lady Millamet," she whispered in Rosaline's ear. "See how she stares daggers at me? Well, 'tis not my fault our dresses are the same color. Perhaps I shall push her into a wine barrel. Then we will have quite different hues."

Rosaline smothered a smile. The ball had thrown Livia into a frenzy of excitement. Attending was worth it if only to see her sister so happy. "Lady Millamet is unlikely to fit in a wine barrel," she whispered to Livia.

"True," Livia reflected. "She is quite fat. Oh! It's us."

As they reached the doors, Rosaline took a deep breath. Too late to turn back now.

The Great Hall was a blaze of light. Every lamp was lit; every chandelier glowing. Livia and Rosaline were two of the last to arrive, and as the butler's voice boomed, "Lady Rosaline of House Tirimo and her sister, Livia," it seemed to Rosaline that the face of every noble in Verona was turned toward them. To her right, Rosaline saw her uncle Capulet give her a scowl and a "Hmph" as she passed by. A cluster of Montagues stood near the prince's throne, Benvolio among them. Rosaline found her eyes locked on his cool dark ones as she wondered what he thought of her now. Was he relieved that she'd managed to break off their disastrous match? Or had her antics merely humiliated him?

A subtle tug at her elbow from Livia brought her attention back where it belonged. As they reached the end of the long red carpet, they came before the prince and his sister, enthroned side by side. Princess Isabella's polite smile became warmer as Livia and Rosaline sank into deep curtsies before them. The prince looked on coolly. But as Rosaline rose to her feet, he too allowed them a smile. "Welcome, ladies," he said. "We cannot tell you the joy we feel to have you in our house."

Rosaline released a breath she didn't know she'd been holding. Perhaps this evening really would be all right.

Tomorrow it would be three weeks since Romeo's and Juliet's deaths. Tonight was the first major social event since the summer tragedies, and the relief of the city's nobles at a chance to take off their mourning clothes and be merry again was palpable. The evening soon dissolved into a whirl of dancing, wine, and gossip. Rosaline tried to stay clear of the latter, as she was sure she was the subject of much of it (she half overheard Lady Millamet whisper something nasty). She had no interest in satisfying Verona's curiosity about the goings-on at House Tirimo.

Instead, she danced until she was out of breath, drank chilled white wine, stole a few minutes to speak with Isabella of their plans for the morning, and kept an eye on Livia— although, in fact, Livia seemed to be behaving herself. Normally she was a scandalous flirt, but tonight, though Rosaline watched her laugh and tease a succession of boys, she was no worse than the other young ladies. It seemed her heart was not in it. Odd.

So distracted was she by Livia's unheard-of decorum that she failed to notice that Orlino was drawing near to her side until the steps of the dance had landed her in his clutches. She tried not to wince as the young Montague's fingers dug into the fabric at her waist. His handsome face was still marred with an angry red cut.

"Good e'en," Rosaline said coolly. "Your face is healing, I see."

He smirked. "Ah yes. Your champion's handiwork." He leaned closer, his hot hideous breath brushing her face. "How did you repay him for his service after he left? I can think of but one way a Capulet wanton could turn a brave man of Montague against his own kin. Didst thou thank him upon thy knees atop his cousin's grave?"

Rosaline gasped and tried to pull away, but his painful grip on her stayed firm as he whirled her about the dance floor. "Orlino, only you would think that bare courtesy needs to be bought so dear," she hissed. "Now, let me *go*."

"Ah, but the eyes of every Montague and Capulet are on us, dear kinswoman," he said. "We must finish our dance so the world may see what a happy family we are now." His fingernails, she was sure, were about to break the skin of her hand. But 'twas true, she could feel the hard stares from her cousins and his. She would simply have to wait till the dance was over to escape him. No matter what poison he poured in her ear.

"May I?"

Orlino stopped. In their path stood Benvolio.

"My apologies, dearest cousin," he said to Orlino, loudly enough for the crowd to hear. "My friend Rosaline promised me a dance. I am sure you will not mind if I collect it now." He extended a hand, and Rosaline, after extracting her fingers from Orlino's talons, took it. "Thank you, lady. Orlino, our uncle Montague would speak with you." He gestured with his head to where Lord Montague waited, arms crossed. Before Orlino could respond, Benvolio had swept her away in his arms.

Rosaline felt the tension at her neck ease slightly. Benvolio was a much better dancer than his cousin, his hand feather-light at her waist as he guided her gently through the steps. Of course, anyone who did not view dance as a sort of weapon would be better than Orlino.

"It seems I've rescued you again, lady," he said, his dark

eyes locked on hers. Orlino's cruelty might be absent from Benvolio's face, but there was no kindness there either.

Rosaline gave him a mocking smile. "And for that you've my gratitude, as usual, my lord," she said. "Of course, I've rescued you as well. Am I not owed thanks?"

His eyes narrowed. "Rescued me? From what?"

She raised an eyebrow.

Understanding appeared in his face. "You mean—" He leaned in closer so he could speak in her ear, below the hearing of the crowd. "You mean our betrothal?"

"Our attempted betrothal. The prince shall trouble us no more."

He chuckled softly near her ear. "If you've managed to save me from the terrible spectre of yourself, you've my gratitude indeed, lady." Rosaline resisted the unholy urge to tread on his foot. "Indeed, not having to marry you would be the greatest boon anyone has ever done me—"

To hell with resistance. She gave him a healthy stamp. He jumped. "But art thou so sure of your triumph, Rosaline?"

She pulled back to frown at him. "What do you mean? I'm here, am I not? Think you that I would show my face without my house were there any chance of this forced union going forward?"

"I am quite prepared to believe that a lady as curst as thee would happily stay within her walls until she died a withered crone. I meant merely that if you think our prince so easily defeated, you have underestimated him."

The dance came to an end and Benvolio pulled away to

bow to her. As he did so, there came an attention-seeking little cough next to them.

"Pardon, Signor Benvolio," Chancellor Penlet said. "Lady, the prince would speak to you."

"Of course." Benvolio lifted her hand to kiss it in farewell, and gave her an *I told you so* look over her knuckles.

Churl. Rosaline retrieved her hand and followed Penlet across the hall to where the prince was surrounded by a knot of nobles and flatterers. When he spied her, he waved them off with a flip of his hand so she could make her way to his side. "Ah, Lady Rosaline," he said. "Your beauty graces our house. Gentlemen, if you'll excuse us, my lady and I have matters to discuss." With that, he took her arm and led her away.

A hush fell in their wake as the crowd saw the prince offer his arm to a shabby little half-Capulet. Rosaline's nervousness grew as she realized he was drawing her not to some quiet corner of the ballroom, but out of the Great Hall altogether, toward his private study. "Your Grace?" she whispered. "Perhaps we ought not—"

Escalus merely drew her arm tighter around his. "Peace, Rosaline. We'll not cause a scandal. I promise."

Rosaline swallowed. In truth, it was not unheard of for the prince to draw this noble or that aside for a private word during a ball—but said noble was normally not an unmarried young girl. Uneasy as she was, though, she could hardly refuse her sovereign in front of all Verona. And no matter how they had quarreled, she still knew Prince Escalus was an honorable man. Surely he would not do anything that would besmirch her honor. A few minutes couldn't hurt.

Besides, the touch of his arm at her elbow had kindled a shy, fluttering warmth in her belly. Even if she should, she did not want to draw away.

As they drew near the top of the staircase, the crowd's hush was broken by a sudden commotion in the back. A loud crash was followed by a female voice calling, "Oh, Lady *Millamet*, you *fell*, you poor thing, let me *help* you. . . ."

The prince craned his neck back to see what was going on. "What in the world was that?"

Rosaline, for her part, had no need to look. "Lady Millamet being pushed in a barrel of wine," she said. "Shall we?" Escaping the ballroom had suddenly become much more attractive.

The air in Prince Escalus's study was cool and quiet after the press of bodies in the Great Hall. Lamps hung around the walls, but when the prince released her arm, he lit only one, leaving the room filled with ruddy light and black shadows. He took a bottle of wine from the cupboard and poured himself a glass and, without asking, one for her as well. Rosaline took a polite sip, though she'd already had as much wine this night as she thought wise.

Escalus drew her down to sit on a chaise by the window. He leaned easily against the arm; she sat so straight her spine ached. With a deep breath, she said, "My lord, I hope you do not take my attendance here tonight as a sign that I have changed my mind. I assure you, I am as adamant as—"

He laughed at her. "*Peace,* my lady Thorn, for God's sake."

He took her hand when she tried to rise, pulling her back down. "Did you never imagine that I might have invited you here to ask your forgiveness? That I might truly hate forcing such a dear friend as you to marry against her will?"

He had not let go of her hand. Between that and the wine, she was having trouble thinking. "*Trying* to force me to marry, Your Grace. You've not succeeded."

"Of course." He leaned back, gazing at her with a warm, lazy smile she had not seen on his face since he took the throne. His eyes, however, were as sharp as always. "Isabella said to give thee her regards, by the way. She regrets she had not more time to speak with thee tonight, but she had to retire early, since she is to leave in the morn."

Rosaline smiled. She and Isabella would have plenty of time to speak on the way to Arragon. Escalus was staring at her glass, so she took another sip. "'Twas wonderful to see her tonight. If only because you had to stop tormenting me while we were all in the same room. I am sure that had she learned what you are about, she would shave your stallion's mane again."

"Ah, so that *was* she. She always denied it."

Ought she to admit it? The bravery of two glasses of wine said yes. "Well—not she alone. I had a hand in it."

"You too?" Escalus shook his head. "Trouble even in the nursery. And you looked so innocent. I should have known."

"You deserved it," she said. "You were forever pulling our hair."

He threw his head back and laughed. "So I was. Well, were there more in this tiny conspiracy? Or just you two?"

"Oh, no, just me and Isabella," she said. "The little girls were far too in awe of you."

He sighed. "Well. Juliet, at least, learned to flout my will."

"Aye. I would she had not, poor wretch."

Silence fell. Through his open window, laughter and music drifted up from the party below.

Rosaline tried again to rise. Again, he pulled her down, holding one of her hands in both of his. His smile was gone now; his gaze lost somewhere in the darkness. "Sit thou with me, Rosaline," he said. "Just—sit with me awhile. Be not afraid of your old friend."

She returned to her place. "Very well, Your Grace," she said. "Just for a moment." He said nothing else, but refilled her wine glass.

Livia was growing rather bored.

Now that the grand feast was nearly over, she was no longer sure what it was she had been so looking forward to. Her feet aching from dancing, she slipped outside to wait for Rosaline to reappear from wherever she'd got to. Livia was ready to go home.

She smothered a yawn, nodding and smiling to the stream of nobles leaving the feast. Their aunt had long since returned to her house, leaving Livia with a few coins to hire a carriage. Thus discharging her financial duty to her nieces for the summer, Livia supposed. *Good,* Rosaline would say.

We've no need of her help. The less we are under the Capulet thumb, the better.

Livia wondered, occasionally, if the Capulets' neglect of them was really as much of a snub as Rosaline believed, or if it was also a response to Rosaline's own fierce independence. Rosaline might not need the Capulets, but Livia was not sure what she needed. Certainly Lady Capulet had been nothing but kind to her these past two days that she'd helped to nurse Sir Paris.

She'd been surprised tonight at how often her thoughts returned to him. She had always loved feasts—dancing and flirting and fashion, and the notion that she could at any moment meet her one true love and be swept away to a life of riches and ease.

But now it all seemed so frivolous. Livia heartily approved of frivolity as a rule, but spending the last few days trying to save a dying man took some of the joy out of fancy clothes. She could not smell the ladies' perfume without remembering the scents of the sickroom. And her handsome young dance partners only called to mind the heat of Paris's cheek against her fingers as his feverish eyes burnt into hers.

She sighed at the remembered romance of the moment. What was a dance compared to *that*?

Rosaline had made her promise to meet here when the clock struck midnight—she said they had an early morning on the morrow, but she would not say why. And now it was nearly one and Rosaline was nowhere to be found. The stream of guests leaving the Great Hall had slowed to a trickle

111

before Livia realized that Rosaline wasn't coming out. She must have gone home without her. Oh, spite.

"Another Capulet harlot," a voice slurred behind her. "Waiting for thy strumpet of a sister?"

Livia turned to find a young man with a jagged scab across one cheek. This must be he who'd attacked Rosaline. "Indeed no, Orlino," she said. "I wait for a physician to sew up that ugly hole in your face. But I fear that if he mends the ugliest one, 'twill leave you unable to speak."

Orlino's face darkened with drunken fury. "You little shrew!" He raised an arm. Livia took a step back, heart pounding. Would he really strike her on the very steps of the prince's palace?

"Let her be, Orlino!"

Livia looked to her left. Her cousin Gramio was there, hand on his sword, glaring at Orlino. To her right stood Lucio and Valentine, two more young Capulet kinsmen. "Leave her alone," Gramio repeated. "Get thee gone. And the next time you speak a word of discourtesy to one of our kinswomen, 'twill be your hide."

Orlino barked a laugh at that, but he was clearly outnumbered. With an obscene bite of his thumb at Livia, he turned and ran off into the night. Young Lucio made to pursue him, but Gramio seized his arm.

"There's naught to be done so near the prince's palace. We'll see to him anon." He gave Livia a smile. "For now, let us see our sweet cousin home."

Livia's cousins had not taken such notice of her in years. Apparently all it took to be valued as a Capulet was to be threatened by a Montague. She allowed Gramio to help her into their carriage, but when they set off, the thought of going home to her dark house was suddenly frightening. "Would you take me to our great house, please?" she asked. "I shall spend the night with my aunt Capulet." Rosaline had slipped off without her, after all. Let her sit at home and worry about Livia in turn. She would spend the night at Paris's side.

Rosaline, the prince realized, was drunk.

That had not, strictly speaking, been his intention. But he'd simply had to distract her somehow, so that she would not insist on returning to the ball. The maid had a very overdeveloped sense of honor.

The danger of her departure was quite past. The stiff, cold woman of two hours ago had melted once he'd poured a bottle of wine into her. She was now ensconced on his chaise, giggling into the arm, feet tucked beneath her. Her curls had come unpinned, and they tumbled over her shoulder.

A knock on the door was quickly followed by a cough before it opened to reveal Penlet. His eyes widened when he saw Rosaline, but if he had any opinion of the scene before him, his years of service kept him from revealing it.

"Your Grace, your guests have all departed," he reported. "Your sister is abed. Shall I arrange a carriage for the—ah—" His eyes landed on Rosaline. "The young lady?"

"That shall not be needed. Thanks and good night, good

Penlet. That will be all." Escalus ushered him out, ignoring the disapproval emanating from the prim little man, and shut the door behind him.

When he turned back, Rosaline had risen from the chaise. Most of the musicians had left, but a lone lute was still picking out a melancholy air. The song drifted up through the open window, and Rosaline stood before it, dancing in the moonlight.

Escalus caught his breath. He knew, of course, that Isabella's little friend had grown into a woman. But it was only now as she twirled, humming to herself, that he truly realized how lovely she'd become. Curls loose and wild, skin silvered by the moon—she was a captivating creature.

When she caught him looking, Rosaline smiled and extended a hand, and before he knew it she'd drawn him into her dance.

His feet followed the familiar steps as his eyes locked on hers. "I did not think thou wouldst grace me with a dance, lady."

Her eyes were soft now. "'Tis lucky thou art to have it, scoundrel that thou art."

"Scoundrel, am I?"

"Aye, 'tis the kindest word for thee, for thou didst break a young lady's heart most grievously." She twirled away before turning back into his arms. "Mine own, when I was seven. Never did a lady weep harder for a lost lover than I did when thou didst go away to study."

He laughed. Her hair smelled of something sweet and

springlike. Escalus wished he could pull her closer. "Thy pardon, dear playfellow. I never knew thy little heart was mine to break."

"Oh, it was," she said. Gaze catching his, she whispered, "It is still."

Escalus's eyes widened. "Rosaline—"

She kissed him.

Since the moment Escalus took Verona's throne, practically every waking thought had been devoted to the care of his city. Even momentary pleasures, like riding Venitio, he only permitted himself so that he could attack his work with more vigor afterward. God knew Verona required all he had to give. But this was the first moment in memory when he realized just what he had given up.

Brawling families, aggressive neighboring cities, the thousand headaches Penlet brought him daily—all of it melted away, leaving nothing but the press of her lips and the warmth of her body and her arms winding round his neck. He knew she was drunk, he knew he was being dishonorable, and, God, he knew what he was going to do to her on the morrow—but still, Escalus found himself wrapping her in his arms, and, just for a moment, pulling her closer.

It was over as soon as it was begun. Rosaline pulled back, and "Oh," she said. "Oh, I do not think I can stand anymore."

He steadied her swaying body. "That is because you are drunk, lady."

She blinked at him. "Oh."

With a sigh, he tucked her against his side and helped her

carefully up the stairs to his bedchamber. True to her word, she could not keep to her feet, and Escalus had to scoop her up and carry her.

As he laid her in bed, her eyes were already drooping shut. Escalus brushed a few stray curls from her cheek before stepping away. He would pass the night on the chaise downstairs. But first, he spent a few moments watching her as she slipped into a deep, trusting sleep.

When she woke, he would shatter that trust forever.

Livia slipped into Paris's room.

She'd hoped for a few minutes alone with him, given the lateness of the hour, but as usual, her aunt was by his side. Her dark, glossy head was bent over his, murmuring something to him as her long, pale fingers stroked soothing patterns over his arm.

She looked up at the door's creak. "Niece," she said, not looking best pleased to see Livia. "Why art thou here so late? I thought thee at the ball."

"'Tis done," Livia said, pulling up a seat next to Paris's bed. "'Tis past midnight. You ought to go to your bed, Aunt. As for me, a horrid Montague has given me such a fright that I shall have no sleep."

Paris started at the sound of her voice and tried to sit up. "Montague? What—"

"Peace, gentle Paris." Lady Capulet's hand pressed him

back into the bed. "Livia, what have the Montagues done this night?"

Livia helped change Paris's bandages as she related Orlino's offense, and the bravery of Gramio and her cousins, noting as she did so that his wound looked much better. His skin had lost its feverish heat, thanks to her care. He would soon be on his feet again.

"Gramio is a coward," her aunt said. "He ought to have run that scoundrel through."

Livia frowned, smoothing the edge of the bandage on Paris's chest with her thumb. "The prince would have arrested him."

"He should have done it in any case," Paris's hoarse voice said. "'Tis no worse than Orlino deserves." He seized Livia's hand, his eyes burning into hers. "When I am well again, Lady Livia, your honor shall be better defended. I swear it."

Lady Capulet gasped. "He knows thee!" she whispered. "Oh, sweet Paris, thy wits return at last."

Livia clutched his hand, and smiled. Out of the corner of her eye, she saw her aunt smile too.

The morning sunlight sliced through Rosaline's eyes.

With a groan, she rolled over. The sun had never seemed quite so painful to her closed lids before. Why was it so bright? And what was the matter with her blanket? It didn't feel like hers at all—

Rosaline sat up. This wasn't her room. This wasn't her *house.*

She was still at the palace.

With a sinking stomach, Rosaline threw back the coverlet. She was relieved to find herself still fully clothed in her red silk gown, now quite wrinkled. What had happened? She remembered leaving the ball with the prince, and after that her memory began to falter. But they had not—surely, he would not—

"Good morrow, my lady."

She turned with a gasp. There, dressed for the day and quite composedly eating a piece of bread and butter, sat the prince.

"Set your heart at rest," he continued. "Your honor is quite intact. Not that the rest of the city is likely to believe that." He nudged a second slice in her direction. "Breakfast?"

Rosaline raised a shaking hand to her curls, finding them in hopeless disarray. "Esc—Your Grace, what happened?"

He looked at her over the rim of a steaming mug. "What has happened," he said, "is that I got you shamefully drunk and put you, quite chastely, to bed. Oh, I was a perfect gentleman, and you were the very picture of an honorable maiden— but Verona knows not that, do they? All they know is that you accompanied me to my private chambers. And that you were not seen to leave."

Rosaline swallowed. Women had been driven out of their families for less. A noblewoman's chastity was sacred. Even the hint of an indiscretion was enough to shame her forever.

What was worse, her shame would not only fall on her. No family would permit their son to marry Livia.

"My sister is long gone, by the way. 'Tis nearly ten o'clock. Very clever of you, trying to escape into her court, but her servants told mine that she was bringing two Verona sisters home with her, and it was not hard to guess whom they were. When I saw Isabella off I told her you had admitted all to me last night, that you had changed your mind about leaving Verona, and I sent her on her way. She shall miss you, but sends her love, and she is glad you have found some way of remaining in Verona."

"Oh God. Oh God." She buried her face in her hands. "We are ruined. Unless—" She looked up at Escalus. "You can save us. Please, my lord. You can, can—" She tried to stand, but a wave of nausea swept her back to the bed. "Tell the city—" What? That she had passed the night in his bed, drunk?

"I shall let it be known that you passed the night with my sister," Escalus said. "'Tis well known you are friends. 'Twill be believed."

He was right. That would work. Rosaline hated to lie, but for Livia, she would. "Thank you, Your Gra—"

"Or," he said, "I could say nothing. And let Verona think of you what it will."

An icy fist seemed to grip Rosaline's heart. Slowly, she sank back down to the edge of the bed. Suddenly this strange morning began to make a terrible kind of sense. "You planned this."

"Yes."

"What do you want?"

119

"You know what I want."

Rosaline laced her fingers together. She stared at her white knuckles and said not a word.

"I will tell your uncle this afternoon that you have agreed to wed Benvolio," her sovereign said. "In a fortnight, I will formally announce your betrothal before the city. Shortly thereafter, you will wed him. If you do this, I will save you and your sister from dishonor at your hands."

Rosaline pressed her eyes shut. In her mind, she could see the little dark-haired girl who had loved her prince with all her might—who had never quite stopped loving him.

When she opened her eyes, the little girl was gone for good.

Did Escalus see some of this in her face? Did he care? She thought he flinched when their eyes met, but before she could be sure, his cool, regal mask was back in place.

"As my sovereign commands," she said with a deep curtsy. *False-faced cur.*

Part 3

Knavery's plain face is never seen till us'd.

—*Othello*

$\mathcal{B}$ENVOLIO OF MONTAGUE. BETROTHED. He could scarcely believe it. He'd tried to prepare for it—he'd known that Rosaline's fit of temper would come to naught in the end, for what citizen of Verona, no matter how curst and shrewish, could flaunt the prince's will? But in spite of himself, the obstinate gleam in Rosaline's eye as they danced at the prince's ball had given him hope that she would succeed in destroying the match.

Now two weeks later they stood in the town square, before a crowd of merchants, nobles, and peasants. Benvolio wore his best doublet; at his side Rosaline was still as a statue in a pale green gown, white flowers in her hair. Beside her, looking no happier than she, was her great-aunt. The Duchess of Vitruvio stood straight and haughty, eyes scanning far out into the crowd, as if by ignoring everyone gathered on the dais for the betrothal, she could prevent it from happening. They were also flanked by their uncles, perhaps for appearance's sake, perhaps to ensure that they did not try to run. Benvolio could not speak for the lady, but he for one had certainly tried to calculate how quickly he could make it out the city gates. But unlike the Capulet shrew, he knew his duty. If the prince and his uncle said he must marry, marry he would.

". . . And so Rosaline, niece to Lord Capulet, shall wed Montague's heir, Benvolio," the prince was saying to the assemblage below them. "And their love shall kill their families' hate. Their wedding day two weeks hence shall be a feast day for all Verona."

A great cheer went up at that. Benvolio glanced at his bride. Rosaline looked fairer than ever, but her eyes were like two agate stones. *Their love.* Hah. If neither of them slew the other in their sleep, Benvolio would count his marriage a great success.

Rosaline's eyes met his for a moment, then slid away. Beside her, her great-aunt's jaw was clenched grimly. Then her eyes narrowed, fixed on the distant corner of the market square. Puzzled, Benvolio followed her gaze. At first he could not see what had drawn her eyes, but then he saw something stirring. Something was happening in the rear of the crowd. The cheers were giving way to shouts of confusion. As they surged forward, Benvolio could see what the commotion was about.

A cart with three passengers drove through the crowd. The driver, who wore a black mask over his face, struck the onlookers mercilessly with a whip till he could push his way through the square. As the cart drew near, Benvolio drew in a sharp breath. The other two passengers were actually dummies made of tarred rags, one in bridal white—cruel effigies, he realized, of himself and Rosaline.

"A wedding gift to bless this foul union!" the masked driver cried. He threw a torch down on the cart, which burst into flame, and then leapt out into the crowd. The square filled with cries of terror as the flames crackled across the wooden frame, engulfing the two effigies. The flaming figures melted toward each other in a ghastly embrace.

"Montague treachery! Seize him!" a voice called.

"Liar! To arms, Capulets!"

The prince raised his arms. "People of Verona—"

But the crowd, roiling with panic and rage, was beyond even the prince's ability to control. The smell of fire mingled with the stench of fear as they stampeded forward over the dais. Benvolio saw a flash of green and turned in time to see Rosaline fall beneath the racing feet of what was quickly becoming a riot. Shouldering his way through the press of bodies, he managed to pull her back to her feet, only to have her ripped from his side immediately.

As Benvolio turned, seeking her, he spied a black-clad figure disappearing onto a roof.

With a curse, he pushed his way to the edge of the square. How had the devil—he looked up. Ah. The stalls that lined the square were overshaded with cloth awnings. Seizing a corner over a fruit stall, Benvolio hauled himself up, using it to clamber onto the roof. Several buildings away, the man in black ran.

Benvolio pelted after him, his hands and knees soon covered in orange dust from scrambling over the steep slants of Verona's close-set rooftops. The man he chased was fleet of foot, but he was no match for Benvolio's determination.

When the man stumbled, Benvolio leapt across the alley and was upon him.

"Now," he panted, ignoring the man's muffled curses as he wrestled him over, "let us see what knave—"

He ripped the mask off. It was Orlino.

Benvolio growled. "Is there no end to your treachery, cousin?"

Orlino fought like a wild beast beneath him, pausing only to spit in his face. "No cousin of mine are you. You sully the name of Montague, you craven dog-hearted foot-licker!" A crazed grin appeared on Orlino's face. "'Tis why I agreed to give my aid."

Benvolio gave him a shake. "Aid to whom? Who guided you into this mischief, Orlino?"

But Orlino's struggles had crumbled the masonry beneath them, and suddenly they were sliding toward the edge of the roof. They were atop a church, and its steep roof offered nothing to stop their slide. Benvolio's feet scrambled for purchase. One crash sounded, then another, as the bits of masonry he'd broken fell to earth far beneath them. Orlino took advantage of Benvolio's imbalance to throw him off and gain a grip on his sword. Benvolio, clinging to the roof with both hands, could not reach his own. Orlino staggered to his feet, pointing his blade toward Benvolio.

A flash of green below him on the street was all he saw before something flew through the air and struck Orlino hard on the side of the head. Benvolio did not stop to wonder what it was. In the moment that it distracted his cousin, he managed to hook a foot in the eaves and hoist himself back onto the roof. Orlino tried to dance back out of his reach, but he'd forgotten how close the edge was. For a moment he seemed to hang suspended, eyes wide and locked with Benvolio's. Then he plunged out of sight and Benvolio shuddered as he heard him hit the ground in the alley below.

"B-Benvolio?"

Benvolio crawled toward the front of the roof. Below him on the street, white-faced, wide-eyed, and dirt-streaked, stood Rosaline. She wore only one shoe. That explained what had hit Orlino.

When she saw him, she waved, then disappeared from sight. Half a minute later, she reappeared when she opened the shutters to an upstairs window.

"Benvolio, come to me. Canst thou climb safely in here?"

"Aye, I thank thee, lady."

He made his way over to the window, crawling in to find himself in a small attic chamber hung with dried herbs. Rosaline gave a shaky sigh when his feet landed solidly on the floor. "Thou art well," she breathed. "Oh God, sir, I thought—"

He shook his head. "I am unhurt, thanks to thee."

She leaned out, trying to crane her neck to see where Orlino had fallen. "Is he—"

"Look not." Benvolio reached out a hand to cup her brown curls, turning her face away from the unmoving body below.

"Heaven help us," Rosaline whispered. "It begins again."

Benvolio nodded. "Like before." Death, treachery, endless hate. It was hard to breathe at the thought.

Rosaline turned wide eyes to meet his. "No," she said. "Not like before. Didst thou not note how Orlino decried us both without naming himself a Montague, so both families would believe they were under attack from the other? Someone did this on purpose. Perhaps the same soul who defiled Juliet's grave."

"Orlino—"

"Not Orlino. He is a hothead, nothing more. Someone else is rekindling our family's war."

She was right. Orlino was not clever enough to plan something like this. Benvolio stood beside her at the window as she stared out over the city spread beneath them. A cool breeze ruffled his hair. Somewhere below was someone who planned to destroy them—no, someone who had already begun.

"I'll not allow it," Rosaline said.

"What?"

Rosaline turned to him, her chin raised. "Our families have sworn peace. Whether these vicious mischief-makers be within our ranks or yours, they speak not for us. Only if we can reveal their treachery may this war truly end."

Benvolio shook his head. "And how are we to find them, pray? And if we do, why should they heed the protestations of a callow youth and a shrewish virgin? 'Tis folly, lady."

"Marry, is it? I shall make no protestations, I, but throw them to the prince's justice, whosoe'er they may be."

He barked a laugh at that. "Of course you will, sweet, gentle Rosaline. But pray do not assume that your frigid disdain for your kin is how I feel toward the Montagues. I've no interest in sending my blood to the prince's jail like common criminals."

"Your devotion to House Montague is nothing if you willfully harbor poison within its walls. Or are you too much a coward to cast it out, Montague?"

Dear lord, the woman could talk a man into believing day was night. He turned away from her, scrubbing a hand over the back of his neck. "No coward I, and were you a man I'd cross swords with you for saying so."

She waved this off. "If your duty to your much-loved Montagues is not enough to move you, consider this," she continued. "If we can bring a natural peace betwixt our two houses, what need will there be to force an unnatural one?"

He turned to her, puzzled. An unnatural peace? What did she— Ah. "We'd not have to marry."

Rosaline's arms were crossed, one delicate eyebrow raised. "For that boon, I think," she said drily, "you'd send a dozen Montagues to the gallows."

"I had rather 'twere Capulets." He grinned. This plan had suddenly grown more attractive. "Very well, sweet unloved bride, what are we to do?"

"Well, detested husband," she said. "Firstly, we are to get out of this attic."

He nodded and made for the door. But Rosaline cried out before going three steps, crumpling to the ground. He darted back to her side. "My lady?"

She shook her head, trying to straighten up. "I twisted my ankle in my flight. 'Tis nothing." But when she tried to put weight on her bare foot she hissed in pain.

Benvolio slid an arm about her waist. "Lean on me."

Their trip down the stairs became a slow progression as

Benvolio half pulled and half carried her down. He could feel her quick breaths jerking unevenly against his hand whenever her left foot touched down, but she uttered not a sound of complaint.

He felt a twinge of shame at what the feud had made of him. Who was he to spurn someone like her? His family's hate was jealous. It demanded as much devotion as a lover. Benvolio was not blind; he knew it was no common armful of beauty pressed against his side. Truly, most young men of Verona would envy him his luck.

But most young men's dearest friends were not slain by the Capulet she-wolf's pride, his mind whispered in Mercutio's voice. *Thou art no unskillful lover of women, Benvolio. Go and find thee out one that never killed your cousin. Better yet, find a dozen.*

And there it was, he thought, trying to ignore the feel of her body against his as he slid her to the ground. Clever she might be, and beautiful—but were it not for her, Romeo would live still. He would ally himself with her for the moment only to ensure that they could soon dissolve their betrothal and part ways for good.

As they made their way down the stairs, he thought he heard Romeo's laugh.

Rosaline seized the first opportunity to shed his arms. As soon as they reached the bottom of the stair, she pushed him aside and started forward on her own—whereupon her ankle gave out immediately. Benvolio sighed and tucked her under his arm once more.

They had just passed the chapel doorway when a voice within cried out, "Halt, scoundrels!"

Turning, they found a monk in a brown cassock hurrying toward them. His normally gentle face was set in a scowl. "What mischief have you and your kin been at this time, Benvolio?" He glanced at Rosaline. "And what poor maid is now entangled in it?"

Benvolio gave a tight smile to his old schoolmaster. "Lady Rosaline," Benvolio said, "may I present Friar Laurence?"

Rosaline narrowed her eyes, but swept him a curtsy as best she could. "Good morrow, Father, I have heard tell of you."

"And I of you, my daughter."

Benvolio could see at a glance that each of them knew the other's role in the summer's violence. Friar Laurence had taught all the Montague boys, and had been a special confidant of Romeo's. It was he who had secretly married Romeo and Juliet—and, Benvolio suspected, he who had listened to Romeo's earlier moonings over Rosaline, probably more patiently than Benvolio had. "Father," he said, "we mean no mischief. 'Twas my kinsman Orlino who caused this morning's strife in the square, but he, poor wretch, will trouble the world no more."

"Will he not?" The friar glared. "Was't not he, then, knocked me from my feet not five minutes since?"

Benvolio froze. "Orlino lives?"

"Aye, though he did run from this place as if all the hounds of hell pursued him."

He must have been just stunned, then, when he fell from the roof. Benvolio didn't know whether to be glad or not that his villainous kinsman's life had not been cut short. "I promise you, Father, his discourtesy will be added to the lengthy ledger of his crimes when I catch him." He tried to stride forward, but he'd forgotten Rosaline's injury. She could not match his pace and stumbled, clutching his doublet as she hissed in a pained breath.

"Your pardon, lady," he said as he righted her.

Friar Laurence hurried over, pulling Rosaline from him. "Come inside. You had better tell me all."

The throbbing in her ankle soon died down.

By the time they had told the friar what they knew of Orlino's treachery, the cool poultice he had applied to Rosaline's foot had sapped the pain. She wished the nurse would take some lessons from him.

"And so the poisonous flower of your families' hate buds once more," Friar Laurence said quietly as he bent over her, gentle hands wrapping a bandage around her foot. "'Tis no surprise, when it has always had such diligent gardeners." One of his brothers had retrieved Rosaline's shoe from the roof, and now he slipped it back on her foot.

Benvolio had not ceased pacing since they had arrived in the friar's cell. "Is she sound, Father? If so, prithee see her home so that I may be off. With every moment, Orlino puts more distance between himself and justice."

The friar shook his head. "I cannot, my son. Thou must needs see thy betrothed home thyself." At the sounds of disgust from both Benvolio and Rosaline at the word *betrothed*, he laughed. "Such a pair you are," he said. "'Twas but weeks ago, in the heat of July, that just such a young Montague and Capulet stood before me, mad to be married. And now August wanes and Providence has sent another pair, just as mad not to."

"Aye," Benvolio said, helping Rosaline once more to her feet. "We're as different from Juliet and Romeo as night from day. For one thing, I've heard Juliet had a civil tongue in her head."

Rosaline tossed her head. "'Tis true, I've none of my cousin's fatal weakness for Montagues, and thank God for that."

"Nor for any other man. For what man of Verona could warm thee so well as thy darling pride does?"

"None, for men of Verona have far more skill at leaving ladies cold in their graves." She looked at the friar, who was giving them a rather cryptic smile. "What?"

"As different as night from night," he murmured.

Benvolio frowned. "What mean'st thou, Father?"

He shook his head. "Nothing. I am sorry, young Benvolio, but I must go. In two days' time shall I depart Verona." He stood, wiping the medicine from his hands with a cloth. "The prince has made it clear that, for my part in this summer's sad events, I am no longer welcome here, so I shall join my brothers some leagues off at a monastery in the countryside."

"Thou, Father?" Benvolio said. "Of all of us, thou art the least to blame."

Father Laurence gave him a weak smile and squeezed his shoulder. "Thanks, my son." He sighed. "But the prince blames me far less than I blame myself. 'Twas mine own pride that led me to believe I could end the feud simply by marrying Romeo to Juliet. Their youth, which sped them to such a rash and hasty union, ought to have been tempered by my wisdom; instead, I spurred them on. Exile is the least that I deserve."

"If you deserve exile, so do we all," Benvolio said.

But Friar Laurence merely shook his head. He led them to the doorway of the church, grasping each by the shoulder. "God be with you," he said. "If, whether by marriage or some other design that you pursue, you can heal this breach within your families, the shades of Montagues, Capulets, and Mercutio will thank you."

"Paris too," pointed out Rosaline.

The hand on her shoulder stiffened. "Aye," the friar said after a moment. "Paris too. Fare you well now, and take heed of what passed today—one who could set your effigies aflame is not likely to hesitate to cause you real injury. You know not where the adder hides her sting."

Benvolio and Rosaline made their way out into the street, turning up the hill toward her home. Benvolio looked back over Rosaline's head to where the friar stood in the doorway, watching them. There was something strange about his old teacher's manner. Probably it was just the grief that afflicted them all—but it occurred to Benvolio to wonder if the friar was hiding something.

Deep in Verona's night, Orlino laughed.

Verona was still in chaos after the day's events. The prince's guards had calmed the worst of the unrest, but it was a momentary respite. Throughout in the city, hands rested on swords, and *Montague* and *Capulet* were on everyone's lips. It was only a matter of time before the two families threw off this womanish peace forced on them by the prince and went to war. Then he and his brethren could crush the treacherous Capulets once and for all.

Orlino could not go home, for he was sure that his cousin was waiting for him. Benvolio, who soiled the very name of Montague. Orlino would enjoy striking him down just as much as he would the Capulets.

So he continued to wander the streets, keeping to the shadows. Unmasked, he was merely one more black-clad noble. Verona's citizens took no notice of him except to give him a wide berth.

As the clock chimed midnight, the streets at last were empty. Orlino thought about contacting his benefactress—surely she could shelter him in her home, wherever that might be. But no, she'd said not to contact her this night. And Orlino's blood was still too hot for sleep, anyway.

He wondered once again who she might be. Some great and noble lady, of that there was no doubt. They'd met but once, and he'd not seen her face. *Come to Friar Laurence's closet when he is at Mass,* her note had said, slipped under his door by unseen hands. He'd arrived to find her already in the confessional, in the priest's seat, so that he could not see her face.

"I am one who knows well how right the Montague cause is," she'd said. *"And how much you are an honorable young soul, Orlino. I believe we can help one another."*

"Orlino."

Orlino started, his hand flying to his sword. His wanderings had led him back to the cemetery where he'd first encountered the Capulet wench Rosaline. Peering into the darkness where the torches barely reached, he saw another black-clad figure, masked as he had been.

"Who goes there?" Orlino called. "Are you one of her—"

"Draw your sword."

"What?"

The slither of steel, and then a glint in the darkness. "Draw your sword, Montague."

Orlino's sword was scarcely unsheathed before the stranger's steel rang against his. Stumbling backward, trying to keep his footing, Orlino quickly realized himself outmatched. He was a skilled swordsman, but his opponent seemed not even human, hand and arm and sword all part of one night-born creature.

"Who are you?" Orlino panted, desperately parrying the stranger's thrusts. "Show yourself, devil."

The masked man made no answer, except with his steel. Orlino cried out as the blade pierced his belly. The last sight his dimming eyes ever saw was his unknown killer, vanishing once more into the shadows.

Said Livia, "My lord, thou must be still." She put a hand on his chest and pushed, sending him back into his pillows with a groan. She took off his linens, freeing him from the sweat-dampened bedsheets that clung to his frame. "Thy fever may have broken, but thou art by no means out of danger. Stay abed or I shall tie thee down."

"Forgive me, lady." Paris smiled up at her. "Canst thou blame me? These four walls grow ever more wearisome. 'Tis unnatural for a man to so rely on women's aid, when 'tis I who ought to protect thee."

"All the more reason to rest, so thou canst leave these four walls without swooning after a half-dozen paces."

He gave her a pleading look but said, "Wisdom I shall heed. Now tell me, lady. What news from Verona?"

His eyes were clear and bright, his gaze steady. In the fortnight since the prince's ball he'd steadily climbed back toward health. His wits had returned and his wound was healing nicely, though he was still as weak as a child. Settling herself by his bedside, Livia told him of the skirmish in the marketplace at Rosaline's betrothal earlier that day.

"By my troth," Paris said, "a spectacle unfit for a lady's eyes and ears. Thou and thy sister were unhurt?"

Livia sighed. "I' faith, Rosaline's betrothal gown shall

ne'er be worn again, which I count a shame, for I had hoped to make it over for myself. And some clotpole trod upon her ankle, but Friar Laurence gave her a poultice for it. He says it is only bruised and she shall be able to walk tomorrow. And as for me, I was not even there. She told me she'd no wish for me to see her yoked to the Montague and bade me stay at home." She pouted. "And hence I missed all the excitement."

Paris lay back against the fresh pillow she'd laid for him, a faint smile on his face. "Thy honorable sister is right to keep you as far from all Montagues as possible. I would not have thee come to any harm."

Her cheeks warmed, but she replied only, "Rosaline says our own dear Capulets have just as great a part in this deviltry."

He sighed. "Perhaps she is right. This feud of yours is a hard knot to untangle. And those it ensnares are hard pressed to escape." He brushed a hand over his bandages. "As I know well."

"Thou'lt go, then?" Livia swallowed. "When thou art well— dost thou plan to leave Verona, as my aunt Capulet suggests?"

Paris laid gentle fingers against her hand. "Let us talk no more of such sad matters." Reaching for the chess set at his bedside, he hid two pieces within his closed fists. "Black or white?"

"Well, Rosaline, where are we to begin?"

Rosaline leaned out of the window of her cottage to find

her betrothed lord awaiting her below. When he looked up and spied her, he grinned and waved, his other hand shielding his eyes against the morning sun. Rosaline could not help but smile in return. Swiftly, she ran down to the front hall and joined him. "Good morrow, Benvolio. Why so pleased, pray?"

"Not pleased, my lady, but eager." He bounded into her hall. "This plan of yours I like more and more. 'Tis the first moment I have had any profitable occupation in weeks." If he found it strange to make a social call on a cottage tucked at the back of the Duchess of Vitruvio's lands, he did not show it, but looked around her bare hall in appreciation. "I like well your house. 'Tis not so crowded with knacks and trifles as my mother's." He unsheathed his sword, doing a few exuberant passes with an invisible opponent.

A scream issued from the stairs. Benvolio ducked as a chair came flying at his head. Rosaline turned to find Livia glaring at him, hands on her hips. "Back, villain!" she yelled.

Rosaline sighed. "Benvolio, may I present my sister, Livia." She looked at the shattered chair. "She is the reason, as thou canst see, that our house possesses such a pleasing lack of furniture."

Benvolio turned to Livia, who had seized another chair and seemed prepared to drop it over the banister, and carefully sheathed his sword. "Your pardon, lady, I pray. I meant no harm."

"Hmm." Livia's eyes narrowed, but she withdrew the chair, muttering something in which Rosaline could discern the word "Montague."

Gathering up the pieces of the chair, Rosaline turned to Benvolio. "Let us start with Orlino. Has he been found? If we can speak to him—"

"Orlino's dead."

"What?"

Livia was coming down the stairs, her narrowed eyes still fixed on Benvolio. "Orlino's dead," she repeated. "Did you not hear, Montague? His sword-slain body was discovered last night near the cemetery. I heard it in the market this morning."

All the mirth drained from Benvolio. He leaned against the wall. "Dead," he repeated. "Orlino dead. Slain."

"I shall not mourn him," Livia said, arms crossed. "Another Montague the city is better without."

"Livia!" Rosaline scolded. "Speak not so of his kin."

"I shall speak however I please of one that has done you such dishonor, Rosaline. He was a scoundrel and I hated him. Those who will not admit Orlino's villainy, kin or no, deserve no better than he." With a final glare at Benvolio, she turned and went back upstairs.

Rosaline pinched the bridge of her nose. "My lord, my sister means no harm—"

Benvolio held up a hand to stop her. "She's right. 'Twas quite clear my cousin would come to no good end." He drew a deep breath. "And this changes nothing. We must still start with Orlino, must we not?"

"Aye," Rosaline agreed. "With his death."

Accordingly they made their way to the cemetery. Rosaline hid a shiver as they passed through its gates. She had not

140

been here since Orlino had attacked her; by day it looked quite different than it had that frightening night, but still, she could almost feel Orlino's hands upon her as she spied the crypt he'd dragged her behind. Benvolio glanced at her sidelong. He said nothing, but drew her arm through his.

"Where do you suppose it happened?" he asked.

Rosaline looked round. The cemetery seemed tranquil and calm, no sign that it had ever been disturbed by the strife of the night before. The city's dead slept quietly in a grave-yard quite deserted. Or—no, not quite deserted, or entirely quiet.

"In youth when I did love, did love,

Methought it was very sweet;

To contract, O, the time for, ah, my behove,

O, methought there was nothing a-meet."

"Hark," Rosaline said. "Hear you this song?"

"Aye." They made their way toward the voice, walking up a little knoll toward the Montague sector of the cemetery.

"But age with his stealing steps

Hath clawed me in his clutch,

And hath shipped me intil the land,

As if I had never been such."

No figure appeared even as the voice got louder, and for a fearful, idiotic moment Rosaline thought it must belong to a ghost. Then as they surmounted the hill, she realized why she had not seen anyone: The voice issued from an open grave, singing in time to upflung shovelfuls of dirt.

"A pickaxe and a spade, a spade,

For and a shrouding sheet;

O, a pit of clay for to be made

For such a guest is meet."

"Good morrow, master gravedigger," Benvolio called. "We would speak a word with you. Pray, will you spare us a moment from your song?"

Half of a dirty face peered over the rim of the grave. "'Tis a jolly song, is't not, masters? I had it from a cousin of mine who lived among the Danes. Ah! He has gone up in the world, for he has buried princes and queens, whiles my humble self has never buried better than a count. And when I did so, the coffin was delivered closed, and I was not considered fit to see the noble body." He looked affronted.

Benvolio looked rather taken aback at this, but Rosaline laughed. "Well, all men are equal in heaven," she said. "He that interred our Savior buried not a king."

"No, nor did he do the job right," grunted the gravedigger as he hoisted himself out of the hole, "for his work undid itself afore a month was out. Ah!" His eyes lit up as his gaze landed on Benvolio and Rosaline. "My patrons! Your pardon, lords and ladies, I knew not that I addressed my benefactors." He bowed and swept off his hat, clods of earth showering from the brim.

Benvolio cocked his head. "Patrons? What mean you, sirrah?"

"Marry"—the man beamed—"does not the poet live through the patronage of great nobles, who do commission him to write sonnets to their beauty and wisdom? Does not the painter earn his bread through flattering portraits of lords and ladies? Well, here in Verona, those who practice the grave arts have no greater or more generous patrons than Houses Montague and Capulet."

Benvolio was scowling beside her, arms folded across his chest, but Rosaline found herself rather amused. At least someone had found some small share of joy among the misery their families had caused. "I suppose we have given you a great deal of trade this season," she said. "You should tell the prince of your love for our houses' feud. He is certain it benefits none in Verona. 'Tis clear he has quite forgotten the gravediggers."

"Aye, lady," the man said solemnly, "but by the time I meet with such a great one, he'll have no use for conversation but with Saint Peter." He sighed. "And truly, I doubt I shall even have a chance at that, for the prince is a young man. But there again, this is Verona. Nobles die young."

"Master gravedigger," Benvolio interrupted, "we come to ask you—"

"Young master Benvolio, well met!" The gravedigger shook him by the hand. "I recall you carrying your friend's coffin into his grave. A fine funeral, that. Sometimes your houses use those crypts, which leaves my hands idle but for sweeping out a clean place for the fresh bones. But young Mercutio had a proper hole in the ground. Such weeping there was for him! But you, sir, you were ever strong, even as those around you wailed and moaned. If I meet with a family looking for a steady coffin-bearer, I'll tell them, call on young Benvolio. He'll do you proud."

Steady Benvolio might be, but Rosaline thought she could see the Montague temper begin to rise. She laid a calming hand on his sword arm. "Good master gravedigger, we thank thee for thy kind words. For the sake of the love thou bearest our families, wilt thou help us now?"

"Aye, lady. Anything for such a frequent mourner. What's your will?"

"We are told Benvolio's cousin was slain here last night."

"Oh, aye," the gravedigger said, pointing up the hill. "'Twas the fiercest fight that e'er I saw."

Benvolio clutched Rosaline's arm. "You were there?" he demanded. "Pray tell us what passed."

The gravedigger cast a dubious glance at his half-dug grave, and Rosaline plucked Benvolio's purse from his side and offered the man a few coins. "There's for thy pains, sir-rah. We shall not keep thee long."

"Well," the gravedigger said as he pocketed the coins, "the dead are nothing if not patient," and he led them up the hill.

"Here," he said as they reached the summit, where a small grove of trees shielded the place from the rest of the cemetery. "I was a-digging for the grave of a young lady lately dead of consumption and I had stopped to sup, when young Montague comes from yonder"—he pointed back the way they had come, toward town—"with a frightful look upon his face. I had thought to call out, to pay him my respects as I did you, my lord and lady, but he walked on without seeing me. Before he had gone ten steps the other man was there, sword a-waving."

"Thou saw'st him, then," Rosaline said. "Who was he?"

The gravedigger shrugged. "Who can say? He was masked, and all in black. He could have been this one here, for all I could tell." He nodded to Benvolio. "Though you've never killed a soul, have you, Master Benvolio?" He looked disapproving at the lack of murders to Benvolio's name.

"Did he speak?" Rosaline said.

"But to say, 'Draw your sword, Montague.'"

"Naught else?"

"Nay. My lord Orlino did as he was told, they had at it, and then the masked one slew Orlino as quick as you could spit and went back the way he'd come."

"Which way?"

The gravedigger waved toward the main entrance to the cemetery. "And that's all I saw, gentles."

Rosaline nodded. "Our thanks."

The gravedigger doffed his cap again before returning to his grave. Rosaline and Benvolio made their way toward the gates, which stood open and unguarded as usual. "And hereupon, our attacker vanished." Benvolio sighed as they surveyed the gates from the hill up above. "Without leaving a hint of his identity."

Rosaline shook her head. "He did leave us a trace or two. Orlino was a strong swordsman, was he not?"

"Aye, he was a fair hand with his steel, though he had not the wit to know when to draw it."

"And yet the stranger slew him. Therefore we may surmise the killer was one supremely skilled with the blade. How many men of Verona could best Orlino, think'st thou?"

Benvolio shrugged. "Perhaps a dozen or two, lady. Andreus of Millamet, Viscount Matteo—Sir Valentine on a good day."

She frowned. "Fewer than that, I think. Marry, thou wast thyself injured in tangling with Orlino. If Orlino could wound the finest swordsman in Verona, there cannot be many who could best him." She realized that Benvolio had stopped walking, and turned to find him looking at her oddly. "My lord?"

He was trying to hold back a smile. "The finest swordsman in Verona, lady?"

Rosaline felt a slight heat flush her cheeks. She'd been so deep in her pondering that she had not realized she'd accidentally given the Montague a compliment. "I have seen you defeat four men at once," she said stiffly. "I speak not to flatter you, sir."

"I know it well, and I am all the more flattered by praise from one who had rather tear out her own tongue than ascribe to me any virtue."

She narrowed her eyes at his impertinent grin and started to retort, but something over his shoulder caught her eye. She gripped his arm, turning him. "Benvolio—"

"I see it." All mirth abruptly left him.

They were standing at the top of the hill overlooking the cemetery's gates, framed by the statues of Romeo and Juliet. HARLOT was once more painted across Juliet's face.

It was suddenly too much for Rosaline. Rage boiled within her like a pot overflowing. Wrenching free of Benvolio's restraining arm, she tumbled down the hill. Once she had reached the gates, she clambered up the base of Juliet's statue, whipping her scarf off and using it to scrub at Jule's face.

"Rosaline," Benvolio said behind her. His gentle plea only infuriated her. She scrubbed harder until he firmly pulled her down. "Rosaline, 'tis no good, the word is dried fast."

The sensible part of her knew that he was right—her pains were for naught. But, as she was beginning to realize was quite common when Benvolio was by, the sensible part of her was drowned out by something fiercer. She rounded on him, shoving ineffectually at his chest as his arms drew her down to earth.

"Who did this?" she demanded, still trying to fight her way free of him.

"Faith, I know not—"

"Lies! Didst thou lead me to this place on purpose to mock me with this latest outrage? Wilt thou carry the tale of my distress back home for the Montagues to laugh over at the supper table?"

"Thou knowest right well I'll do no such thing—"

"I know not the depths Montague duplicity may plumb—"

"Rosaline!"

His abrupt bark froze her hysteria for an instant, but it was his hands gripping hers that silenced her tirade.

"I am innocent of this slander, lady," he said softly, eyes burning into hers. "And well dost thou know it."

"They will not let her rest," she whispered. "Little Jule's end was so terrible, and they will not let her rest."

"I know. And thou hast my word that I will make them pay for it."

She shook her head slowly. "Who would do this to poor Jule?"

Her fury drained as swiftly as it had come. He spoke the truth. Despite her momentary fury, she knew it was not Benvolio who had done this to her cousin.

When had she come to trust him, she wondered? Benvolio, who had, on the day they met, all but called her a murderess—when had he become something like a friend?

In confusion, she pulled her gaze from his, and something caught her eye. She fell to her knees at the base of Juliet's statue, motioning for Benvolio to follow her.

"No, you did not do this," she said. "Nor did any other man." She pointed to a corner, where a bit of the paint that marred Juliet's face had spilled, staining the white marble. Imprinted in the paint was a pattern of smudged bumps and depressions, like a footprint. But it was no footprint.

Benvolio knelt at her side, running his fingers over the marks. "What is it?" he said. "I've never seen aught like it."

"I have," Rosaline said. "In mine own kitchen, when I spilled a jug of wine on the floor. 'Tis such a pattern made by the beaded trains upon the dresses ladies of Verona are wearing this season. The statue's defiler was a woman. And if 'tis so, I know where we must go next."

Benvolio could not stop fidgeting.

Rosaline shot him a quelling look as they waited at the gate. "Be still," she hissed.

"'Tis all very well for you," he whispered in her ear. "She's your great-aunt. You live here."

Rosaline shook her head, clasping her hands in front of her. "As you saw, the cottage I share with Livia is tucked away in the back of my aunt's lands. I rarely come up to her house, and never uninvited."

"Still, you've Capulet blood. I may be the first Montague in a generation to beg an audience at this house."

The Duchess of Vitruvio had ruled Verona's elite social circles for decades. Rumors, secrets, scraps of gossip—all of it found its way to her. If anyone had a notion of which of Verona's ladies had defaced her granddaughter's statue, it would be her. Rosaline had pointed out that she was their best chance, and Benvolio had been forced to agree. But not happily.

"Then you'd better make a good impression, had you not?" Her hand gripped his to stay his nervous jingling of his change purse. "Be *still*, I say."

He gave her a glare, but subsided. "Harpy."

"Clotpole."

He slumped sulkily just to vex her. Rosaline gave him a sharp dig in the ribs. He straightened just as the gate opened. The hulking manservant announced, "Duchess Francesca will see you now, Lady Rosaline." Throwing Benvolio a wary look, he added grudgingly, "And your companion."

As they trailed him into the house, Benvolio shot her a glance and was surprised to that find her eyes now held a spark of mirth. "Doth my cold welcome amuse thee?" he whispered.

"Not the welcome, sir, but the aggrieved look upon thy face. Poor hurt fowl."

"I am, after all, a bloody-minded Montague," he whispered back. "Perhaps I am unused to being insulted by one I may not correct with my sword."

The servant looked over his shoulder in disapproval as Rosaline endeavored to turn a snort of laughter into a cough, then sent Benvolio a reproachful look. He smirked. As they drew to the end of the hall, she leaned in close to whisper, "If you feel the need to slay Duchess Francesca, I for one shall not stay your hand."

He drew back to find her looking at him, one eyebrow raised, a small merry smile on her lips.

"Well, come in, stand not whispering outside the door."

Benvolio gave one last tug at his doublet, self-consciously smoothing the Montague crest on his sash, and then followed the imperious voice's command, trailing Rosaline into one of the grandest parlors he'd seen outside of the prince's palace. The duchess had been a Capulet herself, before she'd wed the Duke of Vitruvio, now long dead. Her branch of the family was not quite so wealthy as that she'd wed her daughter to, and her husband's wealth was his title, not his lands. But his was an old and venerated line, and the greatest of their remaining glory seemed to be gathered in this one room—silken and velvet pillows piled on mahogany chairs, a gilded mosaic on the floor, and the walls adorned with enormous portraits of the duchess's ancestors, each frowning more severely than the last.

The haughtiest face of all belonged to Duchess Francesca

herself, ensconced in an enormous brocade chair at the center of the room. She regarded them, unmoving, as Rosaline made her a curtsy and Benvolio bowed.

"Well, niece?" she said. "Why hast thou brought this creature before me?"

Rosaline smiled. Benvolio was beginning to admire her ability to do that when she so clearly longed to strangle someone. "As well you know, Your Grace, 'this creature' is to be my husband."

The duchess's eyes narrowed. "That's as time shall try."

Rosaline's face was all innocence. "Know you of some reason we may not be wed?"

"When a betrothal celebration ends in flames and a riot, 'tis natural to wonder if the wedding day will ever arrive. Go to, girl, do not waste my time. I know right well thou lov'st not this Montague. Indeed, I loved thee the better for thy defiance. Why didst thou agree to wed him, in the end? How did the prince persuade thee? 'Twas ne'er for the sake of duty, nor for thy family, thou sly thing." Her gaze raked down Benvolio's form. "He's handsome enough, I suppose. But wert thou a maid to be swayed by a handsome face or by pretty words of love, thou wouldst have wed his cousin Romeo. He was the handsomer, and the richer too."

Rosaline and Benvolio exchanged glances. As they'd expected, the duchess knew all. "My reasons are mine own," Rosaline said.

"Aye, thou keep'st ever thine own council. 'Tis why I have let thee live so long upon my charity. Thou and thy sister need less care than my hounds."

"You are kind indeed." Rosaline gave her the sweetest of smiles. Benvolio wondered at her patience. "But, Aunt, we come to you for help with another question. Know you any lady who might have cause to do injury to the Capulets?"

Duchess Francesca jerked her chin toward Benvolio. "Any lady of his family might. Wherefore?"

Swiftly, Rosaline described the latest defacement she and Benvolio had found on Juliet's statue. "In short, we believe some lady of Verona may be behind all this deviltry," she concluded. "We thought perhaps you might have heard some whisper of it."

"Suppose I had," the duchess said sharply. "What would you do? Thou art scarce more than a child, Rosaline, and little regarded even within your own family. Why meddle in the affairs of thy betters?"

"Unimportant though we may be, we may still expose these malefactors to the prince's justice."

The duchess's piercing gaze swung to Benvolio. "The prince's brand of justice showed itself when he let thy cousin Tybalt's murderer walk free," she told Rosaline.

Benvolio's jaw tightened. "No murderer was Romeo. He did only what he had to to avenge Mercutio's death."

"Murder is murder. He should have hanged for what he did." She shook her head. "The guilty must be punished by the law."

"Then help us see them punished!" Rosaline said. "Help us to expose the miscreants who defile your granddaughter's grave! Tell us who is behind all this."

"Tell you?" the duchess said. "You? The prince hath already made puppets of you both. How did he compel thee to marry, Rosaline? I suppose he told thee the truth about House Tirimo, though he was sworn he'd never breathe a word. Men's oaths are easily broken, even princes'."

Benvolio had no idea what she was talking of, and a glance at Rosaline showed she was equally confused. Benvolio started to ask, "What—"

Rosaline nudged him. He fell silent. "The truth about House Tirimo," she said. "Aye, Aunt, you have hit it. He told me the truth."

The old woman snorted. "I knew it. When thy mother died and the prince called me to the palace to tell me he would supply enough gold to keep thee and Livia in honorable state until you were both married, he bade me swear to keep it a secret from you for all my days. He even disguised the funds he sent to you as rent for House Tirimo. He invented a merchant from Messina for a tenant, for he claimed his honor would not allow him to accept your thanks." She shook her head. "As if that house could ever fetch enough to succor two gentlewomen. 'Tis on the unfashionable side of the hill and its stables are terribly small."

Rosaline had gone white. Had she truly not known of this? Her aunt looked on quite placidly, despite the news she'd just delivered. How could she keep such a thing a secret, even at the orders of the prince? By heaven, the things these Capulets wrought upon each other were almost worse than their treacheries to Benvolio's house. "Of course, you are right, Aunt," Rosaline said. "He had only to tell me of this great kindness and he could ask of me any boon."

"Kindness indeed," the old woman said. "I warrant he plotted all along to yoke thee to such a knave. "

Rosaline shook her head as though to clear it. "This matter with the prince is not our business today," she said. "If you would not see me so yoked, once more I pray you, tell us who defiled Juliet's statue."

"Heavens, girl, I've no notion," the duchess said. "If I had, would I have kept it a secret? For, as I have told you, I am a great lover of justice. Yes, what is it, Lucullus?"

The duchess's servant had entered on silent feet and reached her side without Benvolio noticing. For a big man, he was terribly quiet. Benvolio supposed someone in this house had to be. He bent over his mistress, murmuring something in her ear. The duchess stood. "My daughter's servant is here on some errand. Why she keeps her dead child's nurse about I cannot imagine. Get thee gone, Rosaline, and take this miscreant with thee. Thou art grown forward and impertinent. Ask no more questions of this house or any other. I'd lock thee up in this house, but 'tis clear the rash youth of Verona do not scruple to clamber over gates locked by their elders."

Benvolio got to his feet in frustration, blocking her path. Rosaline laid a restraining hand on his arm, but he shook her off. "You disparage the prince, forbid Rosaline to act, and of course, I and all my family you consider scoundrels," he said. "Pray tell, lady, who is to stop this mischief, then?"

The duchess looked at him—a more appraising gaze than the dismissive glances she'd so far offered him. "You are new to this earth, young Montague. Think you truly that your elders are unpracticed at protecting our families? The Capulets are old. We know how to survive."

Benvolio had any number of things to say to that, but Rosaline sent him a warning glance, and with an effort he held his tongue. She took his arm and led him out into the corridor.

Her head was held high, her fingers light on his arm, her steps measured, as much a model of maidenly decorum as if he were escorting her from a royal audience. But the moment the front door had shut behind them, her pace increased almost to a run. Her hem acquired a coat of red dust as she hurried up the long red path to the front wall of the duchess's estate. He caught up to her just past the gate, where she stood staring back over the wall and up the hill. He followed her gaze to the small house she shared with her sister. Which the prince's largess had made possible.

"Thou truly didst not know that the prince—" he began.

"'Tis no matter," said his betrothed. She did not meet his eye.

"But how came it that—"

"I thank you, but you need not concern yourself with it, signor."

Benvolio had any number of concerns, actually, not the least of which was that Rosaline seemed unaware that her hands were so tightly bunched into fists that her knuckles were white. But he took his cue from her sudden brittle formality and let the matter drop. It was probably wise that a Montague not insinuate himself into Capulet finances.

Instead he leaned back against the wall, trying to look as though the odd mood that had overtaken her was not making him nervous.

She turned to him then, an over-bright smile on her face. "The day grows hot," she said. "Let us dine before we continue our search."

He shrugged. "If it please thee. Wilt thou come to my house? My mother has some fine cheeses."

"Nay, I'll go home. Shall we meet in the square at two o'clock?" Without waiting for a response, she turned and headed down the road without him.

Benvolio sighed, and wondered if he ought to ignore the fact that she was walking in the opposite direction of her little cottage.

Her father's house seemed small, thought Rosaline.

In her memory it was vast, but of course she herself had been smaller when last she lived here. She had been inside House Tirimo only a few times since her mother had died. Although her tenant never seemed to occupy the house, still it was his by right, and she could not intrude. But now that she knew the merchant from Messina to be imaginary, she felt no qualms about letting herself in.

The house was bare, but not choked with dust—she'd arranged with her aunt's servants to keep it clean. She shook her head at herself. How grown-up and wise she'd thought she was, taking care of her family's house and fortunes, when all along, she and Livia had been living on the prince's charity. It made her cheeks burn.

She wandered from room to room, choked with memories. Here was the small, sunny sitting room where her mother had taught her to sew. Here was the closet where she'd run and hid after her father shaved his beard and she thought him a stranger, until he'd coaxed her out by singing her favorite song. Here was the nursery, where, family legend had it, a four-year-old Rosaline had taught two-year-old Livia to open the latch and escape. Even when Livia was just a tiny bundle of dimples and blonde tufts, Rosaline had considered her sister her particular responsibility.

All this could have been lost. Had the prince not decided to grace them with a small fortune, the house would have been sold by now, and she and Livia might have already been forced to take holy orders. Instead, they had a home, a monthly income, and a house still to sell for Livia's dowry when the time came. The magnitude of his gift took her breath away. There was no way she could begin to repay it.

What a strange man Escalus was. There were two versions of him that lived in her mind: the handsome, brave prince she'd idolized and adored with all her childish heart, and the cold-hearted villain who had so cruelly blackmailed her into doing his bidding. Now she had to admit that neither vision was precisely correct. Why had he chosen to manipulate her so brutally? Surely he knew that if he had simply revealed how he'd helped her all this time, honor would compel her to repay his kindness with any favor he pleased, up to and including wedding Benvolio.

For that matter, why had he done this in the first place? She had thought he'd quite forgotten his Tirimo playmates. Why help them? And why conceal it? Was he ashamed to admit any connection to them?

Her wanderings took her back to the front hall. While not nearly so grand as her uncle's house or the duchess's mansion, Rosaline had always considered it one of the most elegant rooms in Verona. A wide staircase opened onto a floor of creamy white marble. Sunlight poured through the wide windows. A rug lay in the center of the floor. Rosaline smiled. This was probably her aunt's doing. With her foot, she flipped a corner of the rug over, and glimpsed a bit of the blue and gold mosaic below. Her mother had been mortified that her father had installed a large mosaic of the Tirimo family crest on the floor, but Rosaline had thought it beautiful.

She rolled the rug up, then kicked it over to the wall. Once more, the crest was bright and glittering in the sun, welcoming any who might enter to House Tirimo. She stepped back, wrapping her arms around herself as she admired it.

She would never forgive Escalus for what he had done, but he gave her this, and for that she blessed him.

"Rosaline?"

For a moment she thought the subject of her musings was behind her. But when she turned, she found not her sovereign, but her betrothed hovering in the doorway. "Benvolio," she said. "I thought we were to meet in the square."

"Aye, at two. 'Tis nearly three now." He said nothing of

how he had known she would be here, but she supposed it was shamefully obvious, after the way she'd run off.

She closed her eyes. "Your pardon. I lost track of time."

He shrugged. "I thought perhaps thou wouldst. Didst thou dine?" She opened her mouth to lie and say she had, when her belly gave an unladylike growl. Benvolio grinned. "So I thought. Therefore I bade our cook make me this." He held up a basket. Before she could say a word, he lay a little blanket on the floor, and then spread out a feast. Bread, cheese, sausage, even a little bag of cherries. He waved a hand. "Fall to."

Yet more charity. Why did all the men around her seem to think she must be coddled like a baby? But Benvolio had already plumped himself down on the floor and begun eating with a boyish appetite. It did look good. She supposed it would be rude to refuse. She sat down across from him and began to eat.

Benvolio looked around with frank interest as they dined. He was especially captivated by the crest on the floor. "By my sword! Is that a sea serpent?"

She smiled. "Aye. My father hailed from the Western coast, and his lands were by the sea."

He looked it over, asking questions about the meaning of each element in the crest, its history, whether the family had ever fought any interesting wars. She answered as best she could, and for once she found that speaking of her family did not pain her.

The confused ache in her chest was replaced with a

companionable spirit. After he'd reduced her to giggles with an imitation of the duchess's haughty voice, she realized that this was one of the first hours of simple joy she'd passed since Juliet's death. She wondered if it was the same for him.

"Thank you." She waved over their repast. "This was kind."

"We Montagues know what it is to be subject to the prince's whim. Forgetting meals is the least of it." He tossed a cherry in the air, caught it in his mouth, and grinned at her around the stem. "I still hate thee deadly, of course."

She stuck out her tongue. "Of course."

As they finished their meal, conversation turned once more to business, and to the parts of their conversation with the duchess that did not pertain to Rosaline's house. "Didst thou note it?" she asked. "I'd warrant the duchess was hiding something."

"Think'st thou so? It seemed to me she merely wished to be as unhelpful as possible."

"Perhaps," Rosaline said slowly. "But she truly hates the Montagues. For her to tell me to leave them alone—" She frowned. "'Tis strange, that's all."

"Think you your aged aunt leapt out into the night with her sword and slew Orlino?" he asked, packing their dishes away in his basket.

She laughed. "Aye, she's a master swordswoman, no doubt. 'Tis why she wears such wide black skirts—to conceal her blade beneath."

Benvolio shuddered. "A fearsome thought indeed. Come, let's away and seek this swordsman." He gallantly offered her his arm. "I shall protect thee from any and all murderous old ladies we meet."

She started to take his arm, then stopped, taking him by the shoulders and turning him away from her. He craned his neck back to look at her. "My lady?"

She was frowning at his back, fingers tracing over his doublet. "After we left the duchess's house, you leaned against her wall."

"Yes. Why?"

Her fingers scrubbed against his shoulder blade, then she extended her hand to show him what she'd found. Paint. Half-dry black paint.

"It can't be she."

"It must be she."

"It *can't*."

Rosaline ground her teeth in frustration. Hours had passed since they'd left House Tirimo. The sun had set, her feet ached, the hem of her dress was thick with dust, and they had had this argument up and down Verona. "Why would my aunt deface her own granddaughter's statue?" she demanded. "Use your wits."

"That old termagant would do anything to be disagreeable," Benvolio said darkly. "Besides, what say you of the black paint?"

"I say she had her wall painted," Rosaline retorted. "A crime dozens in Verona are guilty of."

"And 'twas thee who said she was hiding something."

"Aye, *something*. I am not ready to accuse her of murder."

Benvolio shook his head. "You take such pride in holding yourself loftily above our skirmishes. But you are just as quick to leap to the defense of a fellow Capulet as any of your eager-bladed cousins."

"What do you suggest we do, then?"

"Go to the prince," he said promptly. "Tell him what we've found."

"Tell him what?" Rosaline laughed. "Your Grace, prithee, clap the matriarch of the Capulets in irons, she hath an impatient air and a black wall?"

Benvolio ducked his head, conceding her point. "To my uncle, then. We can gather the men of my house, return to the duchess, and find the proof we need, whether she will or no."

Rosaline rolled her eyes. "If a throng of Montagues invades her house, no proof will be strong enough to calm the passions roused thereby. The city will be in flames within the day."

"What, then?" He threw up his hands.

"We continue as we have been. Even if the duchess is somehow involved, she cannot have slain Orlino. If we can find the swordsman, we may unravel her secrets too."

"We have visited half the passable swordsmen in the city today. None of them could have done it."

"Then tomorrow we visit the other half."

He shook his head. "Thou hast more patience than I, lady."

"Not so much as you may think," she snapped.

He looked up, startled at her waspish tone. They both began, reluctantly, to laugh. "You are right," he admitted. "I just wish we could stop this. A murderer walks free; I hate to waste even a moment."

"I know."

He extended his arm in apology, and she took it. They walked on in silence through Verona's lengthening shadows. Rosaline leaned gratefully upon him. She was unused to walking so much, but she had been loath to contradict his assumption that she could keep pace.

The moon hung over the eastern wall, huge and nearly full. As they walked on, Rosaline found herself staring at it, lost in its glow. "Romeo compared me to the moon," she said suddenly.

The arm under hers grew tense. But Benvolio said only, "Oh?"

"Aye." Rosaline found herself smiling. "I used to tell him he must mean to insult me, to call me after something so round and pockmarked."

Benvolio chuckled. "He never heard a sonnet but he rewrote it ten times worse. Apparently execrable poetry was pleasing enough to Juliet, though."

"No," she said. "No, I doubt it. Romeo had wit aplenty. But 'twas not I who was destined to ignite it. I am sure whatever he told Juliet was beautiful."

"He never spoke of her," Benvolio said quietly. "Never confided in me."

Rosaline sneaked a glance at him. He was lost in thought.

She rubbed a bit of his sleeve between her finger and thumb. "I truly thought 'twas for the best, you know," she said hesitantly. "I knew he did not love me, for all his torrent of gifts and sonnets and declarations. Spurning him I thought a boon."

He said nothing, but gave her arm a squeeze. Rosaline was almost ashamed of the warmth that burst through her. Had she been waiting so pathetically for his forgiveness?

He pulled away, and Rosaline looked around, startled to find they'd arrived at the door of her cottage. The sun had set now, and she suppressed a shiver, surprisingly cold without his warmth at her side.

Benvolio's arm was still half extended toward her. "Well," he said. "Until the morrow, then." He started to say something else, then stopped. Staring at her, he swallowed hard.

"Aye, until tomorrow." Seized by a sudden impulse, she raised herself on tiptoe to press a kiss against his cheek. She felt his breath hitch in surprise against her temple. Cheeks flaming, unable to meet his eyes, Rosaline whispered, "Good night," and slipped inside her door.

"I swear, Your Grace, I know not who it was."

Escalus rubbed a hand over his eyes. The darkness would hide his weariness from young Truchio's earnest gaze.

The Palace Guard were not best pleased with his decision to take Venitio and ride the city streets. But he knew not what else to do. Yesterday, the betrothal ceremony, meant to dampen the flames of the feud, had ended more disastrously than he could have imagined. Then young Orlino had been slain in the night. Tempers were higher than they had ever been. His city was about to explode, and if the sight of its stern-faced sovereign was enough to dissuade even one impetuous young man from drawing his sword, it was worth the danger to himself.

He was holding Verona together with all his might, but he did not know how long his grip could keep it from flying apart.

"I'm sure you know who scrawled insults on the Capulet wall today," he said. "And I am sure 'tis no coincidence I found you lurking so near the house of the Duchess of Vitruvio. Come, Truchio, I tire of your kin's false stupidity. Who but one of the Montague youths would do such a thing? Was it you? Young Marius? Marcellus? Tell me."

Truchio raised his chin, remaining silent. Escalus sighed. In truth, he had expected nothing else. "Young knave, you help neither yourself nor your family by hiding treachery in your midst," he said.

"I hide no treachery, I, upon my life," Truchio whined. "Ask Benvolio. He'll tell you."

The prince followed his gaze and drew in a breath, drawing Venitio to a halt. Sure enough, Benvolio was there.

This was not the first time today that the prince's wanderings had carried him to Rosaline's house. The duchess's estate was near the outskirts of town, but Venitio's steps seemed to point that way without Escalus's direction. He had seen no one there before. Now Benvolio stood before the gate, looking up at the cottage. After a moment, light was kindled within. Benvolio, the prince realized, had been seeing his betrothed home.

He ought to be pleased, if Benvolio's feelings for Rosaline were growing warmer. He was requiring them to marry, after all. But telling himself that did nothing to soothe the urge to seize Benvolio and drag him away from her.

Rosaline was within. Rosaline, who loved him. She had told him so. Escalus had only to go inside, to tell her that she need not wed the young Montague on her threshold, and she could be his.

By God, he wanted to do just that.

He drew in a sharp breath as it washed over him. Finally, he admitted to himself what Isabella had tried to tell him. Renting Rosaline's house, arranging her marriage, even the drunken evening he'd spent with her—she'd captured his attentions not because she was a Capulet useful to the Crown, but because he desired her.

And it mattered not a jot. This marriage was more essential than ever. He could not disrupt it for the yearnings of his own foolish heart. Damn these two houses. They would never know what they had stolen from him.

Venitio snorted and stamped, drawing Benvolio's attention. His eyes widened when he saw his sovereign staring at him silently. He made him a bow. Escalus nodded but said nothing, nor did he approach.

He wheeled Venitio about, pointing him back toward the palace. "Hie you home, Truchio," he muttered. "Get back to the streets where the Montagues live. Here's no place for you." But he did not wait to see if the boy complied before he rode for home himself.

On the morrow, he would wonder if he had sealed the boy's doom.

Once more, night's torches lit Benvolio's steps.

It was becoming a habit, he acknowledged wryly to himself. This time, at least, his sleepless wanderings through Verona's streets had less to do with grief than confusion. Rosaline's keen green eyes haunted his thoughts.

The idea of marrying her had grown no less absurd. If Benvolio married a Capulet lady, he'd never have a moment's peace, from her or from anyone else. The prince and his uncle were foolish to think otherwise. And yet, what if they succeeded in breaking the betrothal? The thought of her vanishing from his life caused a strange pain in his breast.

Benvolio had never been in love, and he was certain that he was not now. When he compared the turmoil Rosaline provoked in him to Romeo's sighing, poetical ardor, he found they had little in common. He felt no urge to write sonnets, nor to moan her name and weep. *That* was love. This was— irritating.

No less so because it seemed to have displeased his sovereign too. What had been the meaning of that encounter by Rosaline's door? Why had the prince looked at him so coldly? How could he be displeased if they were together? He had betrothed them, after all. Did he think he meant Rosaline some dishonor? He thought perhaps he ought to go to the palace, to explain, but he could not explain his feelings even to himself.

And so he wandered, for hour upon hour, as the night grew deep and the streets empty. He hoped Rosaline's sleep was peaceful, for he'd be little use tomorrow if, as he thought likely, he walked till sunup.

"Yahh! Halt, Montague! Your house's defeat is at hand!"

Benvolio drew up short when he suddenly found the tip of a sword wavering before his nose. Following it down to its owner, he found a young man in Capulet garb, wavering excitedly before him, scowling and fierce as a terrier.

Benvolio sighed. "You were in the graveyard three weeks ago when Rosaline was attacked. Hail, fellow."

"Aye. Gramio is my name, and I shall be your doom!"

"Will you?" Benvolio inquired, stepping out of reach of the erratic blade. "I defeated you and two of your fellows together that night. Have you grown a better sword arm since?"

"Capulet fortunes have changed since then," the Capulet blustered proudly. "Thy cousin Truchio was as arrogant as thee, till he met our guardian spirit's blade. Draw thy blade and give me satisfaction!"

Benvolio had been struggling not to laugh at this fierce little fowl. Now he grew sober, his hand drifting toward his sword. Unlike Orlino, Truchio was a good-hearted lad and had stayed out of trouble since that night in the graveyard. "What mean you?" he said. "Where is Truchio?"

"Dead," Gramio laughed. "The spirit clad in black, the guardian of the Capulets, ran him through on the Eastern road, two hours after sundown. 'Tis the ghost of Tybalt come again to restore our house's honor." He brandished something—a bit of cloth—and Benvolio grew cold. It was a Montague sash.

His sword was in his hand before he knew what had happened. "Give me that," he said quietly.

Gramio grinned fiercely. "So thou art no coward after all. Have at it."

"What," Benvolio growled. "Art thou a savage, taking trophies from the dead? I said give it to me!"

The first hint of fear showed in Gramio's face. "Montague—"

Benvolio brought his sword crashing down against Gramio's. There was a fierce rushing in his ears, drowning out everything else. The street, the torches, the night air—all of it ceased to exist. He could have been fighting atop the church altar on Sunday, for all he cared. He would get back Truchio's sash, or one or both of them would die in the attempt.

Slash. He opened a cut in the Capulet's left shoulder. *Slash*. He nicked his sword arm. *Clang*. He parried Gramio's attempt at an attack so fiercely that the scoundrel cried out in pain, clutching his wrist. Gramio was dodging left and right, employing every paltry trick he knew to stay out of Benvolio's reach, but none of it would be enough. Benvolio was sick of bowing and scraping in the face of Capulet insults while his family died around him. Tonight it ended.

Coldly, he evaluated the series of maneuvers Gramio had begun, parrying them almost lazily as he waited for the mistake he knew was coming. Gramio was panicked and sloppy;

in just a moment he would fall slightly off balance, forcing him to step back and leave his left side open—right—now.

Gramio's poor swordsmanship saved his life. Had he recovered from his falter with slightly more grace, it would have fallen out as Benvolio had predicted, and his sword would have buried itself in Gramio's heart before he'd had time to think. Instead, Gramio fell backward, sprawling to the ground, his sword spinning out of his hand.

It only put him out of reach for an instant. But it was long enough to pierce the red haze that had descended over Benvolio's gaze. Though anger still screamed in his veins, reason was beginning to reassert itself. The short mop of dark curls that flopped across Gramio's face with every frightened breath were much the same as those he'd earlier struggled not to draw his fingers through. This was Rosaline's cousin.

Planting a foot on Gramio's chest, he pointed his blade at his throat. "The sash. Now."

Gramio's eyes flicked toward his sword, lying just out of his grasp. Benvolio's jaw clenched, his hand tightening on his sword. *Yes. Reach for it. Please.*

But for all his bloodlust, Gramio valued his own life. With a sulky glare, he held the sash up to Benvolio. His fingers were about to close around it when something slammed into him from the side, hard, sending him flying across the cobblestones. He did his best to roll and control his fall, which was probably all that saved him from serious injury. As it was, he hit his head on the wall so hard that he saw stars. Rolling over, he saw another swordsman standing above him. He was masked, and dressed all in black.

Beside him, Gramio gave a savage cheer. "Ha! Vengeance has found thee, foul Montague! Behold our guardian spirit!"

Whoever the masked man was, he had no interest in a swordsman's honor. He gave Benvolio no chance to regain his bearings or even to raise his sword before his own was slashing downward in a deadly arc. Benvolio scrambled backward, trying to avoid the man's blade, but not fast enough. He hissed as he felt a vicious slash across his chest.

"Who are you?" he panted. "What is your quarrel to me and mine?"

"Vengeance," whispered the stranger, and struck Benvolio's blade with his. Weakened by his injury, Benvolio could not prevent him from knocking the sword from his hand. He flinched, waiting for the killing blow.

But instead, the masked swordsman picked up Benvolio's sword, turned, and plunged it straight into Gramio's chest. Gramio's cry became a gurgle. He died with a look of shock frozen on his face. The man in black retrieved his own sword, bowed to Benvolio, and walked back the way he'd come, soon swallowed by the shadows.

Recovering from his shock, Benvolio hauled himself to his feet and gave chase.

"Halt, villain! Coward!" he screamed. "Will you murder a man who never raised a sword to you and flee under the cover of darkness? Come and face me like a man!"

He reached the intersection and turned a circle, searching for any sign of the murderer. But he was gone.

On unsteady feet, Benvolio returned to slain Gramio's side. The lad's eyes still stared at where his phantom killer had been. Benvolio fell to his knees. What manner of demon was this who cut down Montague and Capulet alike? Numbly, he reached for the hilt of his sword.

A scream broke the air. Looking up, he found a laundress had dropped her basket and was pointing a trembling finger at him. "Murderer!" she screamed.

"I—no, I—" Benvolio realized as he climbed to his feet, hand still resting on the sword's hilt, how this must appear. "'Twas not I, we were both of us attacked—"

But now a crowd of merchants and early market-goers were gathering in the gray pre-dawn light.

"Murderer!"

"Villain!"

"Halt, in the name of the prince!"

Much later, Benvolio realized that if he had stayed, if he had gone to the prince and explained his innocence in Gramio's death, he might have avoided much that followed. But after the night he'd had, all he could think was *run*.

And as the sun rose on another bloody Verona day, he did just that, leaving his sword where it was, pinning a Montague crest to poor Gramio's chest.

Part 4

O, a kiss
Long as my exile, sweet as my revenge!

—Coriolanus

"Come, Rosaline! Come, Livia! Nieces, wake!"

Rosaline gasped and sat up in bed. Someone was pounding on her door, yelling loud enough to wake the whole of the duchess's estate. Pulling on a dressing gown, she leaned out the window. The sight below made her gape in surprise.

"Uncle?" she called. "By heaven, what—"

"No time, child!" Lord Capulet roared up to her. "Wake your sister, gather your gowns, and hie you both to House Capulet, an you value your lives and your maidenheads!"

Rosaline ran down the stairs, opening the door to her uncle. "Calm yourself, good my lord. What is it?"

He entered, mopping at his brow. He looked as though he'd run to Padua and back. "'Tis the Montagues," he said. "They make open war upon us. Every Capulet lady and child is to withdraw within the safety of House Capulet's walls, so that I may protect you."

"Rosaline?" Livia, sleep-mussed and yawning, was stumbling down the stairs. "What's that noise?"

"Uncle," Rosaline said firmly, "I thank you for your pains,

but if this is another street brawl, I'm sure there is no need for your protection."

"Gramio was slain last night," Lord Capulet said.

Next to her, Livia gasped. Rosaline gripped her hand as their uncle related the circumstances in which his body was found. Rosaline pressed a hand to her mouth, trying not to be sick. Livia wrapped her in her arms and guided her to the couch.

"I pray your pardon, Rosaline," her uncle said heavily as she clung to a shaking Livia. "You saw the blackness of this Benvolio's heart long ere I could. I should never have agreed with the prince's foolish scheme to marry you with him."

Rosaline felt as though her stomach had dropped through the earth. "Benvolio?" she whispered.

"Aye," her uncle said, grim-faced. "'Tis he slew Gramio."

Rosaline shook her head, clutching Livia closer. "Ah! No, not he, Uncle. Some kin of his perhaps, but not he—"

"Was not this his sash?" Lord Capulet said, producing a torn length of crimson cloth.

Rosaline closed her eyes. Benvolio had worn just such a sash the night before. Had any of his other kinsmen worn them? She thought so, but could not be sure. "I know not," she whispered.

"Marry, you may not, but the sword that pierced it, and Gramio's chest, is known to be Benvolio's."

Could Benvolio really slay her kinsman on the street?

She recalled the fury in his eyes as he'd slashed his blade

across Orlino's face, and shivered. Aye, he could. If roused, he could.

"Very well, Uncle," Rosaline said, meeting his gaze steadily. "We'll away to House Capulet."

He gave a short nod. "Good. There's one there who would speak with thee."

"Curst girl, I'll punish thee if thou speak'st not!"

The prince winced as Lord Capulet thundered at his niece. It was a familiar scene, if missing a few players: Rosaline sat, hands folded, staring at thin air; her uncle Capulet was seated behind his desk, growing ever more red-faced. And Escalus himself, watching. Just as they had been the night he'd told Rosaline she was to marry Benvolio.

Circumstances had changed, but the obstinate tilt of her chin had not.

"I have told you, Uncle," she said calmly. "I know not where Benvolio may be found, nor anything of last night's slaughter save what you yourself have told me."

So she had been saying this past ten minutes, and though the prince could see her growing irritation, still her voice remained even and low. Her curls were pinned neatly back, her green dress spread carefully over her knees. Like a statue in a hurricane, battered but unmoved. Rosaline could not be made angry unless she chose to be, quite possibly the only Capulet ever born with such control. It was that, he supposed, that had made her an object of such fascination to him, that had made him so hell-bent on using her in his scheme. He'd been certain that that captivating mix of wisdom and beauty was just what Verona needed.

Now he wondered if it was Verona he'd really been thinking of.

"I mean not to accuse you, Rosaline," Escalus said. "I seek only to keep you and yours safe from Benvolio's bloodthirsty ways. I know you have kept company with Benvolio of late—"

Narrowed green eyes flashed to his. "How know you that?"

"I saw him outside your house yesternight."

"Why hast thou passed thy days with thy cousin's killer?" Lord Capulet blustered. "Tell thy betters, or it shall fall heavy on thee."

"'Tis none of your affair, Uncle."

"We'll be the judge of that."

"Your judgment, gentlemen, betrothed us in the first place. I'll keep mine own counsel, I thank you."

"Insolent girl!" Lord Capulet heaved himself to his feet, glaring at her.

Escalus laid a hand on his shoulder. "Signor, might I speak with your niece alone for a moment?"

Capulet squinted at him. "Why?"

Escalus merely offered him a thin, polite smile. Capulet threw up his hands. "Well, she's at Your Grace's disposal. If you can get any sense out of her, I thank you."

He left, slamming the door behind him. Rosaline turned to Escalus, squaring her shoulders, preparing for a fight. The prince held up a hand. "I told thee, I mean thee no harm. I wish merely to capture thy cousin's killer."

"And I have told you, I know nothing that might help you," she said. "Two Montagues are dead as well. Why seek you not their murderer?"

"None saw who slew Orlino or Truchio, but Benvolio's guilt is proved."

Her gaze was glacial. Rosaline might not be quick to anger but nor was she quick to forgive. "Nothing is proved."

Escalus sighed. Why was he taking her down the same path they always trod? "Thy pardon, fair maid," he said.

This startled her icy composure. "What?"

He knelt and took her hand. "I cry thy pardon for the unwilling betrothal I forced upon thee. Had I had any inkling of Benvolio's true nature, I should have cut him down myself before allowing him within a mile of thee." He swallowed hard. "Tell me he hurt thee not."

Her eyes were wide, lips parted in surprise as she gazed down at her sovereign abasing himself before her. "I—I—" She shook her head slightly. "He was ever a gentleman."

"Thank heaven." He gripped her hands in his.

But she slowly drew back, eyes clouded with confusion. "If you mean to once more use our former friendship to compel me—"

He shook his head impatiently. "Thou hast my word, I shall never do so again. It was the worst choice that ever I made. No, speak or speak not, the choice is thine."

"I thank you." She hesitated. "And—while you are here—it seems Livia and I have much more to thank you for."

Her face flamed bright red. Ah. She had found out. He rocked back on his heels, trying to keep his face an innocent blank. "I know not what you mean."

"You do. 'Tis thanks to you we've been able to live in honorable state." She shook her head. "Why did you not tell me?"

In his mind's eye, he saw the black-clad, solemn young maid she'd been when he'd come back to Verona. At thirteen she was already a beauty, but she seemed not to care how the eyes of the young men of the court followed her. His own parents were recently dead too, and he did think of speaking to her, of sharing their grief. But princes did not show friendship to penniless maids, did they? He was not sure, and there was no one he could ask. His parents were dead, his sister gone away. His new crown was heavy on him. Would she think he was courting her? No, surely she would be more sensible than that. Would Verona think he had taken her as a mistress? The Montagues would certainly say so, if they saw him paying special attention to a Capulet maiden. That would not be good for Verona. He must think of Verona.

He was sixteen, and still outgrowing his doublets every two months. It had been easier to give her some money, and say nothing.

"I never intended you should know of the gold I give your aunt for you," he said. "I did not do it to compel you to my will."

She shook her head. "And did you never consider that I might prefer to be compelled by such kindness than by that jade's trick the night of the feast?"

"No," he admitted. As usual when he thought of that night, a great wave of shame and confusion overtook him. "Canst thou forgive me for what passed that night?"

She stood and moved away from him. "I remember little of it. How can I know whether to forgive?"

He drew a deep breath. "I brought you to my study," he said. "We drank some wine."

"Some wine." Her arms were crossed.

"A great deal of wine," he allowed. "Virtuous thing that you are, I had to give you enough to keep you still." Her eyes went wide. "That is, to persuade you not to return to the ball."

"What then?"

"We spoke of our days together," he said. He took a step toward her. "Of our childhoods, before there were such troubles in the world."

"I had thought you had forgot all."

"Never, Lady Thorn." He took another step.

Silently, she mouthed the old nickname. "What then?" Her eyes were locked on him, big and green as the sea.

"I danced with thee," he said. "We danced beneath the moon, and I wished that we might never cease." He was close to her now, and her lips parted as though to prompt him again, but no sound issued from them. "Then we stopped, and thou told'st me—" And here he could go no further.

But there was no need, for Rosaline knew, and covered her face with her hands. "Oh God."

"No, no, 'tis no matter—"

"No matter! To drunkenly confess my greatest shame? Oh

God! To my *sovereign*. Your Grace, I pray, if you have any friendship left, leave me, let me no more show my face to you. You cannot have any wish to be reminded of this foolish passion I allowed to grow above my station."

His heart grew sore as he listened to her panicked babbling. "If thou dost wish it so, I'll quit thee, but," he said, gently drawing her hands from her face, "I would not desire that."

Hope and fear warred in her eyes. "Your Grace?"

He stroked a curl back from her face. "Passion cannot be shameful if its object shares it."

He had her for an instant. Then her face hardened and she fled him again, going to lean against the window's sill. "This is some trick."

"Thou art too cautious, maiden. Shall thy proud heart never soften?"

"No, never, and certainly not for you, for you will not use it honorably. You think of naught but *Verona*." She spat their city's name like a curse.

"Not today," he said. "In truth, though this treachery of Benvolio's pains me, I cannot help but rejoice that thou canst not wed him. I swear, my love, I'd throw my crown away and tear Verona stone from stone if it would win thy heart."

At last his arrow hit its mark. She turned to him, the anger that had been in her eyes since the feast now replaced with shock. He was just about to fly across the room, to take her in his arms, when—

"Your Grace, the watch are here." Lord Capulet stood in

the doorway, looking quite ignorant of what he'd interrupted.

Escalus fought the urge to shove him backward and lock the door. "What news?"

"There's no sign of young Benvolio, but horses are gone from his stables. They think he's fled the city."

Oh hell. Could not the city stop disintegrating for five minutes? "Then they'd better search the countryside. Bring the captain in. I'll give him his orders."

Rosaline, who had been frozen in place since her uncle had barged in, put her head down and hurried for the door. "My lady Rosaline," he blurted.

She turned. "Your Grace?"

He was all too aware of the curious gaze of her uncle. "I shall have more to speak to you anon."

She made him a curtsy. "I am ever at Your Grace's command." Her eyes, though filled with confusion, were considerably warmer.

"Good. Tomorrow, then." He kissed her hand and let her go.

Livia felt as though she might run mad.

She had arrived in her uncle's house just a few hours before, and already she felt ready to scream. Living alone with Rosaline had made her accustomed to silence and solitude, both of which were now in short supply. Every niece, nephew, aunt, and cousin had descended on House Capulet, sealing themselves within its walls. Her uncle's home was large, but even his household groaned to accommodate so many. In the parlors, the women clung together in bundles of two and three, weeping for Gramio. In the courtyard, the young men practiced endless passes with their swords, making dark promises to each other of death to the Montagues. The nurse ran from one room to another, striving to meet demands for food and drink and handkerchiefs.

In short, the house was so full that Livia could not safely steal away to see Paris. She was dying to tell him all that had happened, but every time she turned around, some infernal cousin was underfoot. She tried to seek out Rosaline's company, but her sister was shaken by Gramio's death. Livia would have thought her sister would be pleased, at least, to have broken her betrothal for good. Livia certainly was. But when she'd said as much, Rosaline had merely nodded absently. She'd hidden herself away by a window, and made only distracted answers when Livia tried to talk to her, choosing instead to sit frowning at the Montague sash, which she'd taken from their uncle.

And so Livia wandered the house, sullen and irritated, as the day wore on. Gramio's mother was nearly mad with grief; a half-dozen older wives and mothers had ushered her to a private bedroom, from whence issued from time to time heartrending wails. Livia shivered late in the afternoon as yet another cry broke the air. How many such had reverberated through House Capulet's walls over the years? The weeping of feud-widows and newly sonless mothers must have watered the foundations of the place. She found herself on an upper landing on the back stair, and she leaned out of the window, looking down on the courtyard below. Her uncles were carrying something out, a long, dark shape. They laid it on the cobblestones. Gramio's coffin, for his entombment on the morrow.

Enough. She had to speak to Paris. Below, she could hear the servants summoning everyone to supper. That ought to give her enough time to slip up to his room.

She went up the stairs. A group of girl cousins passed her. "Come you to sup, Livia?" asked little Jessica.

"By and by," she said. "Go on."

They nodded, heading downstairs without another thought. Their noise died down, and she was alone. Livia stole down the corridor and around the corner, to the little door that led to the wing where Paris was hidden.

"Whither goest thou?"

She whirled around to find Duchess Francesca standing behind her. "Your Grace," she gasped. "I—I—" She covered her confusion with a curtsy.

Her great aunt ignored it. "Why, 'tis young Livia," she said. "Why art thou here, my ward? Beyond that door lie only rooms unused for years."

"Is't even so?" Livia asked, in what she hoped was a carefree tone. "The nurse bade me go and fetch Cousin Giacentio and his children for supper. That is not his chamber?"

Her great-aunt regarded her with narrowed eyes. "Nay. They are to sleep in the north chamber, on the second floor." She reached out a hand to the doorknob and Livia's heart leapt into her throat, but she only gave it a rattle. "See? 'Tis locked."

God bless the nurse. "I've been so little in this house these last few years I've quite forgot my way. Your pardon, Aunt." With another curtsy, she went back the way she had come. A glance over her shoulder revealed the duchess still staring at the closed door.

It seemed Livia would not see Paris any time soon.

In Juliet's chamber, Rosaline slept not.

Beside her, Livia's slow, even breaths counted away the minutes. Livia had objected to sleeping in Juliet's bed, fearing her shade might still haunt the chamber she'd occupied in life—the chamber where, they said, she'd consummated her love to Romeo. But for all her fear, Livia had quickly fallen asleep, untroubled by their cousin's ghost. Rosaline was glad that Livia, at least, could rest, since she'd been restless all day. She'd been badly rattled by Gramio's death, which made sense, since she'd spent so much of her time of late at the Capulet house, tending to their aunt.

A strange occupation, since they'd never been terribly close before. But Livia sometimes fixed odd ideas in her head. Perhaps she was trying to insinuate herself in the Capulet inner circle—not the worst idea, if she was to find a husband. Of late Rosaline had been too occupied with her own troubles to speak much with Livia; she promised herself that on the morrow she would.

She shifted, shielding her eyes from the moonbeams streaming through the doors to the balcony. Faith, how had Juliet ever slept with so much light pouring into the room?

Thoughts of the living, not the dead, kept Rosaline awake. Could Benvolio really have done what they said he had? True, he'd had no love for the Capulets—but Rosaline had been so certain that he was an honorable man. The thought that she could have been so wrong about him made her feel as though the ground had dropped away beneath her.

But then how came his sash and his sword on Gramio's body? That was damning enough to hang any man. Who slew Gramio, if not he? And, if he was as innocent as her aching heart wished he was, why had he fled the prince's men?

And what was it about that sash that kept niggling at her mind?

She sighed into her pillow. Thoughts of Benvolio and Livia were a welcome distraction from what weighed on her most: what had passed this afternoon with Escalus.

She had longed for this day to arrive since she was a little girl. For her beloved prince to look at her and say she was not alone, that he returned her ardor. She could not count the number of times she had pictured that moment. When she was a child, and even during the long, lonely years after her parents died, she used to lull herself to sleep imagining it. She had never thought it would actually arrive.

Was it that shock that accounted for her uneasiness? Was it lingering anger at how he'd tricked her the night of the feast? Her fury at that had faded since she'd learned how he'd saved her and Livia. And yet, his confession did not warm her as much as the pleasant dream that used to carry her into sleep had.

She rebuked herself for her foolishness. Her family was in the midst of a crisis. Her friend stood accused of murder. His city stood on the brink of civil war. Of course Escalus's confession of love had not been exactly the stuff of romantic dreams. Besides, he was right: She was inherently cautious. It was difficult for her to enjoy any good fortune.

She closed her eyes. Forget the Capulets. Forget Livia's odd behavior. Forget Benvolio's troubles. Escalus loved her. What said she to that?

There was only one thing she could say. He was her prince. Her savior. His love was a dream come true, and when she thought of the soft, anguished pleading in his eyes, her whole body shivered with an emotion so strong she could not put a name to it. Oh God, Escalus. Her Escalus at last. If, when he returned tomorrow, he asked for her hand, she would grant it.

"Rosaline!"

Rosaline sat bolt upright in bed, heart pounding. She was sure she'd heard a voice whisper her name, but there was no one there. Surely the chamber was not haunted after all?

"Rosaline, I say!"

The voice came again, and this time she realized it came from outside. Slipping quietly from the covers so as not to wake Livia, she hurried out to the balcony.

There, clinging to the ivy that mounted the balcony railing, was Benvolio.

"Benvolio!" she hissed. "Why art thou here, Montague? If they find thee here, they'll kill thee!"

"I'm here for thee, Rosaline."

Rosaline swallowed and took a step back. "What mean you, sir?"

"I need thy help. I know not where to turn. House Montague's barricaded, our young men arming themselves, the prince's men seeking me in the streets." He hoisted himself over the railing, dropping onto the balcony. Rosaline flinched, drawing away.

"Why draw you back, lady?" He stepped closer, trying to meet her eyes, but Rosaline dropped her gaze, her heart pounding so that she thought it might burst through her chest.

"They say you murdered Gramio," she whispered. "That the Montagues will make war on our house."

Benvolio looked grim. "I'm afraid 'tis true that the Montague men make ready to avenge the deaths of Orlino and Truchio, for the which they lay the blame at Capulet's door. I know not whether my kin believe I killed Gramio, but if so, many of them likely celebrate me for it. I'd hide me within their walls, but I will not give the Capulets any more excuse to blame my family for my supposed crimes. But, Rosaline, I am innocent of your cousin's blood, by my life I am."

"But your sword—your sash—"

The sash.

Suddenly she realized what had been bothering her all day about the sash found on Gramio's body. "Wait there."

On silent feet, she returned to the bedroom and took the sash from her bedside table. Returning to the balcony, she scrutinized it under the moonlight. "No paint," she said. "This cannot be your sash."

"No, 'tis Truchio's. Gramio took it from his body."

"And the sword?"

"Stolen by the man who gave me this." He pulled down his doublet and the rough bandage he'd fashioned to show her a jagged cut across his chest.

Rosaline's eyes went wide. "Get thee gone, Montague," she said. "Fly this place ere thou art discovered."

Benvolio seized her hand, pulling her back to his side. "Yea, I shall go, but not without thee."

"Me?"

He seized both her hands in his. "Aye. We must go to Friar Laurence. I feel certain he knows something of this confederacy."

"Friar Laurence? Why?"

"Send your mind back to the day we told him of Orlino's treachery," Benvolio said. "He said—"

Rosaline gripped his hands. "He said, 'You know not where the adder hides *her* sting'! He knew a woman was involved in this strife! We knew not so ourselves. He must know something of this."

"Aye." Benvolio's smile was relieved. "Friar Laurence's monastery lies some leagues without the city. I intend to fly there tonight. Wilt thou come?"

Rosaline hesitated. A cool night breeze raised gooseflesh

on her exposed arms, and she realized that she stood before a man in nothing but her nightgown.

She pulled away, wrapping her arms around herself. If she left with Benvolio, there would be nothing to stop him from doing whatever he liked to her when they were alone on the road. True, the sash was not his, but he could have fought Gramio for Truchio's crest. For just such pretexts were duels fought. She'd be putting her life in his hands. But then, she'd already done that, had she not?

What would Escalus think?

He stepped toward her. "Rosaline," he whispered, cupping her face in his hands, "you must trust me, sweet friend. You must. I beg you."

Rosaline couldn't breathe. His pleading gaze was so desperate that she couldn't look away. This must be the selfsame balcony where Juliet had trysted with Benvolio's cousin. Had Romeo's eyes ever yearned as Benvolio's did now?

A noise in the courtyard startled her. There was no time to think. She must decide. When she had proven Benvolio's innocence and uncovered the true culprit, Escalus would understand. He would thank her for it.

"Let me dress," she said. "We'd best be away before the sun rises."

Benvolio's relieved grin was like the sun breaking through the clouds. "I've horses waiting below. I hope you ride well, lady."

She tossed her head. "Well enough to leave thee and thy mount in the dust, sir."

Rosaline hurried into a clean dress and cloak before returning to Benvolio. He helped her over the balcony, supporting her body with his own so she would not fall as they climbed down to the ground.

Neither noticed a pair of eyes gleaming in the moonlight, watching their flight.

"Sweet Livia, what is wrong? Why so afear'd?"

Livia tried to calm her breathing long enough to tell Paris what had happened. She had dashed across the house and up the stairs without pausing to draw a breath—the duchess had ceased her lurking, thank God—and now her heart thundered deafeningly in her ears. Paris looked at her, concerned, and cupped her shoulder as she pressed a hand to her mouth to keep a sob from escaping. She would *not* cry, she told herself fiercely. She'd displayed enough cowardice for one night already. Rosaline would be brave. So would she.

"He took her," she managed to get out. "He stole my sister away!"

"What? Who?"

"Benvolio," she said around the lump in her throat.

Paris's eyes widened. "What? It cannot be."

"I saw it with mine own eyes." Livia drew a deep breath as Paris guided her to sit on his bed, taking her hand soothingly as she continued. "Rosaline and I slept in Juliet's chamber. I woke to hear noises outside the window. I looked over to see him taking her off the balcony. Oh God, what will he do to her?" She shook her head fiercely. "Such a fool was I. I should have cried out, I—"

"Nay, lady, you did right. The villain would have slain you both." He tenderly brushed a tear from her cheek, and Livia's heart gave a flutter despite her fear.

"What villain?"

Paris jumped, withdrawing his touch. Livia looked up to find her aunt standing in the doorway in a long white night-gown, holding a candle.

Paris gave her hand a squeeze. "Benvolio hath stolen her sister," he said.

"What! Oh, Livia!" Her aunt hurried to her side. She put an arm around Livia's shoulders, pulling her into an embrace. "My poor niece."

Livia buried her face in her aunt's sweet-smelling shoulder for a moment. "What am I to do? Is there any hope for her?"

"Fear not, sweet," Paris said. "I'll see thy sister is returned to thee." He turned to Lady Capulet. "Go and rouse the household. Every man must search high and low for my lady's sister and this scoundrel. And I pray you, have your stables saddle a horse."

Lady Capulet stiffened. "Do you mean—? Paris—"

"Aye," he said. "It's time."

She'd spoken true. Fair Rosaline could ride.

Benvolio had not been sure what horse to bring her when he'd stolen into the stables disguised as a servant for his own mount, Silvius, and a spare sword. Some ladies were afraid of all but the smallest, gentlest mounts, but such a delicate animal was not suited to the hard ride they had before them.

He needn't have worried. The bay mare he brought her was instantly smitten with her, and she had a good, confident seat. They'd ridden slowly through the darkened city, hoping to avoid attention, but as soon as they'd crept past the city gates, Rosaline leaned forward, raised her face to the eastern wind, and urged her horse into a gallop.

With a laugh of surprise, Benvolio nipped his heels in, sending an eager Silvius in pursuit. He found her waiting for him over the next hill, windblown, rosy-cheeked, and looking lighter than he'd ever seen her.

"Free of Verona at last," she said.

"By heaven, lady," he said, reining back on Silvius, who would have preferred to keep running to the horizon. "Who taught thee to ride so well?"

"My father. We rode often. Tirimos are noted horsemen, and as he'd had no son, he took me instead." She gazed out over the countryside. The rolling hills were tinged with pink from the rising sun. "Since he died, running a household leaves me little time for it, nor the money to keep a proper stables—but oh! It's lovely, is it not?"

"I think I remember thy father. Everyone envied that white mare of his. How did he die?"

Her eyes met his swiftly before she urged her Hecate into

a walk. "You do not know? 'Tis not a tale that will make us better friends."

Ah. "A Montague slew him."

"Several Montagues." A bitter smile twisted her lips. "No one has ever thought the entire tale fit for my ears, but from what I have gathered, 'twas thine uncle Signor Valentio, and Signor Martino. Marry, 'twas no unjust fight. There were at least three other Capulets in it too."

He cursed himself for asking. "I am sorry, lady."

"Oh, be not so," she sighed. Again, that mirthless smile. "My kinsmen saw to it that several Montague babes were left fatherless too, so what have I to complain of?"

Sooth, 'twas no wonder she so longed to escape Verona. He began to think she was right to do so. "It seems mine own father was quite inconsiderate to die of the ague when I was two," he told her. "There was no one to kill in his name."

He was rewarded with a laugh. They rode on, and as dawn turned to day, Benvolio told her what he knew of Gramio's death at the hands of the masked man.

"And thou hast no idea who he could be?" Rosaline asked.

"He was masked. His voice seemed familiar, but—ah, by my sword, I know not. He was a fearsome swordsman, though," Benvolio said. "'Tis no surprise if 'twas he who overcame young Truchio, and even Orlino. An inch closer to my heart and he'd have killed me too."

Rosaline drew to a halt. "Aye, I had forgot thine injury. How is it?"

"Well enough." He tapped a hand on his chest, then could not suppress a groan.

Rosaline shook her head. "Faith, Benvolio, I know not how you've managed to keep all your limbs attached to your body. Come, dismount."

They let their horses graze as she washed her handkerchief in the stream. Benvolio doffed his doublet and she cleaned the shallow cut the killer had left across his chest. He winced as she dabbed the dried blood away.

"Ay!"

"Be still," she ordered. "Unless you wish to take blood sickness."

"I hope you're as good a physician as you are a rider."

"I am, though my sister Livia's a better. She tended to our mother when she was dying of the fever, and the physicians taught her much," said Rosaline absently as she rebound his bandage as best she could. He wondered how many of her handkerchiefs he was destined to ruin with his Montague blood. "How didst thou get our mounts and your new sword, by the way?"

He struggled to be brave under her capable but not especially gentle touch. "I stole a groom's cloak and slipped into the Montague stables. The servants may have seen me, but they'd not give me up."

"At least Montague loyalty is good for something." She drew his shirt back over his bandage. "There. The monks will be able to do better for thee, I hope, when we reach the monastery."

"I am well enough. If Friar Laurence can guide us to the villain we seek, I shall ask no more of him." Rosaline started to rise, but Benvolio caught her arm. "I would speak one more word with thee ere we go."

"Yes?"

"Orlino was a scoundrel," Benvolio said. "For his death, I grieve only that he died before I could chastise him myself. But Truchio—he was little more than a child."

Rosaline turned away. "Man enough to draw his sword against an unarmed lady."

"I know, and much did I upbraid him for it. But he was under Orlino's sway when he attacked thee. He'd never have offered thee an unkind word, else." He got to his feet. "And, lady, I give thee fair warning—when we find the culprit, whether he be Montague or Capulet, my kinsmen's death shall fall heavy on him."

"You will not give the culprit over to the prince's justice?" Rosaline demanded. "I know he slew your kin, but if a Montague flouts the law yet again to slay an enemy, 'twill be no aid to the peace we seek. And the prince is like to turn the weight of his law upon you in turn. I thought you wished to end this cycle of death, Benvolio."

Benvolio narrowed his eyes. "Why speak'st thou so fawningly of the prince's justice? Thou wast no great admirer of his before. Has he bought thy allegiance with thy house?"

She gave him a glare that seemed fiercer than the question warranted. "Speak not so of our sovereign."

Benvolio sighed. "To oblige thee, lady," he said, "I will yield the villain or villains up to the prince. But if he puts them not to death, I will."

This concession did not appear to win him back into her good graces. Jaw set, Rosaline went back to Hecate and remounted. "I suppose that is the least amount of violence I can expect from one of our bloody-minded families. The hour grows long, let's away." And without waiting for him, she rode on.

"Rosaline, tarry—Rosaline!"

But she did not look back.

Prince Escalus was staring at a ghost.

He had seen County Paris's blood-covered corpse with his own eyes. Yet now his cousin stood before him on the rug in his study, thinner and paler than he had been, but very much alive. He was dressed in a dark gray velvet doublet, its elegance understated but clear. His stance was relaxed, giving no hint that a few weeks before he'd been wounded almost to death.

"You have been at *House Capulet*?" Escalus asked again. "Why on Earth? Why sent you no word? Every palace physician would have attended you."

Paris gave him a slight smile. "I was not only injured, but sick at heart as well. Had your beloved slain herself for love of another, would you have wished to expose yourself to Verona society?"

"I suppose not, but still—" Escalus cut himself off with a laugh. "Why stand I babbling about that? Paris, you live!" He leapt from behind his desk to clap his cousin in his arms. "Ah! 'Tis the only happy piece of news I have had this season."

Paris put out a hand to push him gently away. "Right glad I am to cheer you so, but I fear 'tis not only glad tidings I bring. Benvolio has abducted Lady Rosaline from House Capulet."

A chill washed over Escalus. He knew he should not have left her alone in that den of vipers. "What? How came this to pass?" he demanded.

"He climbed to Juliet's window and stole her away in the hours before dawn."

Oh God, Rosaline. If this cursed feud took her from him, woe to both houses. "Why would he so?"

"I know not. But Livia saw him take her, not three hours ago. Her cousins have since searched the streets. They're nowhere to be found. Could he have taken her to House Montague?"

Escalus shook his head. "My men searched the house at dawn."

Paris looked grim. "Then I believe he's taken her without the city walls. Your Grace, I beg your leave to go and search for them."

"You, Paris? Wherefore?" He shook his head. His hands were trembling with rage. "No. I'll go and seek them myself."

"What? Your Grace, you know you cannot."

"I'll not let him escape with her."

"Leave that to me." His cousin clapped a reassuring hand on his shoulder. "But this is a dark hour for Verona. Your city needs you here, Your Grace."

With effort, Escalus pushed the image of his hands

wrapped around Benvolio's throat from his head. "Why wish you to go?"

"Rosaline's aunt, Lady Capulet, has sheltered me these few weeks. In saving her kinswoman I hope to repay the boon." He hesitated, then continued, "Rosaline's sister nursed me with great care too. Poor Livia's quite distraught. I—I would not have her come to any grief."

It looked as though fair Livia had healed his heartsickness as well. At least some good had come of this horrible passage. "Very well, cousin. I shall send you with a company of my best men."

But Paris shook his head. "I am sure you know there's a traitor abroad in Verona," he said. "Benvolio may not have acted alone. I cannot risk having such a villain hidden among my company. I'll take but a few men of my house, loyal guards I've known since boyhood."

"Aye, that may be best. I know not who to trust of late." He gave his cousin a nod. "Very well, tell Penlet to outfit you with any supplies you and your company require. And I pray you, make all haste."

Paris made him a quick, crisp bow. "As you say. I'll away within the hour. The villain's lead is already too long."

"Good man. Pray bring them home. And, cousin—"

"Yes?"

"I should like to have Benvolio alive so that he may face the Crown's justice. But the safety of the lady is paramount. He that brings her home safely will deserve much of me."

Paris gave his cousin a long, searching look. But he said nothing, merely gave him a short nod, then turned and left.

Livia nearly did not say goodbye.

When Paris left House Capulet to go to the prince, she had wanted to go with him, but Lady Capulet forbade it. "'Tis not safe without our walls for a young lady of our house," she said.

"Nor within them either," Livia pointed out, but her aunt raised one delicate eyebrow, and Livia subsided, grumbling.

Only until her aunt turned her back, of course. They might have grown closer these last few weeks, but that did not make her aunt her mother.

When word reached House Capulet that the county was to leave immediately to seek Rosaline and Benvolio, Livia donned a dark cloak and slipped from the house through the servants' entrance. None saw her leave, and she sped through the streets unhindered to the city's east gate. Paris was half hidden deep in the shadows of its arched stone walls. The walls were fifteen feet thick, but as usual the gate stood open during the day, guarded by the prince's men. Paris stood with one hand on the reins of his horse. With him was Lady Capulet. They were deep in conversation, voices low.

"'Tis good to see you by daylight," Livia called.

Paris and her aunt started, leaping apart. "I told you to stay at home," Lady Capulet said crossly.

Livia's eyes met Paris's. "I could not let my sister's savior take his leave without offering him my thanks."

"Thou foolhardy child—"

"My lady," Paris cut Lady Capulet off, eyes never leaving Livia, "might I speak to your niece alone for a moment?"

Lady Capulet's eyes narrowed, but she bowed her head in assent. Paris took Livia by the hand, leading her just outside the city walls. The eastern road stretched out before them, a dusty ribbon among rolling green hills. Paris looked out over it, his face brooding.

"Truly, torchlight did not do you justice," she said. "Thou art twice as handsome in the sun."

Normally her flirtations made him laugh or blush. Now he looked at her solemnly. "Livia, I will do all in my power to wrest thy poor sister from Benvolio's clutches. Whatever has befallen her, her honor shall be avenged. But thou must needs prepare thyself for what I may find."

"Thou wilt find her safe and well when thou sav'st her from captivity," Livia said firmly.

He ducked his head with a mirthless smile. "Thine innocent faith in me is perhaps mislaid."

"Innocence has nothing to do with it." Raising on tiptoes, she leaned forward and brushed a soft, brief kiss against his lips. "Go forth, my champion, and take this token with thee."

Paris stared at her in shock, a hand to his lips. For a split second, Livia regretted her forwardness. She could practically hear Rosaline's *tsk* of disapproval.

But Rosaline was not here. These were strange times, the future uncertain, and Livia was tired of secrets.

She placed her hands on Paris's shoulders, giving him a gentle push. "Go," she said. "Find my sister. Please. She's all I have."

Paris stroked her hair back off her face. "Not all."

Livia cupped his hand against her cheek for a moment before he drew away, mounted his horse, and set off down the road. Her aunt came to her side, and together they watched until he was out of sight.

Rosaline avoided him till dark.

When Silvius galloped, Hecate walked; when Benvolio slowed his pace to return to her side, she declared Hecate anxious and bade her run. She knew she was being childish, but the fear he'd stirred in her breast left her unsure what to say.

The prince did not look kindly on those who took the law into their own hands. He'd exiled Romeo for slaying Tybalt, though the entire street had seen Tybalt kill Mercutio. Even if they came riding back to Verona with ironclad proof of Benvolio's innocence, Escalus might still punish him if he did not yield up the true killer to the prince's justice.

And what would she be in Escalus's eyes?

And then again and again, her mind flew back to those stolen moments in her uncle's study, and she felt as though the ground was sliding away beneath her.

Finally, she resolved to think of it no further. Her prince was miles away, and growing farther by the minute. Prove Benvolio's innocence. Find the true killer. All else could wait.

The sun was setting when she mounted a hill to find Benvolio waiting for her. "We'll camp here," he declared.

"Why? It cannot be more than a few hours farther."

"There are bandits on these roads. And since your ladyship objects to me drawing my sword on any man, no matter how villainous, I would fain avoid them."

Rosaline rolled her eyes at his snide tone. "Very well, if thou art afear'd of bandits. By all means let us stay here, an 'twill set thy fluttering heart at rest."

"Call'st thou me a coward, lady?" Glaring, he unbuckled his scabbard, throwing it at her feet. "If thou be so stout of heart, perhaps 'tis thee who should defend us."

"Be not a fool. Thou art like to a sullen child, determined to take every word spake to thee as an excuse to begin wailing again." She tried to lift his sword to throw it back at him, but the weight made her stumble. Benvolio gave a cruel laugh.

They made camp in angry silence, Rosaline grooming the horses as Benvolio lit a fire. They had no blankets, so Benvolio lay out their cloaks to sleep upon. Rosaline sighed when she turned to find he'd laid both cloaks out by her pack for her.

"Take one for yourself," she insisted.

He left his cloak where it lay. "The nights are cold in the hills, lady."

"And 'tis you whose chest gapes open to the air. Take a cloak or you'll catch your death."

He sulked away from her, sitting on a log near the fire. "Murderous Montague I may be, but I'll not deprive a lady."

Shaking her head, Rosaline plucked up his cloak and laid it about his shoulders. When she felt how he trembled beneath her touch, she knew his injury had weakened him more than he would admit. But still, he'd planned to pass the night on the damp ground for her.

Idiot.

"Montague though thou art," she said, still fussing with the hem of his cloak as she settled it about his shoulders, "murderer thou art none."

He looked up at her. The sun had set, and the firelight played over his face, hooding his dark eyes and throwing sharp shadows across his face. "Are you certain?" he asked. "For all others in Verona, save you alone, believe me a cold-blooded killer."

And she'd acted all the day as though she shared that opinion. She was not sure the Montagues would so quickly condemn him, but after the way the city had turned on him, he had earned a bit of self-pity. "Thy pardon," she murmured. "I am oft told my scorn is roused too easily."

He smirked. "Why, who has slandered my lady's sweet and gentle tongue so?"

She laughed. "One who spoke naught but truth. But, Benvolio, if I gave thee cross words this morn, 'twas because thy words struck cold fear into my breast."

Benvolio frowned. "Fear? Of what?"

She settled on the ground beside him, gazing into the fire. "After my father died, the Capulets nearly disowned us," she said. "Livia and I had no more money, so they ignored us. That little cottage was all any of them did, and we would not have got so much had the prince not given his aid. Livia cried, but I was glad. I wanted no more to do with them. I never again wanted to see someone dear to me bleed his life away on the streets." She could feel his gaze on her, but she stared at the fire, refusing to meet his eyes. "This feud of ours—'tis like to a savage beast. Its thirst for blood is never slaked. And if thou dost feed it, I fear thine own life will be the next sacrifice it demands."

Benvolio's hesitant hand came to rest between her shoulder blades. "I would never wish to cause thee grief, sweet friend," he said softly.

Rosaline rubbed angrily at her eyes. "The grief of wives and sisters and daughters is always forgot when these brawls arrive, though, is it not?"

"Perhaps."

She turned to look at him. His eyes were solemn, his handsome face less boyish in the ruddy light. "Thou art the best of them, Benvolio," she told him. "Wise and strong and slow to anger. I pray to God to keep thee so."

Benvolio ducked his head, and Rosaline was amused to note that his ears had blushed bright red. "We'd best sleep," he said.

Rosaline nodded and returned to the cloak he'd laid out for her. Benvolio curled up on the other side of the fire, apparently quite comfortable sleeping out of doors.

Rosaline, on the other hand, had never slept out in the wild. When a twig snapped, she sat bolt upright. "Is it highwaymen?" she hissed.

Benvolio's sleepy chuckle drifted across the fire. "'Tis a rabbit, lady."

"Oh." She settled back down. "Art thou certain?"

Benvolio heaved himself up, dragging his cloak around the fire and resettling himself a few feet behind her. "There," he said. "Now any highwaymen or villainous rabbits will meet my blade ere they encounter thee."

She ought to object to his lying so near, but he had already begun to snore softly. Rosaline's own eyes grew heavy. With Benvolio's steady warmth at her back, sleep soon found her.

Benvolio found it hard to wake her up.

In the night Rosaline had drawn close—or perhaps, he acknowledged, it was he who'd reached out and drawn her against his side—and he'd woken to find her warm body pressed against his, her hair tickling his nose. He gently drew a few modest inches away, and as the sun rose he lay watching her, sleepily distracted by how its rosy hues played in her hair, smiling at how she twitched and snuffled as the smoke of the dying fire reached her nose. But he'd promised her they'd make an early start, so he squeezed her shoulder.

"Leave off, Livia, 'tis not near day."

He chuckled. "Day is here, lady. Dost thou not hear the lark?"

She rolled over, her arm flopping across his face. "Hush," she mumbled. "'Tis not the—"

She froze, perhaps realizing that she was not in her bed and Benvolio was not her sister. She cracked one eye open. "Perhaps 'tis the lark," she acknowledged.

Benvolio grinned. "I am ready to declare it any bird thou say'st, lady."

Narrowing her eyes at him, she sat up. "How close are we to the monastery?"

"Eight leagues off, I should say." He rose and stretched, wincing at the protests from his saddle-sore body. After breakfasting on some bread and cheese from Benvolio's pack, they broke camp and set off, riding together this time. Just after midday, they turned a bend in the road, and a large stone edifice rose before them, surrounded by farmland. There was a smaller gray building off to the side.

"Montenova Abbey," Benvolio said. "And the nunnery of Saint Cecilia lies beside it. I'll go and tell them we're here. Prithee stay and let the horses graze."

"Aye."

Benvolio walked up the road and raised the heavy iron knocker. The hollow thump was so muffled by the large oak door that he wondered if it could be heard inside at all. But a moment later a voice called, "Who is here?"

"I am Signor Benvolio of Verona," he called. "I seek an audience with Friar Laurence, late of our fair city, now resident among your brethren."

There was a pause, then the door creaked open. A small, white-haired monk came bustling out. "Brother Laurence, you say? Wherefore?"

Benvolio was not inclined to lay the whole sordid tale at the feet of a stranger, even a holy friar. "He was my schoolmaster. I crave his counsel," Benvolio said.

"I am sorry, good signor, Brother Laurence sees no one.

He is but newly arrived, and he has been deep in prayer and speaks little. He wishes no company."

Benvolio hid a frustrated sigh under a polite smile. The monk at the door returned it gently. "Only tell him I am here," Benvolio said. "I am sure he will change his mind. I pray you tell him 'tis a matter of some urgency, touching the House Montague."

"As you wish," the monk said doubtfully, and withdrew.

He returned a few minutes later. "As I told you," he said, saintly smile still in place, "my brother Laurence abjures earthly company. Good day to you, my son."

"Wait! It's urgent. Please—"

But the door shut in his face. Sighing, he returned to Rosaline's side. "What did they say?" she asked.

"Their door is barred to us." Benvolio swore, then said, "Your pardon, lady."

She shrugged. "An 'twere ladylike to swear . . ."

"We came all this way! I was so sure he'd help us." Benvolio cast a longing glance at the doorway. "What are we to do?" His hand strayed toward his sword.

"Benvolio!" Rosaline grabbed his arm. "Thou'lt not draw your sword on men of God. There must be another way." Rosaline frowned, twisting one curl around her finger. "Sanctuary," she said finally. "Go thou back there and claim sanctuary. At least then thou'lt be within their walls. Friar Laurence cannot escape thee forever. He'll have to emerge to eat. Then canst thou force him to acknowledge thee."

Benvolio shook his head. "Sanctuary is for those in peril of their lives," he said.

"What think'st thou that *thou* art?" Rosaline pointed out.

"Fair enough. But what of thee?"

"I'll to Saint Cecilia's. They will let a maiden pass the night there, 'tis certain."

Benvolio frowned. "I like not that thou shouldst be so far. But I suppose thou shalt be safe enough among thy future sisters."

She looked startled. "What?"

"When you take holy orders, I mean."

"I— Of course." She nodded to the monastery. "Thou hadst better go."

Odd. For a moment she'd looked like she'd altogether forgotten her plans to become a nun. She had not changed her mind, had she? That thought was surprisingly welcome—for her sake, not for his, of course. How could such a fair and witty maid hide herself away from the world, allowing her bloom of youth to wither unadmired and unloved?

But he knew his advice on the subject would hardly be welcomed, so he said only, "Very well."

Returning to the monastery, he rapped once more on the door. When it opened, the monk sighed. "My son—"

Benvolio had never shoved a man of God in his life, and he endeavored to do so now as gently as possible. The monk gave a squawk as Benvolio strode past him into the hall.

"What in the world!"

Benvolio held up a placating hand. "I claim sanctuary within these walls."

The monk's eyes narrowed. "Sanctuary is not for children

who have not got their way. 'Tis a haven for those desperate souls in mortal danger from without."

Benvolio gave him a mirthless smile. "Holy father," he said. "'Tis clear you know little of what has passed in Verona of late. Mortal danger is an apt description of my circumstances."

The monk threw up his hands and scurried off. After a few minutes he returned, and Benvolio was conducted to the abbot's study, where he was once more told that Friar Laurence was unavailable.

"Then I will simply stay until he is free to see me," Benvolio said firmly. "Are there any chores an able-bodied man may perform for your holy order, Father? I would be happy to help for as long as I remain here."

The abbot sighed. "Well, son," he said, "it seems you shall have your will. Master Montague, you may pass the night here, if you'll consent to take your leave at daybreak."

Benvolio smiled. "I'll do so happily, if I have done that I came for. Where is Friar Laurence?"

"I told you, he'll none of you!" But the abbot's eyes flicked toward a tower at the northeast end of the building. Benvolio smiled inwardly. Rosaline's plan showed wit indeed.

A convent such as this could be her home.

Saint Cecilia's was rather less grand than the monastery, though constructed of the same cold gray stone. Many ladies of Verona took orders here. She had long thought she would be among them. But of course, the prince had changed everything. Rosaline knocked on the large wooden door and a small window opened. "Who goes there?" said the rectangular section of nun that appeared.

"One who would shelter with you for the night," Rosaline called. "My name is Rosaline, daughter of Niccolo Tirimo. I am a lady and a maid."

"Come in, my child," she said to Rosaline.

She did, looking around as she followed the nun to the abbess's chambers. The convent was plain but well kept, echoing with the sounds of prayer and the quiet steps of its black-clad occupants. Some of them darted curious glances at Rosaline, probably thinking she was a new postulant. Benvolio must be wondering why she had forgotten that she was one day to join such a cloister. In truth, she had not given a thought as to what to say to her traveling companion. Should she tell him that her heart was the prince's now? There was no official understanding between her and Escalus, and in any case, what would Benvolio care? The only reason they'd passed so much time together was to escape their own betrothal. If he heard that another man had now spoken for her, he would probably cheer. Yes, it would probably be a great relief to him to be rid of her for good, even though she had helped him at every turn, had believed him when no one else would, had even fled the city to help him. But what of that? He would always—

"My lady?"

She turned to find her guide hovering uncertainly behind

her. In her anger she'd outpaced the woman without noticing.

She was tired from traveling. That was the only reason that the thought of Benvolio blessing her love for Escalus had driven her into such a fury. She carefully declined to consider any other explanation.

The friar was not easily tracked down.

Benvolio spent the day helping the monks, chopping wood, hauling water, and tending to their livestock. They gave him a poultice for his wound, which was already healing—luckily, it was not too deep. But no matter how much he tried to ingratiate himself, none of them would usher him to see the man he'd come for. He had a feeling that the abbot was assigning him outdoor tasks to keep him far from his quarry.

Growing impatient, on the second day he took his supper early and then waited outside the dining room, standing in a corner where he was not easily observed. The monks flowed in and out in twos and threes, supping for an hour or so before heading to their evening prayers. Finally, as the night hymns began to echo through the stone halls, he spied a lone figure hurrying from the dining hall.

"Good e'en, Father," he said, stepping out to block Friar Laurence's path.

Friar Laurence started, clutching a hand to his chest. Glaring at Benvolio, he crossed himself, then moved to step around him. Benvolio stepped aside to block him again. "I bade you good e'en. Have you no kind word in return for your old pupil?"

Friar Laurence merely scowled and hurried past him. Apparently his silence would not be broken so easily.

Nor was Benvolio easily discouraged. He hurried after him. "Very well, I shall accompany you. I am sure you are famished for news of home, banished as you are." The friar tried to walk faster, but Benvolio's long legs easily kept pace. "Another of your old pupils is dead, did you know?" The friar looked pained at that. "Aye. Truchio is slain. They say it was a man clothed all in black. Know you who Verona's deadly shadow might be, Father?" His voice had grown loud. The monks they passed looked rather scandalized at such earthly tidings being shared under their roof. Friar Laurence, now muttering a Hail Mary, gave him a tight shake of the head. "Come, I am sure you know, sir. You were ever at the center of my family's bloody doings. Why, Romeo slew himself nearly beneath your nose!"

A wide-eyed young monk crossed himself as they passed him. Benvolio cared not. Unexpected anger was building in his chest. Verona was burning, and the friar had cloistered himself in this sleepy place. What a coward.

"Well," Benvolio continued, "if you know not who the man might be, what about she who aids him?"

A ripple of shock passed across Friar Laurence's face. "Aye," Benvolio said. "There is a woman involved in all this, as well you know."

They had reached the base of Friar Laurence's tower. After pulling the heavy wooden door open, the friar at last turned to look him in the eye. "Stop," he hissed. "I cannot help thee. I swear I would if I could, but I cannot. Go home."

He tried to draw the door shut, but Benvolio wrenched it from his grasp. "I have no home. If once I set foot within Verona's walls, I shall be killed. I stand accused of the death of Gramio, a young Capulet." He followed the friar up the winding stair to the summit of the tower. The friar was a learned man, and it seemed his brothers had honored him with rather fine quarters. He had been here only a day or so, but he must have sent his things ahead, for he was as comfortably ensconced as though he'd been here for years. His chamber was small but airy, with windows on three sides. His books lined the shelves, and Benvolio recognized many of the volumes of Latin and mathematics that had tortured him and Romeo as small boys. A desk was scattered with papers and ink pots. Plants overspilled their pots and twined over the windowsills. This must be heaven on earth for the retiring, scholarly friar.

"A fine chamber," Benvolio said. "I shall not find the prince's jail so comfortable, I fear. Does my fate not trouble you at all, my old teacher? Or will you idle away your days here till all your pupils are slain and none of us remains to remind you of your sins?"

Friar Laurence turned to look at him at last, and the grim set of his jaw reminded Benvolio of his school days. The friar had been a gentle, tolerant teacher, but on the rare occasions when the small Montagues had reached the limits of his patience, his fury had awed them. Benvolio could still feel the sting of the switch on his hand.

But he was not a child anymore.

"Attend and mark, young scoundrel," said the friar. "Much as I might wish to stop your kinsmen's slaughterous ways, my loyalty is to a higher power than the Montagues. Even for my dearest pupils, I will not break my vows."

Aha. A clue at last. Benvolio seized on it. "Break your vows?"

Friar Laurence closed his eyes. "I have spoke rashly."

What part of his vows could prevent the friar from saving lives? Benvolio puzzled as the friar went to the window, stooping over the sill, his body an arc of defeat. Benvolio pushed aside a pile of papers to perch on a corner of the friar's desk. Then it struck him: A friar was privy to all sorts of information, very little of which he was at liberty to share.

"Someone told you something in confession," he realized.

Friar Laurence said nothing, but the slump of his shoulders told Benvolio he was correct. "Who was it?" he asked.

"Well thou knowest, boy, I cannot tell thee."

"Father, lives are at stake. Give me a name. Some hint at least. God will understand."

"Knowest thou God's plan, now?" The friar gave a bitter laugh. "Nay, I have sinned enough in thy family's name."

Benvolio's fist clenched in disappointment. In doing so, he nudged one of the piles of papers, which began to slide off the desk. As he righted it, he noted a small red book beneath it. It was open, both pages covered with the friar's tiny, neat writing. A passage caught his eye.

. . . fear if she stoppeth not, Romeo shall soon . . .

Benvolio frowned, intrigued. Friar Laurence still had his back to him, head bent in prayer. Praying that Benvolio would let him be a coward in peace, no doubt. Discreetly, Benvolio tugged the journal toward him, so he could see the full page.

> *A came to me again today for confession. Sweet soul, she little understands the intelligence she possesses. Her loyalty does her credit, even if those she grants it have little merit.*
>
> *The attacks continue, and of course none shall suspect their culprits, for the villainess is too highly placed. I fear if she stoppeth not, Romeo shall soon be joined by the greater part of his kin, and by the Capulets too, strange though that seems. But I cannot speak to stay L's murderous arm. What can the vixen have done to earn such fanatical following? And how can a mother so persecute her own daughter's—*

Before Benvolio could read on, a hand slammed down upon the pages of the book. Friar Laurence snatched it from beneath his nose, snapping it shut. "How dare you!" he snarled, peaceful face twisted with fear and rage.

"How dare *you!*" Benvolio cried, stabbing a finger at the book. "Enough, Friar! I know right well that the Duchess Vitruvio is behind all this, and there's the proof!"

The friar drew a sharp breath. His nostrils had gone white. "You know nothing."

"L. Who is L, Friar?" He saw suddenly, in his mind's eye, the duchess's hulking, silent servant bending over her. Lucullus. Her manservant. It was he who wore the mask. Benvolio extended his hand. "Give me the book. The prince shall know of this."

But Friar Laurence ran to the window and rang a bell that hung there, the clangor echoing through the courtyard below. Seconds later, three of the monks' servants burst through the door. "Seize him," he said. "Escort him without our walls. His sanctuary is at an end."

Prayer, then cooking. Prayer, then laundry. Prayer.

The day was long, the work hard, the food sparse, and the bed cold. The abbess was a cold-eyed woman of fifty, clearly contemptuous of soft noble hands. To appease her, Rosaline had insisted on joining entirely in the life of the nunnery for as long as she stayed there, just as a postulant would, but as she knelt in the garden, trying to pry radishes from the ground with throbbing, aching fingers, she was glad she would not be adopting this life permanently.

She paused to wipe her brow. A few feet away, a postulant

bent over her own row of turnips; two more knelt beyond her. In a few minutes the bell would ring, and they would file in to wash and go to supper. In truth, it was not the work that bothered her, but already she chafed against the monotonous tyranny of the hourly bell. The clamor and color of life in Verona seemed as distant as the Orient. Here there was only the murmur of prayer, the gray stone, and always that bell. There was beauty in the order and simplicity of the nuns' lives, but by this day, it was dull.

Still, she'd passed an entire day without once hearing the names *Montague* or *Capulet*. Which was a pleasant change, to be sure. Such a day was unlikely to pass once she was Princess of Verona.

That thought made her freeze. If she wed Escalus, she would be a princess. How had she never thought of that?

Escalus's mother was called Princess Maria, the pretty, birdlike daughter of a Sicilian duke. Her circle had been small and intimate. Just a few ladies attended her, including Rosaline's mother. Every summer, she rode out hunting with Lord and Lady Montague at their country estate. The princess hated hunting. She cried to see the game fall. But that was the price she paid for not having a Montague lady in her inner circle. She could not appear to favor one family over the other.

If Rosaline married Escalus, keeping the peace between Verona's great houses would be as much her task as his. The feud that seemed so distant from this quiet garden would be her daily occupation.

Well, someone had to do it, she thought grimly. Perhaps

Escalus's task would be easier if he was wed to one who already knew the players in this endless game.

"Ah, see how the mighty house of Tirimo is fallen."

She turned to find Benvolio, hands hooked on his belt, staring down at her with a mocking grin. "Good e'en, Benvolio," she said. "Think you that good, honest labor in the service of God is so shameful?"

"I think you look more miserable now than you did with three swords pointed at your throat."

She did not care to tell him that her frown came from contemplating hunting with his kin. Instead she wiped her hands on the apron they'd lent her and stood. "Miserable? Never less so," she claimed.

"Truly? Do you truly think you can forgo the beauty and excitement of Verona for radishes and these infernal bells?"

"The rhythm of the bell is soothing," she retorted, as if she'd not just thought the same thing. "And in any case, what concern is it of yours, Master Benvolio?"

He shrugged. "I think thee much prettier without a coating of dirt." He reached out a thumb, wiping at the side of her forehead.

"Ahem."

They turned to find the abbess behind them, eyes narrowed. Benvolio withdrew his hand.

The abbess put a hand on Rosaline's shoulder and drew her away from him. "We've word from Montenova," she said to him. "Father Laurence says you were turned out of their door and we're to have no traffic with you. Come, daughter, we've a basin for you to wash yourself."

Rosaline followed her to a chamber near the garden. As she splashed frigid well water on her arms and face, Mother Abbess said, "There will be none of that, you know."

"None of what, Mother?"

"You assured me that you were a noble lady of good character when you took shelter beneath our roof," the abbess said. "One who had kept chaste and away from the company of men."

Rosaline laughed. "Do you mean Benvolio, Mother? I assure you, he need not concern you."

"I know what sin looks like, lady." She shoved a towel at Rosaline. "Dry yourself."

She did so, having no more words with the abbess, as she could think of nothing to say that was not unconscionably rude. But it seemed the abbess had no such qualms.

"Benvolio is to return to Verona, the friars tell me," she said when Rosaline had washed and changed. "You will, of course, stay here, until a more suitable chaperone may be found."

Rosaline blinked. "Your pardon, Mother, but I cannot. If Benvolio has what we came for, I must return with him."

"You will not travel alone on the road with a young ruffian whose company even holy brothers cannot abide. Your chastity demands you remain."

Rosaline's gaze followed the abbess's out the window where Benvolio waited on the other side of the garden. When he saw her looking, he waved. Rosaline shook her head. "My chastity is in no danger from him."

"The worst sin is that which the sinner will not see."

Enough of this. With a curtsy to the abbess, she hurried to Benvolio's side. "I hear even monks cannot abide your company," she teased.

But his face was grim. "Come. We must return to Verona." He put a hand on her back, ushering her toward the gate. Knowing the abbess's gaze was still on them, Rosaline felt as though his touch was burning straight through her clothing. She tried to take a modest step away, but he stayed close, hulking protectively around her.

Beyond the nunnery gates, she found Hecate and Silvius saddled and ready to ride. Benvolio turned to her.

"I spoke to Friar Laurence." He sketched out what had passed in the monastery.

"So he did not name the duchess?" she asked, frowning.

"No, but 'tis quite clear, is it not?"

Rosaline had to own that it was. "So L is Lucullus," she said. "That explains how the duchess has been able to manage the slaughter. But who is A?"

"That puzzles me still."

"A. A." Rosaline snapped her fingers. "Angelica."

"Angelica?"

"'Tis the given name of Juliet's nurse. Rememb'rest thou, she was at the duchess's house?"

"Of course. She must have seen something there and told the friar, without realizing what intelligence she possessed." Benvolio looked worried. "I hope the good soul has spake not of it to anyone save her confessor."

Rosaline suppressed a shudder. She hated to think of Juliet's nurse in danger. "Hast thou the book? We'd best show it to the prince."

Benvolio shook his head. "Friar Laurence had me thrown out the door. He'll not let me touch it."

"Very well, we'll just have to tell the prince what thou saw'st." If they could convince the prince to believe Benvolio's story, she added silently. Escalus might love her, but last she saw him, that had not been enough to convince him to trust Benvolio.

Benvolio noticed her discomfiture. "What?"

She shook her head. "Only a Montague could so irritate a company of holy friars that they could not abide him even for holy sanctuary."

Benvolio paused from checking Silvius's bridle to look affronted. "Yonder black-habit looks no more pleased with thee, Capulet wench."

Sure enough, the abbess was across the courtyard, giving her a stare that could powder granite. Rosaline offered her a weak smile and bobbed a curtsy. "True, but it's because she wants me to stay, not to go. She thinks I'll be not safe on the road with thee."

Benvolio frowned. "She may be right. Perhaps thou shouldst stay."

"So the prince's men can kill thee on sight? Be not such a fool. I must vouch for thy honesty, thou knowest it well."

"If I must sacrifice mine own safety to keep thee from harm—"

"Then art thou a fool indeed, and shall vex me greatly.

There is no safer place in Italy for me than at thy side." Without waiting for a response, she took hold of Hecate's pommel and swung herself up into the saddle. "Come. The hour grows long. Let's away."

She wheeled Hecate about, starting down the dusty road back to Verona. After a minute, she heard Benvolio's soft curse behind her and the clop of Silvius's hooves. He, at least, heeded her counsel.

The clouds grew gray above them as they rode.

Benvolio cast an apprehensive glance toward the sky. In the scant hours since they'd left the abbey, the sky had gone from a soft, dusty blue to angry gray, and the air had developed an ominous chill. Ahead of him, Rosaline's hair whipped wildly in the wind as she leaned over Hecate's charging neck.

He drew even with her. "Lady!" he shouted over the wind. "This sky bodes ill! 'Twill be a hard storm! We ought to find an inn for the night."

She shook her head, urging Hecate even faster. "We must press on," she called.

"Rosaline." He reached out and grasped Hecate's reins, pulling both horses to a walk. "We're no good to Verona if we lose our way in a storm. We cannot return tonight."

Rosaline's chin was rising mulishly, an expression that Benvolio was beginning to learn boded ill for his chances of changing her mind. "I beg of thee," he said quickly. "I am already falsely believed responsible for one death. Do not make me truly responsible for thine."

She rolled her eyes. "'Twould not be thy fault."

"Thou told'st me when we left the abbey that thou didst trust me with thy life," he retorted. "If thou shouldst perish on our way, 'twill prove that sour-faced abbess right."

Before Rosaline could respond, they heard a clap of thunder, and, indeed, Hecate began to dance nervously. "Very well," Rosaline called, soothing the trembling mare with strokes to the neck. "At the next village we shall stop for the night."

"Agreed."

They rode on, but their progress was soon slowed as the storm began in earnest. The wind whipped the rain into their faces, the trees swaying above them in the gale as the sky went black. Benvolio rode on Rosaline's windward side, trying to shield her, but there was little he could do. The horses struggled, slipping and sliding as their hooves sank into the mud.

They were less than a league from the village, by his calculation, when his worst fears came to pass. Lightning struck a tree just a few hills away, and at the blinding flash and deafening crack, Silvius reared, shrieking. For several heart-pounding instants Benvolio struggled to calm the terrified animal. Just when he settled all four hooves back to the ground, Benvolio heard another scream. He looked around to find that Rosaline had not been so lucky. Hecate was bolting up the path, Rosaline clinging desperately to her reins.

She disappeared into the trees, but as he dug his heels into Silvius's sides, he caught a flash of her crimson cloak far ahead. The narrow path twisted down the mountain above the bank of a river; yesterday it had been a sleepy trickle far below, but the rain had swollen it to a roar so powerful he could scarcely hear Silvius's hooves strike the ground. His eyes strained through the gloom, but he could not catch another glimpse of her. And then he heard her cry out again. Leaning over his horse's neck, he urged the steed faster, rounding the bend just in time to see Hecate rear. Lightning flashed, and for a moment he saw Rosaline frozen, clinging desperately to Hecate's neck, before her horse lost its footing and horse and rider plunged over the side of the bank.

"No!"

Benvolio was barely aware that the hoarse cry he heard had been ripped from his own throat. He threw himself off Silvius's back, racing to the broken, crumbling spot on the path where she'd vanished. "Rosaline!" he yelled. "Rosaline!" Falling to his knees, he strained his eyes for any sign of her. All he could see was a steep, muddy drop of a hundred feet to sharp rocks and white water below. No one could survive that fall.

She'd been swept away. She was dead.

It was as though Silvius had kicked him in the chest. Benvolio couldn't breathe. Heedless of the rain and the wind, he curled to the ground, hands pressed to his forehead, eyes wide but unseeing. *She's dead, she's dead, she's dead.*

And then lightning flashed again, and a streak of crimson caught his eye.

Crawling on his hands and knees to the edge of the cliff, he peered down over the edge. Yes! There it was, perhaps ten feet below the path. A small rocky outcropping jutted from the side of the cliff, and on it lay Rosaline's crumpled form.

As he watched, she stirred and groaned. Heart in his throat, he called, "Rosaline!"

She struggled to sit up. "Benvolio?"

"Art thou hurt?"

"Not badly, I think."

"Move not." Running back to Silvius, he found a length of rope tied to his saddle. He tied one end to a tree and knotted a loop in the other end, then threw it to Rosaline.

She slipped her head and shoulders through the sling he'd fastened for her. "Hold fast," he called down. She nodded, gripping it tightly. Benvolio went down on his belly, hauling up the rope. His chest burnt—his injury made this far more difficult than it ought to be. He felt his palms begin to slip. He gritted his teeth and pulled harder.

Just as he thought he could do no more, Rosaline's hands appeared, pulling herself up. Benvolio reached a hand out and she grasped it. He hauled her over the edge, and then she was there, she was safe, and they collapsed to the muddy ground in a heap.

Benvolio sat up, pulling her to her knees. "Art thou well? Art thou sound?" His hands chased over her shoulders, her arms, her head, searching for injury.

Her hands grasped his wrists as she managed to give him a shaky smile. "I am unhurt."

He cupped her face in his hands, leaning his forehead

against hers. His breath was coming in deep gasps; he could not seem to calm his racing heart. She was all right. She was alive. She was *alive*.

He kissed her.

He felt her breath catch as his mouth slanted over hers, desperate and possessive. His hands threaded through her hair as hers fisted in his tunic. There was no decision in his mind to pull her closer, no thought except the need to *feel* that she still lived. He crushed her against him, every inch of them pressed together from shoulders to hips to knees as his mouth explored hers.

A crash of thunder broke them apart on a gasp. Her fingertips brushed her swollen lips as she stared at him, wide-eyed. Benvolio swallowed. He had no idea what to say.

He released her and stood. "We'd best away," he said. "We must find shelter."

Rosaline ducked her head and nodded, getting to her feet as well and trying to little avail to clean some of the mud from her gown and hair. "Hecate is gone," she said in a shaking voice. "She was swept away. I am sorry—"

He brushed away her apology gruffly. "Let us begone. Silvius can carry us both." He helped her onto Silvius's back before mounting in front of her. Rosaline wrapped her arms around him from behind, and Silvius set off down the path once more.

Luckily, they had not strayed far from the main road. Even there, though, conditions were treacherous, as fallen branches dotted their path. Keeping them safe took all Benvolio's attention, for which he was grateful. He did not care to examine what in the world he had just done.

Although, with Rosaline's arms about his waist and her warm weight against his back, it was hard not to dwell on it.

After an hour or so he spotted a village ahead. He urged weary Silvius on until they reached it. There was an inn, thank heaven, by all appearances clean and well-appointed. He drew Silvius to a halt outside. From Rosaline's steady breaths at his neck, he knew she was asleep. He squeezed her hand.

"Rosaline," he said. "Wake."

"Mmm," a weary voice came over his shoulder. "Are we home?"

"No, lady. Verona is still many leagues off. Shall we pass the night here?"

Her warmth left his back; he tried not to miss it. "We cannot press on? No, I suppose not. Very well."

They rented two rooms for what remained of the night. The innkeeper was irritated at being woken, but Benvolio mollified him with a generous tip.

After seeing Rosaline safely to her room, Benvolio collapsed on his bed, asleep almost instantly.

Benvolio! She woke up with a gasp.

Rosaline sat stark upright in bed, heart pounding. Before she slept she'd been too weary to give much consideration to the night's events. Now that she'd had a few hours' rest, it weighed so heavily upon her mind that it had woken her up.

He had kissed her. *Kissed* her. And no gentlemanly kiss upon the hand, either. This was a lover's kiss. What was she to do?

Perhaps he had not meant anything by it. Some men, she knew, would take such casual advantage of a lady alone. In some ways, it would be easier to dismiss it as but his momentary whim. But Benvolio was more honorable than that. And the tenderness she'd seen in his eyes spoke of something more than a fleeting fancy.

Rosaline swung her feet onto the floor, wincing at the aches throughout her body. Her fall had left her more bruised than she'd realized. Gingerly she felt the back of her skull; there was a throbbing lump there where her head had struck the rocks.

A knock at the door proved to be the chambermaid with an offering to draw her a bath, which she gratefully accepted. Once the large basin had been filled with steaming buckets of water, she sank into it with a grateful sigh, scrubbing away the mud and fear and confusion of the night before.

If he had merely stolen a kiss, all would be well. But no, God forgive her, Rosaline had returned the kiss, touch for touch, breath for breath. She sank down beneath the water, mortified by her own remembered wantonness. She had rejected Romeo because she'd loathed the idea of involving herself in their families' feud—and then last night found her so entangled with another Montague it had been difficult to say where Capulet ended and Montague began.

She could almost see cousin Juliet's shade laughing at her.

What did he wish from her? More to the point, what did she wish from him? If there was one thing Rosaline thought she knew, it was that she would never love any man but Escalus. Shame shot through her as his face rose in her mind. God, she was all but betrothed to him!

Was she, though?

The last time she had seen Escalus, he had declared his love. He had looked at her with all the tenderness she had ever longed to see from him. He had left her with the knowledge that he would almost certainly ask for her hand the next morning.

And she had fled in the night with another man.

She'd had her reasons, to be sure. But it was high time she faced the truth: A part of her had been glad to escape before Escalus asked for her hand, because she was not certain what her answer should be.

That part of her seemed to grow stronger every time Benvolio's rakish grin kindled a shy warmth in her belly.

What did it matter? He was still a Montague. Even if Escalus had never wooed her, any union between herself and Benvolio could only end in grief. One storm-swept, fear-fueled kiss did not change that, nor did it change what she felt for Escalus. Sternly ordering herself to stop fretting, she turned her attention to scrubbing herself pink.

After a good bath and dragging a comb through her wet hair, she felt a bit more like her old self. The chambermaid had cleaned her muddy clothes, and she dressed and went across the hall to Benvolio's room.

"Come in," he called at her knock, and Rosaline opened the door to find him bare to the waist, wet-haired, dressing after his own bath.

Rosaline gasped, clapping a hand over her eyes. At the sound, Benvolio whipped around. "Rosaline!"

"Pray pardon me—"

"No, no, the fault is mine, I thought you were the groom—"

Rosaline turned, fumbling toward the door without opening her eyes. She knocked something from his dresser and it landed on the floor with a crash. Trying to retrieve it, she smacked her head on the dresser.

"Peace, lady." Benvolio's hand was at her shoulder. "Thou may'st safely ope thine eyes."

She did and found him now fully clothed, retrieving his belt from the floor, looking bemused at her sudden clumsiness. One kiss seemed to have turned her into an idiot.

Enough. She had always been the cooler head between them; now was no time for that to change. She drew a deep breath, but before she could speak, he said quickly, "Lady, last night on the path—I must press upon thee how sorry I am—"

"Thou art sorry for it?"

"I—that is—" His mouth opened and closed. "I know not what to say."

"Nor I."

They stared at each other. Rosaline swallowed. His gaze had once more fallen to her mouth.

There was a clatter of hooves out in the courtyard. Rosaline tensed, eyes flying to the window—that many horsemen were unlikely to be good news. Sure enough, a deep male voice began to roar outside.

"We seek the murderer Benvolio of Montague! In the name of His Grace the Prince of Verona, if the villain or the maid he hath stolen be within your walls, produce them!"

Benvolio cursed under his breath. Rosaline crept to the window, peering carefully out; there were perhaps three dozen liveried men. Curiously, none wore the uniform of the prince's guard; some appeared to be mercenaries and the rest wore green and yellow livery, and a crest she recognized but could not place. As she watched, the innkeeper emerged and spoke with the man who had shouted. She saw the inn-keeper nod and point up toward their rooms. Looking at Benvolio, she mouthed, "They come."

His mouth was set in a thin line. He nodded shortly, buck-ling on his sword. Taking her hand, he jerked his head toward the back stairs. Turning the knob carefully, he opened the door a crack, and they slipped out into the corridor. But they were too late. Rosaline's heart squeezed painfully in her chest as she heard boots pounding up the back stairs. Benvolio's grip on her hand felt as though he might break her fingers as he tugged her toward a vacant guest room. He pulled the door shut behind them just as the guardsmen arrived in the corridor.

"'Tis here the young man slept, gentles," the old inn-keeper said. "The young lady was across the hall. They gave not their names, but they did say they were bound for Ve-rona." Rosaline gave a soundless gasp. Benvolio shook his head at her fiercely. They listened silently as their rooms were searched. Rosaline looked around. The room they were in had a window, but they were far too high to jump—they'd break their legs at best. There was no other way out, except past the men searching for them. She leaned up to whisper into Benvolio's ear, "What are we to do?"

"Perhaps they'll think we are fled and leave," he breathed.

It would be unlikely, except that mercenaries were not exactly known for their intelligence. Indeed, after their rooms were found bare, she heard their seekers have a muffled conference in the corridor, then their boots began to tramp back down the front stairs. She was about to breathe a sigh of relief when one last lone set of footsteps paused outside the door of the chamber where they were hidden. Before she knew what was happening, Benvolio had yanked her into the closet, pulling the door shut.

Just in time, for the guardsman opened the door to the vacant chamber, his footsteps slowly sounding across the floorboards. Rosaline's heart thundered in her ears. The small closet was scarcely large enough for the two of them. Benvolio was pressed tightly against her, so that she could feel every tense rise and fall of his chest. He had one hand braced on the wall behind her and the other covering her mouth to smother any sound. The footsteps came back toward the door. Then, by the closet, they paused.

In the near-darkness, Rosaline's eyes found Benvolio's. As his hand shifted to his sword, they held a silent communion, and Rosaline found that though they spoke not a word, she knew exactly what to do. The handle of the door began to turn, but without waiting for the door to open, they burst out of the closet as one. The startled guardsman gave a shout, but Rosaline had already stepped back and to the side, giving Benvolio space to draw his sword and send the fellow sprawling. "Run!" he roared at her. She dashed into the corridor. The other guardsmen, hearing the commotion, were returning, but Benvolio was in front of her, blade at the ready, as they retreated toward the rear stairs.

Luckily the corridor was narrow, and the back stairs more so, and Benvolio was able to keep them at bay. Rosaline knew they had a minute at best, so despite the terror each clang of steel sent through her, she did not look back to see Benvolio's fate. Instead she flew down the stairs three at a time, scrambling across the yard behind the inn and back to the stables. Silvius nickered anxiously as she threw his stall open and thanked God he was already saddled. Leaping onto his back, she raced to the door and yelled, "Benvolio, hither!"

He came pelting out the door, guardsmen at his heels, and vaulted onto Silvius's back behind her. He had scarce landed before she threw Silvius into a gallop, and Benvolio's arms squeezed her waist as Silvius's surging muscles gathered themselves and he leapt over the stone wall behind the inn, landing with a bone-jarring thump.

"Do not stop!" he shouted in her ear. "They still pursue us." Rosaline hazarded a glance back and saw that he was right. A handful of men had managed to get a-horse and were in pursuit, but their mounts were nowhere near as fast as Silvius and their roars of frustration soon died away behind them. After a few minutes, they reached the edge of the forest once more, and Rosaline gave a sigh of relief, drawing

Silvius down to a canter. "I think we've lost them," she said,
and Benvolio nodded—

Which was when two dozen figures in green and yellow
came pouring out of the trees from all sides, swords in hand.

"Drop your weapons!"

"Unhand the lady!"

"Surrender, Montague!"

Benvolio raised his sword as Rosaline wheeled Silvius,
searching for some weak spot, some hope of escape, however
small, but with a sinking heart she realized their luck had
run out. Benvolio kept a tense, protective arm around her
waist that tightened as their captors drew near. Their nearest
assailant, a blond man of thirty or so who appeared to be the
captain, pointed a sword at him. "Unhand her, sir, or 'twill
be the worse for you."

Rosaline swallowed. It was clear these men, whoever they
might be, would not hesitate to hurt him. "Good sirs, he
means me no harm, let us explain—"

"Silence." The man jerked his head toward the ground.
"Down. Both of you."

She could feel Benvolio's muscles coiling, readying to attack, however suicidal that might be. But she squeezed the
hand at her waist and whispered, "Please, Benvolio," until
his grip reluctantly loosened.

The moment they slid to the ground, dozens of hands
were upon them, pulling them apart, stripping Benvolio of
his sword. Rosaline fought toward him as he was forced to
his knees, his hands bound behind his back. "In the name of
the prince, stop! You know not what you do!"

The next moment her protests died on her lips in shock when she too was forced down, her hands jerked behind her and tied. Benvolio threw himself toward her with a roar. Though his hands were bound, he managed to get past two of his captors before they were able to wrestle him into submission. The captain slammed him across the face with the butt of his sword, stunning him enough for three of the guardsmen to throw him facedown on the dirt. Rosaline screamed as the captain grimly raised his sword over Benvolio's neck.

"Stop," a voice said sharply.

The captain froze, withdrawing his sword. Rosaline drew in gulps of air. She turned to find Benvolio's savior, and saw a ghost. Her eyes widened in shock.

"Paris?"

County Paris looked well for a dead man. His gaze was cool and calm as he took in the desperate tableau before him, his long fair hair tied back with a bit of leather, his pearl-gray doublet pinned with a little green and yellow crest. That, Rosaline realized, was where she'd seen the colors before: these men wore the livery of Paris's ancestral house.

"My lord," she gasped. "What in the name of heaven . . ."

But he ignored her, nodding to the captain. "Take them back to camp," he said.

The nurse knew not if she should hold her tongue.

She frowned as she considered the Capulet courtyard. Her rooms were near the back, but she had a small window through which she could see a sliver of Verona. Most of the servants were quartered in the cellar, but not she. She was no ordinary servant, Angelica was not. Had she not her own manservant, Peter? Had not her lady Juliet loved her as a mother? Was she not by her dear lamb's side every day—yea, even unto her last?

So she knew she must sort out what she'd seen with more wit and delicacy than the average credible chambermaid or footman. No more would she keep secrets from the lady of the house.

But what was she to do, then?

She simply did not know how to tell her mistress that she suspected Paris was deceiving them. Angelica was sure that restoring Paris to health was the only thing that had saved the lady of the house from dying of grief. She was so glad, her sweet lady was, to have snatched at least one young life from the bloody summer that stole her daughter away.

And then there was Lady Livia. It was as plain as day she was in love with him.

Angelica wanted to believe that Paris was as good and noble as they thought he was. Pretty little Livia deserved to have a romance that went right, for once in this family, and Angelica would die before she added to her mistress's grief. But then why, the night Orlino was slain, had she found Paris gone from his room, and nowhere to be found? At the time she'd thought he was merely restless, wandering somewhere in the empty wing of House Capulet. But he had vanished again the night Gramio and Truchio fell. And that night she found a black shirt hidden beneath his mattress, still damp with blood.

It was not possible that the man they'd sheltered was involved in these attacks, was it? That was nonsense. The blood was probably Paris's own—perhaps his wound had reopened. Everyone knew it was the villain Benvolio who had killed the young Capulet, who had stolen away dear Rosaline to God knew where. Perhaps she ought to simply remain silent.

She'd told these things to no one but her holy confessor. Perhaps it was time that changed.

With a sigh, she rose, a hand soothing the twinge at her back as she set out through House Capulet's halls to begin her day. She could not keep anything else from her mistress— but what would Lady Capulet say if the nurse made vague aspersions against the man she'd saved?

Enough dithering. Lady Capulet would be stirring. Now that Paris had gone, she'd retaken her place as lady of the house at last. The nurse would confide her misgivings before dressing her and let her sort it out.

But her mistress's chamber was empty, her bed cold. And the door leading from it to the locked wing was open a crack. Frowning, the nurse went through and felt her way into the dark, dusty corridor beyond. Lady Capulet had used this entrance from her own room to visit Paris without being seen, but why had she used it today?

Light spilled into the hall from Paris's old room. The nurse could hear movement within. "My lady?" she called. "I must speak to you. I—"

She pushed the door open and clutched her heart. Lady Capulet stood bent over a wash basin, scrubbing a black doublet the nurse recognized. It was the one she'd found beneath the mattress—the one she'd hastily shoved back into its hiding place, so her mistress would not see it. The sodden garment had streaked her mistress's hands and arms with blood. Hanging over the chair beside her lay a black mask.

Rosaline was shocked by Paris's camp.

She had expected to see a small encampment near the main road, such as messengers of the Crown often used. Instead, she and a still-dazed Benvolio had been thrown over the backs of the men's mounts and conveyed up a winding track back through the hills. By her estimation, they were now just a day's ride from Verona, but deep in the wilderness where travelers rarely ventured. And then they crested a hill, and she drew her breath in sharply. The valley in front of them was filled from north to south with tents, horses, and campfires.

Paris, for reasons she could not fathom, was gathering an army.

Feeling her wide-eyed gaze on him, he turned back from the head of their convoy to offer her a polite smile.

"What is this?" she demanded.

"Our rebirth," he answered, his handsome face lit with calm joy.

"What? Whose?"

He nodded to the captain. "Lock the Montague away. I will dine with Lady Rosaline." Benvolio groaned softly as Paris's men hauled him none too gently off his horse. Rosaline stifled a cry as they bore him away. His head was still bleeding and he had not completely woken since they'd struck him. Paris watched the proceedings, head cocked.

"Good Sir Paris," she said, "I pray you do not hurt him. Upon my honor, whatever Verona told you of him is a lie. There are traitors about—"

"Pray do not unbind my lady until she is safe in my tent," Paris said to the captain. "I fear her sojourn in the clutches of that villain has addled her wits."

The two men who seized her arms and pulled her from her horse were gentler than those who'd borne Benvolio away, but their grip was still iron, and did not give way when she struggled. Eventually she gave up, allowing herself to be marched toward a large tent at the center of the camp. Once there, Paris nodded to her captors, who withdrew, closing the tent flap behind them.

"Do not take their absence as an invitation to run," he told her, a teasing glint in his eyes, for all the world as though he was admonishing her for treading on his toes at one of the prince's feasts. "They stand guard just outside."

Rosaline shook her head. "I know well 'tis folly to flee straight into a strange army that could be friends or foes."

"Friends, dear lady, friends." Gently, he took her hands in his, then drew a little dagger from his belt and cut her bonds. "I mean thee no harm."

She pulled her hands from his grasp. "Then let us go."

He sounded genuinely regretful when he said, "Would that I could." Two manservants entered bearing steaming trays, and Paris, with a nod, directed them to lay out the repast on the table. Rosaline's stomach, after days of travel rations and nunnery gruel, betrayed her with a growl, and Paris gave a polite wave. "Please, eat. A poor repast compared to what we might enjoy in Verona, I am afraid, but thou art welcome to it, good Rosaline."

Why not? If these last days had taught her anything, it was not to count on her next meal. She took a plate and began piling it high. "Why are you so familiar, sir? In Verona we scarcely knew each other."

He gave her that gentle, inscrutable smile again. "No, but 'twas thy sister's faithful care saved my life, so she and hers are as dear to me as kin."

Rosaline nearly dropped the plate. "Livia?" she whispered. "How is my sister a part of this?"

"Sit thee down peacefully and I shall tell thee all."

"Naught can be peaceful between us so long as Benvolio is in danger."

Paris gave an indulgent sigh. "Thou hast my word, the scoundrel's person shall be safe at least for the length of the meal thou and I share."

In the face of this frighteningly paltry promise, Rosaline sat. "How is it that you live?" she demanded. "What confederacy have you bound up Livia in? What do you want with me and Benvolio? I promise you, he is as innocent as—"

Paris held up a hand. "My tale is long, as I imagine thine is. Prithee, hold thy peace awhile, and then may'st thou explain how thou cam'st to wander so with that Montague. Let me start with my death." He dipped his head with a smile, acknowledging the absurdity of this. "The night my love Juliet died, I believed, as did we all, that she was already in heaven. While I kept vigil at her tomb, another mourner appeared." Finally, a shadow crossed his face, marring at last that strange, charming calm he had developed.

She knew who he meant. All Verona knew. "Romeo," she said.

"Aye." Paris's hand drifted to his ribs. "Had I not been so weakened by grief, so Juliet-mad—but I was, and the fellow ran me through. And then I lay there, and I bled. By and by there were others come—the friar, my cousin Prince Escalus, Montagues, Capulets—some stepped over my very feet, others stopped to minister to me, but I was so near death they thought my soul was fled indeed. But I lived. I could feel everything."

His gaze was distant and unseeing, and Rosaline shivered. She could imagine no horror worse than to spend endless minutes and hours painfully bleeding one's life away, drop by drop. It was enough to make one run mad.

"How were you saved?" she asked.

That smile again. "I met an angel," he said.

The nurse could not believe the sight she saw.

"My lady?" she asked.

Lady Capulet looked up sharply. "Nurse? Thou shouldst not be here."

The nurse's heart pounded in her ears. Her lady was right. She ought to turn around this instant and wipe the scene before her from her mind. Whatever strange doings went on betwixt Verona's nobles, they were not for the likes of her. But her feet carried her into the room of their own accord. *No more secrets.* "My lady, is that County Paris's doublet?"

Lady Capulet snatched the doublet and the mask, whipping them out of sight into a sack. "'Tis no concern of thine."

"They say 'twas one in such a mask who slew young Gramio," she said. "And the young Montague men too."

"Very like it, I suppose," her mistress said, with that sweet, winning smile. "But well you know that Paris was lying ill all that time. 'Twas young Benvolio slew Gramio of Capulet."

But the nurse shook her head. "My lady, I may be an old and simple servant, but pray do not undervalue my wit. Paris was recovered by then, and he was gone from his bed that night. Methinks we have given unwitting shelter to a murderer. We must to the Crown. The prince must know of this."

She turned to go, but Lady Capulet's hand gripped her arm, nails digging into her flesh. "Verona's prince already knows all," she said. "Verona's rightful prince. Prince Paris."

Rosaline soon realized he was mad.

Paris was pacing the length of the tent, his eyes lit with a vision only he could see. His face was flushed with an almost holy joy; his body, lean and strong, moved with grace. He would have been beautiful if he were not so frightening.

"At first I knew not that my savior was Juliet's mother,"

he said. "I lay in pain-racked delirium for weeks as I hovered between life and death. She was nothing to me but a cool hand at my temple, a soothing voice. Her face was so like my beloved's that I believed she was an angel, Juliet come back to guide me to heaven.

"But then my fever abated, and I knew her for who she was. No earthly love, but an angel indeed—a heaven-sent mother to restore me and set me on my path. I would have left then, but in her wisdom she persuaded me to remain hidden in House Capulet."

"Why?"

He paused, fingering the crest at his shoulder. "What knowest thou of Verona's succession?"

"What is there to know? The crown passed from Escalus's grandfather, to his father, to him, and thence to his future son."

He shook his head. "My father and Escalus's were brothers. My claim to the crown is as great as his. The crown of Verona is rightfully mine."

Rosaline's eyes went wide. It seemed she had greatly underestimated her grief-racked aunt. They all had. "Paris, your father was *younger* brother to the old prince. He never made any claim to the throne. Is this the poison she poured in your ear?"

"Not poison. Salvation. Ah, canst thou not see? Escalus has been a blight on fair Verona—his reign has brought naught but strife and pain and destruction. Providence intends I should rule. Surely canst thou see that, from what thine own family has endured."

Rosaline shook her head slowly. "I have said it a thousand times: The Capulets are neither cursed nor persecuted. None can end the feud but the feuders. The prince is not to blame. 'Twould be easier for a ruler to stop the tide than to prevent Montagues and Capulets from brawling."

Paris gave her a pitying look, as though she were a child who insisted that two and two made five. "I love my cousin well, but if he is allowed to continue, Verona will not stand. Your aunt did but show me the truth of this, and helped me to prepare Verona to welcome my succor as it should."

Rosaline narrowed her eyes. "And how did you accomplish that?"

"I'll trouble not the mind of an innocent maiden with the ways of warriors," he said soothingly. "Thy sister, dear to me as she is, knows none of this, and nor shalt thou."

"But my aunt knows. Have you no care for her gentle womanish heart? Tell me, Paris. My maiden's mind is stronger than you think." Paris remained closed-mouthed, but Rosaline's eyes went wide. There was no need to hear it from Paris's own lips—she knew what he had done. "'Twas you who killed Gramio."

Paris's smile was sad. He bowed his head in acknowledgment. "I shall say prayers for his misguided young soul forevermore," he said. "And for Truchio, and for Orlino. I take comfort in knowing that their young lives would soon have been swallowed up by the feud, even had it not been my hand that slew them. I gave their deaths a purpose." He turned and dug through a small chest, emerging with a black mask. "'Tis strange, is it not, that such a small scrap of cloth should strike fear into an entire city? Thine aunt sewed it for me with her own hand. There's another in my room back in Verona, but I brought this one to remind me of all I have done."

"And my aunt, I suppose, defaced her own daughter's statue." The thought made her feel as ill as that of Paris slaying those poor boys.

"My lady was very brave, to make her way through Verona by night and write those things. But she knew this seeming slander was the only way to truly honor Juliet's memory."

"But why? What can your aim be? Why did you two slay young Montagues and Capulets alike?"

"Because I had no choice. Verona must be pushed to the brink of civil war so that I can seize my rightful crown."

Rosaline was numb. "Our houses must be in open war on the streets, so no one will be on guard against your army's approach. 'Tis why you falsely implicated Benvolio."

Paris put a compassionate hand on her shoulder. "Aye. And I am sorry, but 'tis why he must die."

Oh God, oh God, her mistress had run mad.

"Lady," the nurse said, her voice taking the even, low tone that had never failed to soothe Jule from a nightmare. "Lady, Paris is no prince."

Lady Capulet shook her head. "Thou art wrong, nurse. No rightful sovereign could have allowed all that has passed. Dost thou mind the night Tybalt was slain?"

The nurse nodded, shivering. Brave Tybalt, who had toddled hand in hand with her lady Juliet as a babe, lying bloody and rent in the street as Lady Capulet screamed over his body was a sight that haunted her nightmares. After that, she thought her mistress's rage spent, collapsed into all-encompassing grief. It seemed her fury had but been hidden.

"I was as trusting as a child then," her mistress said, her gaze far away. "I looked to the prince over Tybalt's body and asked—*begged*—for justice." She gave a bitter chuckle. "Can you imagine? I, mistress of the ancient house of Capulets, daughter to a duke, begging for the justice that was owed me—and our so-called prince looked at me and offered only to send Romeo into exile. *I* knew, when Romeo slew my dear kinsman and escaped with his life, that vile Escalus would never have my fealty again. When I found Paris, I understood Providence had sent him to me to bring Verona on the right path at last. When he takes his crown, he will crush the Montagues under his righteous fist."

"And our house too?" the nurse whispered. "Paris has already begun the bloody work."

"Fear not," Lady Capulet soothed. "Some sacrifice is necessary to claim our house's due glory. Those Capulets who are worthy shall be saved, even exalted, once Paris has claimed his throne. House Capulet must die to live, but once my husband and his pack of puling, brawling nephews are gone, it shall rise anew from the ashes, without Montague to trouble it. And when Paris takes a Capulet bride, the throne shall be ours as well."

"A Capulet bride?"

Lady Capulet gave a sly smile. "I am not so indifferent to the sweet looks and sighs between him and my niece as they may think. I am quite content to give her to him. Even now, Paris approaches, having gathered an army of his allies. The prince shall throw the gates open for him so that he may bear Benvolio hence, little knowing he is welcoming his own downfall."

"A cunning plan," the nurse said slowly.

Lady Capulet smiled. "I could not have done it without thee, dear retainer. Thy loyalty shall not be forgotten."

The nurse sat down heavily on Paris's one-time bed, her mind in a whirl. Here she had nursed him faithfully—the man she had once helped Juliet to spurn and deceive. She had gotten above her station, taking it upon herself to help Juliet defy her parents, and when the dear child died of it, she had been determined to be ruled by her mistress's wisdom henceforth.

But this—this was too far. Would Juliet rejoice to see her own family destroy her husband's kinsmen? She could not believe it. Lady Capulet was not to blame, of course—grief had twisted her mind down this treacherous path. The loss of Juliet, the nurse thought, was enough to drive anyone mad.

"My lady," she said soothingly, "let's to the palace. I'll tell how Paris hath deceived you. Prince Escalus will have compassion for your grief. I am sure you need not fear our prince's wrath—nay, he will be grateful, if you tell him what is coming." She took her mistress's hand in both of hers. "Come, lamb, let's to the palace and confess all."

Something like rage flashed across Lady Capulet's face.

Then she smiled. "Think'st thou in thy soul this is the wisest course?"

"Aye, lady, I am sure of it."

"I cannot dissuade thee from it?"

"I bow to your ladyship's wisdom in all matters, but in this I must do my duty. 'Tis but for love of you and yours, my lady."

Her lady drew her hand away and stepped behind her, squeezing her shoulder. "Dear, dear nurse. Has House Capulet ever had a more loyal servant? Thy fealty shall never be forgotten."

The nurse patted the hand on her shoulder. "I do but discharge my duty."

"I know." And then a cord was passed about her neck and pulled tight.

"Dear soul," Lady Capulet said in her ear as the nurse gasped and choked and clawed at the scrap of cloth about her throat. "Even in death shall thou serve us. Shh, shh."

I'm dying, thought the nurse.

And, *I do not understand.*

And, *Juliet, I come.*

Soon thereafter, a scream broke the air when the nurse's lifeless body was discovered crumpled near the Capulet doors. A note was thrown on her body like trash:

THUS TO ALL CAPULETS.

Part 5

Cry "Havoc!" and let slip the dogs of war.

—*Julius Caesar*

$\mathcal{B}$ENVOLIO WAS DREAMING OF his wife.

In his dream he was at a great feast. His wife was whirling across the dance floor, her laughter echoing all around him, but no matter how he pushed through the crowd he could never seem to get to her side. Though the room was stuffed from wall to wall with every droning noble he knew, and the heat should have been stifling, somehow the air was cold. Perhaps that was the reason for the ache in his bones.

Romeo and Mercutio were acting the fool, as usual. No matter how many times he told them to stop teasing him, they persisted in mocking his nuptial state.

I' faith, Benvolio, I'd thought not to see you so yoked, said Mercutio.

Aye, said Romeo. *Rememb'rest thou not our oath to remain three bachelors until we die?*

There was something wrong with that, but Benvolio could not remember what. Finally it hit him. *Thou art no bachelor, Romeo. Thou'rt wed.*

Aye, said Romeo. *But I'm no traitor.*

Who have I betrayed? I wed for love.

For love of her? Or hatred for thy friends?

I hate you not! Benvolio exclaimed. *What hath my love to do with you two, pray?*

He's right. Mercutio grinned. *He's just a fool. Some men do bear the yoke, some cuckold's horns, but our Benvolio's the only man whose marriage made him don a cap and bells.*

A cap and bells? No fool's cap do I wear.

A cap at least, Mercutio replied. *And hush! For that same fool-maker draws near.*

And yes, suddenly his wife was just behind him, and he kept turning around and around, trying to draw her to his side so he could present her to his friends, explain them to each other, but she seemed determined to prove their bad opinion of her right. She laughed, darting away from him, never letting him see her face behind her curtain of long dark curls, but for some reason her hand kept reaching out to pinch his hip.

Then he awoke, and he realized that the pinching was real. Rosaline's toes were digging into his leg.

"Thank God," she said. "I thought you'd never wake. It's been hours."

"What—"

"Hush," she hissed. "Be still."

Benvolio blinked his exhaustion from his eyes. He stifled a groan as sensation returned. His muscles were stiff and sore, and the scabbed wound across his chest had begun to throb again. Paris's men had tied him to a post in a tent near the edge of camp this morning, and had left him alone there ever since. Despite the cold ground he sat on, his grumbling stomach, and his worry for his companion, he'd finally nodded off some hours after sunset. Now he awoke to find Rosaline bound to another pole, just opposite his, her lower lip caught in her teeth as she stretched her foot toward him to prod at his belt. Her shoes sat discarded beside her, her dress ridden up to her knees.

"What art thou about?" he gasped, trying to ignore the sensation of her toes creeping along his inner thigh and— God in heaven.

"Freeing thee," she whispered, nodding toward his side, and he realized she was trying to reach his dagger. It was small, and hidden under his sash, so the guards had missed it, but he'd been unable to twist enough to reach it himself. Rosaline's long, flexible legs and nimble toes, however, showed every sign of reaching their prize.

To distract himself from pursuing thoughts of her legs, he whispered, "Why art thou here? I'd not have thought Paris such a scoundrel as to hold a lady in such conditions."

"He did not wish to. He would have held me in his tent, but I had to find thee, so I made him see I was too dangerous not to imprison properly. I tried to stab him with a butter knife," she said proudly.

"Foolish maid! He could have killed thee!"

"Hush." Her toes gave a twist and with a suppressed cry of triumph, she withdrew his knife. Drawing it back toward herself, by dint of much bending she was able to put it in reach of her hands. She went to work on her bonds. As she did so, she related to Benvolio what she'd learned of Paris's plans.

Benvolio set his jaw. So Paris meant not to let him live. "Dear God."

"Aye," she said grimly. "We've no time to waste. They have Silvius tied just outside. The guard is snoring. If we can slip our bonds, we can flee before they know we've escaped."

Benvolio's mind flew over what he'd seen of Paris's defenses. It was possible—*possible*—that she was right. They were near the edge of camp, after all. There was a chance they could bypass the guards outside the tent, sneak past the sentries, and be gone before anyone was the wiser.

But Rosaline had overlooked something. She seemed to think his death was imminent, but if Paris planned to use him to bait a trap for the prince, Benvolio was more valuable to him alive, at least for the moment. Paris could drag him before Escalus himself, and let him rave of an army waiting over the horizon; who would believe the crazed murderer he was thought to be?

Rosaline, on the other hand, was a much greater threat. She had the ear of the prince, who would have no reason to doubt her. Paris would have to find a way to convert her, as he had evidently endeavored to do, but if it became clear that Rosaline was not going to fall in with his plans, Paris would have to silence her.

Benvolio would not permit that.

Aloud he said only, "An excellent plan. What time is it?"

"Near midnight." Rosaline huffed a curl out of her eyes to give him a smile, then returned her concentration to her bindings. After a moment she blew out a triumphant breath and drew her hands from behind the post, the ropes now severed. She quickly crawled to him and bent over his wrists, attacking his bonds with the knife. A strand of her hair tickled his cheek; he closed his eyes, trying to lock the sensation in his memory. Perhaps this was what his dream-friends were trying to tell him—Rosaline had indeed made a fool of him, for he was about to do the most foolish thing he had ever done.

She made quick work of his bonds and helped him to his feet. She started toward the front flap of the tent, but Benvolio shook his head—he did not wish to risk waking the guard. Instead he guided her toward the rear, where the canvas was held together with laces. Retrieving his dagger, he cut enough of the bindings for them to slip through. The rows of tents backed nearly onto each other with only a few feet of space between them, forming a narrow canvas alley. Heart in his throat, Benvolio guided Rosaline along the slender pathway until they were out of sight of the tent where they'd been imprisoned. Then, motioning for her to stay where she was, he slipped back out.

Rosaline had been right, thank heaven—Silvius was hitched to a post not ten feet from where he stood. Sending up a quick prayer of thanks to whomever watched over wayward Montagues, he beckoned Rosaline over. Luckily, they both still had their long cloaks, and he pulled up her hood and his own, tucking her curls back behind her ears. With any luck, they would pass for a groom and a stableboy.

There were a few fires in their death throes at intervals between the tents, each dotted with dozing sentries and idle gossipers. But none seemed to take note of them as they took

Silvius's bridle and began walking him toward the road. As they slipped past the line of torches that ringed Paris's camp, into the enveloping darkness beyond, Benvolio sighed. Perhaps his desperate plan would not need to be put into action, after all.

"The prisoner has escaped! To arms!"

Oh *hell.*

Benvolio seized Rosaline's wrist in one hand and Silvius's reins in the other and ran. Risking a glance over his shoulder, he saw the camp was in an uproar, torches darting hither and thither. Already, mounted men were starting toward the road. "We must mount, we must away!" Rosaline said, tugging at his arm, and Benvolio turned to her, locked an arm around her waist, and kissed her, hard. Then he pulled back, taking advantage of her momentary confusion to seize her by the waist and all but throw her into the saddle. *"Go,"* he said, and smacked Silvius's withers as hard as he could. Silvius reared and bolted, Rosaline clinging to his neck. He had one last glance of her pale, bewildered face staring back at him before he took a deep breath and shouted, "Paris, thou blackguard, face me like a man!" as he charged back into camp.

One man against a thousand was poor odds, even if he had been armed—Rosaline still had his dagger. Still, he laid about him with his fists—no need to make anything easy for these vile traitors. His goal was distraction rather than escape, and he intended to buy Rosaline as much time as he could. It was not until they had him bound once more that the captain thought to ask, "Where is the lady?"

Benvolio grinned around a split lip. "What lady?"

The captain's face reddened. To his men, he said, "Take him before my lord."

Accordingly, Benvolio was hauled into the great tent at the center of camp. Paris, looking less genteel now, was pacing, his hair mussed as though he'd been running his hands through it. When he saw Benvolio he glared. "Where is she?"

Benvolio's only reply was to spit a mouthful of blood at his feet.

Paris's fist caught him across the face. Stars flashed in Benvolio's eyes. He would have fallen to the ground had his captors not held him up. "You should have run when you had the chance," Paris said. "You'll die for this."

"A pity. I hoped you would make me your lord chamberlain."

"Send men out to capture her," Paris snapped to the captain. "The rest of you, break camp. We'll make haste for Verona in the morn." To Benvolio he said, "Tell me where she's gone and perhaps I will spare your life."

"She is somewhere you will never find her," Benvolio said, and hoped it was true.

Rosaline was flying down the road.

Silvius's hooves clattered frantically across the stones, and no matter how she hauled at the reins he would not heed her. He was so panicked that all she could do was cling to his neck and try not to fall. A few endless minutes passed before he even began to slow. When she finally coaxed him down to a walk, she realized she had no idea where she was.

She found herself on a dirt road threading between groves of trees. Off in the distance, she could see the gleam of a light or two—perhaps farms. But where she was now, there was nothing but forest. Somewhere in the darkness, an animal screamed. Rosaline shivered and drew her cloak closer about her. Had they gone north or south when they left camp? She did not know—she had counted on Benvolio to lead her.

What could she do? Go to one of the farmhouses for help? A lady alone took a grievous risk in throwing herself on the mercy of strangers. Press on until she found an inn? That had already led to disaster, and in any case ladies certainly did not do *that*. She shuddered to think of what might befall her if she appeared in an inn on her own.

A thundering of hooves behind her interrupted her whirling thoughts. Rosaline tensed. Paris's men would be searching for her. Slipping swiftly from Silvius's back, she tugged at his reins. He tossed his head and whinnied, as though to ask who this strange, weak little creature was and what she had done with his master.

"I know," she muttered. "'Tis his own fault. Come *on*."

Silvius deigned at last to be led off the road and into the trees. Luckily his coat was dark; he'd be nearly impossible to see. Still, Rosaline held her breath as the riders drew near. Silvius stayed blessedly still too, and Paris's men rode by without stopping. And then Rosaline and Silvius were alone once more in the darkness.

A wave of fear rose up and nearly choked her. *Curse* that Montague! How could he have abandoned her so? If Paris's men did not find her, highwaymen or wolves were sure to do so. There were a million dangers between her and Verona, all of whom would see a young noblewoman alone as easy prey. And they would be quite right—she was defenseless. She laid a trembling hand against Silvius's warm side for comfort, and found that he still wore Benvolio's saddlebags. Apparently Paris's men had not bothered to remove them. Eager for a distraction from her despair, she fumbled them open, taking an inventory. There was little of use. A bit of bread and cheese. A few small coins. An apple for Silvius. And, neatly folded, Benvolio's spare doublet and hose.

Tears sprang to Rosaline's eyes and she pressed her face against the fabric of the doublet. It was laced with his scent, leather and spice and something that was just *him,* and she had to shove a hand to her mouth to hold back a cry of despair. Benvolio was on the way to his death. For her. And since he'd left her on her own, she was probably doomed anyway. His sacrifice would count for naught.

Then make it count, a cool little voice said inside her.

Stop crying.

Look around. You are not defenseless, daughter of Tirimo. You still have your wits.

Rosaline's hands clutched the fabric of Benvolio's doublet. Yes.

Before she could stop to doubt the wisdom of such an outlandish idea, she grabbed the hem of her dress and yanked it over her head. Her shift soon followed, and Rosaline shivered, naked, in the darkness. She tore several long strips from the hem of her shift, tying them about her chest before pulling on Benvolio's doublet and hose. She felt no less naked when she was dressed, for the men's clothes were strangely loose and permissive. One more strip of shift served as a hair tie, binding her curls at the nape of her neck. Benvolio's clothing was much too large on her, but young men of modest means often wore their elder brothers' cast offs. She belted his doublet as tightly as she could and hung his dagger at her waist. One final step was necessary—with a sharp yank, she ripped the crest sewn onto the shoulder of the doublet, the sign of Montague following her female trappings into the darkness. She kept only a handkerchief she'd embroidered with a rose, after her name, which she tucked into her sleeve—all that remained of Lady Rosaline. Then, with a deep breath, she mounted Silvius and turned him toward what she hoped was east.

As the sun rose, a slender youth rode into the inn yard in a small village just outside the forest. He rode a fine horse, but his clothes were shabby, and he had a grim face for one so young. Few took note of him except the innkeeper, who took a shilling for a bit of porridge and directions for the young man, who called himself Niccolo, to Montenova Abbey.

Livia's patience, never great, was frayed.

If one more well-meaning Capulet cousin came to her chattering about how sorry they were that her sister had been sullied by a Montague, she was going to pitch the lot of them down the well. None of them cared a bit for Rosaline, only for the Capulet honor. Her uncle had been on the verge of letting everyone return to their homes yesterday, when the discovery of the nurse's body had thrown the city into an even greater uproar than before. No one had seen which Montague had been cowardly enough to murder a poor servant woman, but her family was ready to slay every last man among them. Livia could not find it in herself to object to such a plan. The sight of the dear nurse's broken body had left her crying all night. Lady Capulet had sat with her for a time and stroked her hair, even as her own tears fell. Livia admired her aunt's strength. Somehow she found time to speak with all the furious young Capulets, even though her own grief must be greater than anyone's.

But with the great families and their allies now making open war in the city's streets and the city consumed by riots, Livia could not so much as set foot beyond House Capulet's walls, and she thought she might go mad. What had become of Paris? Had he found Rosaline in time? Had that bastard Benvolio hurt either of them? She had to know.

So when the gates of House Capulet opened to admit Verona's prince, Livia did not intend to withdraw with the other young maidens to Juliet's nursery as she'd been told to do. Instead, she watched from an upper window as her aunt and uncle greeted Prince Escalus in the courtyard. When she heard her uncle say, "Let's in to my study, my lord," she flew on swift and silent feet to the heavy oak door and slipped inside before they were in sight.

Her uncle's study, though rich, was not large—it contained

a few bookcases, an ostentatiously ponderous desk, and some leather chairs. Nowhere for a stealthy maid to conceal herself. She had the momentary wild notion of hiding under the desk as they had as children, but she suspected that she was too tall now to fold herself beneath it without being noticed. Her uncle's heavy tread was coming up the stair. Any moment now they would open the door and discover her, and her chance would be gone. She looked around again. Ah!

Livia threw herself behind heavy, floor-to-ceiling drapes that covered the windows, managing to still their telltale fluttering just as the door creaked open.

"These are joyous tidings you bring us, Your Grace," her uncle's voice said. She heard him huff his way around to his desk, then the dual sighs of his breath and his chair as he settled his bulk in it. "Please, be seated. You say Benvolio is captured?"

Livia pressed a hand to her mouth to suppress a gasp. Thank God! Did that mean Rosaline was safe?

"Yes," came the prince's reply. "These news are not for any ears but yours, for I've no wish to start a riot, but I've word from County Paris. He says he and his men have captured the scoundrel and they will bring him back to Verona for execution."

"*Ah,*" said Lady Capulet, her voice filled with more satisfaction than Livia had ever heard. "Justice at last."

"Aye. He requests that I ope the gates of the city, so that all Verona may come to Executioner's Hill and see justice done."

"An excellent suggestion," Lady Capulet said. "Young Paris is wise. Will you be guided by your kinsman in this?"

"Perhaps. I am sure, Lady Capulet, that thou hast had ample time to gain respect for my cousin's wisdom in the weeks you kept him hidden from me," the prince said drily. "But I confess I still do not understand why such a thing was deemed necessary."

"Forgive me my womanish fears," Lady Capulet said sweetly. "I should have had more faith in Your Grace's ability to protect him even in these treacherous times. Although our nurse's recent death suggests your forces are, perhaps, overtaxed."

"I am sorry for her death," the prince said with a sigh. "And whatever your motives, I am grateful to those who restored my cousin to health, and I will certainly attend his counsel."

"'Twas our honor to restore him to Your Grace," she said humbly.

To hell with all this chatter about gratitude and honor. Now that Livia knew that Paris was safe, she had but one remaining care: what had become of her sister? Livia scowled, and suppressed the urge to scream that there was a maid in danger out there while they played their hideous adult game of politeness.

It seemed her uncle, at least, shared a bit of her concern. "In any case, what of the girl? That niece of mine. Rosalind. Ruined, I suppose?"

"Rosaline, mean you? I—" A queer tension had entered

the prince's voice. Livia bit her lip. "I know not. Paris spoke not of her in his message. I have writ to him to see. It is my dearest hope that she is safe in his care."

"You know not if she be with him?" Lady Capulet demanded.

"Believe me, no one cares more for Rosaline's safety than I!" the prince roared.

A shocked silence followed. Verona's sovereign was known for his even temper. Livia had never heard him speak so. "Forgive me," he said after a moment. "Your niece and I . . ." He trailed off. "That's for another day. Capulet, I intend to put Benvolio to death with all haste, before the eyes of the city entire. But in return, I expect you to rein in your house. We'll have no more warfare on Verona's streets. I have not forgotten that two young Montagues are dead as well, and their killers not yet discovered. From this minute forward, the life of any Capulet who so much as brushes his hand across his hilt is forfeit."

Lady Capulet's smooth voice cut in again. "I am sure that all young men of our house will be more than glad to withdraw in peace when they see justice wreaked on Benvolio's body."

"They will withdraw now," the prince said. "Do not make me say it again."

A pause. Then: "Forgive my wife. She speaks out of turn. I'll see the lot of our hotheads kenneled within the hour."

"Then," said the prince, "justice they shall see. And right soon. I expect Paris is but two days' ride from the city. And when he arrives, Benvolio shall not see another sunset."

Young "Niccolo" liked riding as a man.

Rosaline had never been the most ladylike of riders, taking more risks and going faster than maids were strictly supposed to. She even borrowed the duchess's finest stallion without permission on occasion. Livia liked to tease her that it was her one vice. But she had never realized how much she'd been constrained by decorum and petticoats until she could throw her tunic-clad self into the saddle, shout "Hyah!" and let Silvius fly. Luckily, Silvius was built for endless speed, and with such a small rider on his back, they ate up the miles.

They met a few travelers on their way; though Rosaline was nearly screaming inside with urgency, she made a point of stopping to pass the time of day with them. One old matron expressed concern that "such a little fellow as thee" should be traveling alone, but none saw through her disguise. Rosaline was tall and thin for a woman, and in Benvolio's doublet, she looked very much like a youth on the cusp of manhood. Niccolo's secret, it seemed, was safe.

Thanks to the storm and the delay it had caused them, Rosaline was only a few hours from the abbey. Soon, Montenova Abbey rose before her once again. Rosaline raised her hood. Now came the difficult part.

After a brief internal debate, she decided not to knock at the front door and claim sanctuary as Benvolio had. Her goal was not to gain an audience with Friar Laurence—quite the opposite, since he would take one look at "Niccolo" and recognize the maid whose ankle he had mended—but merely to insinuate herself into the abbey until she could find the journal Benvolio had spoken of. She prayed it contained the proof of his innocence that they needed.

She had considered riding straight for Verona, but with Paris's army between her and home, there seemed little point. She was sure his men were still combing the countryside for her, but they would be seeking a Verona-bound maid, not a youth riding east. Besides, now that she knew the extent of Paris's betrayal, it was more important than ever that Escalus learn the truth. She now realized that L was not Lucullus, but Lavinia, her aunt Capulet's given name. It was so rarely used that it had slipped her mind entirely. If the friar had been more explicit elsewhere in his diary, his unwilling evidence and Rosaline's own testimony might be enough to save Benvolio's life—and perhaps Escalus's own. If only she had been able to purloin that mask Paris had waved in her face! She would just have to hope that the diary was enough.

Rosaline's steps slowed as she reached the door at the rear of the abbey, where servants and tradesmen were to knock. It was a great deal of hope to place on one little book of monk-scribbles. She prayed it would suffice, and that she could find some way to take it.

She drew a deep breath. No time to think of that. Escalus, Benvolio, herself—she would have to be man enough for all three of them. Squaring her shoulders, planting her feet, and hoping she looked manly, she pounded on the door.

"By and by I come." A monk in a food-spotted brown robe

opened the door, looking startled to see her there. "Who might you be, then, my son? Are you the gentleman of Verona who sheltered here? I'm not to readmit you. They say you struck good Brother Laurence."

Rosaline put on her best look of blank male incomprehension. She found thinking of Lucio and Valentine helped. "Verona? Nay, Father, Niccolo's my name and from Padua come I, seeking a place as a page in Milan. Might your holy brotherhood have a bit of honest work for a man such as I, in exchange for a night's shelter?"

"A man such as you is no man at all, but a half-grown brat," said the friar. "Home to your mother and father with you."

"They're dead, Father." True enough. One less century in purgatory for lying to a man of God.

The monk's face softened. "An orphan, are you?"

"Yes, with nothing in the world but the clothes on my back and Si-Sirius here. But I'm a fair hand in the kitchen, and with horses. I pray you, let me be of use."

He considered her. "Very well, you may help old Tuft in the stables for the day."

Praise be. For one who had once thought to be a nun, Rosaline was deceiving and defying a great many of His servants these days. She sent up a quick, silent prayer of apology, made the monk the best bow she could, and headed for the stables, where she found the aforementioned Tuft, who proved to be a gnarled old horseman who walked with a stoop but led Silvius with strong, capable hands. "A fine piece of horseflesh," he said. "Have I seen him before? I think the young Verona fellow had a horse of such a color, and such a height."

She gave him the stupid look again. "I hail from Padua. Sirius has been mine since he was a colt." Silvius, bless him, chose that moment to give her an affectionate butt with his head, just as though she really were a lifelong friend and not an interloper who'd stolen him from his master. Rosaline stroked his neck and together they turned looks of great innocence to Master Tuft.

Tuft shrugged and lost interest. "Well, I suppose there's gray horses enough in the world." He handed her a shovel. "The cart horses' stalls want mucking."

He gave her a homespun shirt and trousers, which she changed into in an empty corner, out of his sight. She spent the rest of the afternoon shoveling manure. She could not hide her disgust, but she did not suppose that would hurt her disguise—a young gentleman, even one who had come down in the world, would not have spent much more time pitching manure than she had. At least these were not Benvolio's clothes. He would probably have had to burn them.

The thought of Benvolio sent a shot of panic spiraling through her stomach. She set her jaw, forcing her eyes to her task, though it was all she could do not to throw down the shovel and bolt into Friar Laurence's chamber to demand the book that would be his salvation. It galled her to wait here idly when every moment she waited brought Benvolio closer to his doom. What if she waited too long? What if Paris had already killed him? Worse yet, what if Escalus had? She did not think it was possible that they could be back in Verona—it was about a day and a half of hard riding from where she'd left them, and at least a day longer for an army such as Paris's, which could not move as swiftly as two riders alone. Still, the thought was enough to make bile rise in her throat, and she pressed her arm hard over her mouth.

"Buck up, you flap-mouthed baggage, it's naught but a bit of horse-dirt. No puking on Vestiver there."

Rosaline straightened, swallowing with an effort. "Your pardon. I did but pause to draw breath."

"Well, you're a hard-working enough young fellow," Tuft said reluctantly. "That's enough for today. Come, let's wash and sup."

Rosaline looked up and realized the sun was actually setting. She and Tuft left the stables, and she found that the monks had left them several buckets to wash with. She had a moment's panic when Tuft stripped off his shirt and plunged it in one bucket and his head and arms in another, scrubbing himself vigorously. "What are you waiting for?" he asked when he saw her hanging back. "Wash, boy. You cannot dine so among holy men. Nothing brings lofty thoughts to earth like a good stink."

Rosaline fingered the edge of her shirt. He was right, but she could hardly disrobe before him. "I—I—"

Tuft gave a mighty sigh. "You are a soft one, aren't you. Here." He tossed her a change of clothes. "Friar Francis left this for you. Watch out, I think he means to make a monk of you. Take it and go and wash in yonder bushes."

Thank God for Tuft's towering contempt for nobles. It seemed to make him lose any interest in "Niccolo's" eccentricities. Rosaline took the shirt and some water over to the bushes, which afforded her enough privacy to wash and change without fear of detection. Niccolo of Padua would live on for the moment.

Newly scrubbed, she and Tuft made their way into the kitchen. Tuft was right about Friar Francis—he seemed to have designs on "Niccolo," and asked her to join the monks for supper, "to discuss your future." But Rosaline begged off, fearing to come face-to-face with Friar Laurence, and instead ate in the kitchen with Tuft and the other lay servants.

Finally, supper was done, the pots and pans scrubbed, and the monks had found "Niccolo" a place to sleep by the hearth. Rosaline changed back into Benvolio's clothes—she did not intend to pass another day here, and she did not wish to steal from the monks who had been so kind. Friar Laurence was another matter. She lay awake, listening to the pops of the logs and the evening prayers echoing against stone, until at last the noise was still and the abbey was silent. When she was sure that the monks had gone to bed, she rose.

Now or never.

Her heart was in her throat as she picked her way over the snoring scullions, praying for sure-footedness. Once past the kitchen, she found the stone corridor empty and silent, lit only by a few torches. What had Benvolio said? Friar Laurence's study was at the top of a tower? There were two, one at the northeast corner and one at the northwest. She crept toward the northwest corner of the abbey, but found the door there locked.

It would have to be the other one, then. Rosaline slipped into the shadows, pressing herself into the wall to allow a group of sleepy young monks to pass by, before tiptoeing eastward. As she passed the chapel, a light caught her eye. A candle rested on the floor, next to a figure bent in prayer. It was Friar Laurence, though the calm, gentle man she had met a week before was nearly unrecognizable in the desperate figure before her. He was on his knees, rocking, his body a slumped arc of shame, his hands clasped as though he could hold on to God's mercy with the strength of his grip. His mumbled prayers were too quiet to understand, but she did hear the words "Montague" and "Forgive me."

Rosaline hardened her heart against a stab of pity. He could beg for forgiveness until doomsday as far as she was concerned. It was his fault they were in this mess. His fault Benvolio was in danger. Besides, his midnight attack of conscience was good luck for her. It meant his chambers were empty.

She sped toward the east tower. Finding the door unlocked, she slipped up the winding stair and into a small, moonlit chamber. Sure enough, the walls were lined with books, plants, and mathematical models, just as Benvolio had said. Now where was the book she sought? She looked on the desk where Benvolio had discovered it, but found it bare. None of the drawers contained a small red book either, nor any of the shelves. She looked in his closet, even under his bedclothes. In her haste, she no longer tried to leave the place looking undisturbed, throwing books and robes and blankets all around. Nothing.

Despite her growing panic, she paused, and took a deep breath to regroup. The book was gone from its former place. Had Friar Laurence destroyed it? She would have. If you had a secret you feared would be discovered, why keep it writ down? But she suspected the friar was of a more sentimental turn of mind than she. He would not want to destroy it. But he would, perhaps, hide it. Rosaline clasped her hands behind her back, turning a slow circle as she allowed her eyes to drift over the friar's small room. Where could he hide anything?

Her gaze caught on one of the chamber's few bits of adornment: a drawing mounted on the wall. Frowning, she drew nearer. It was more of a sketch than a drawing, really—just a handful of lines and a bit of shading, suggesting its subjects rather than detailing them. The drawing was merely competent, but what the hand of the artist—the friar himself, Rosaline imagined—lacked in brilliance, it made up in affection. The sketch portrayed several small boys of about nine, all of them with slates in their laps. One, a lanky lad, was peering over his mate's shoulder, as though to steal his answer. His neighbor, a small boy with a comical mop of curls, was gazing dreamily off into the distance. Only one serious young figure was bent industriously over his sums, his dark brows furrowed, tongue poking out of the corner of his mouth.

Rosaline swallowed, brushing her fingertips over their young faces. Mercutio. Romeo. Benvolio. She knew she'd found the friar's hiding place.

Sure enough, when she pulled the drawing back from the

wall, she found a small crevice in the stones, and inside it was a slim red book. Rosaline seized it, preparing to run, and then with a surge of irritation turned back and seized the drawing too. The sentimental old coward had no right to such a thing when two of its subjects were in heaven, the third shortly to join them, and he'd done nothing to stop it.

Rosaline ran down the stairs as quickly as she could, not caring so much about the noise now. She was not far from the rear door. All she had to do was get to the stables without being stopped and she and Silvius could be on their way. She had almost reached the bottom when she ran headlong into Friar Laurence.

He stumbled back, nearly falling down the stairs. Righting himself, he grumbled, "Boy, why art thou about? The abbot has promised me that no servant—" He looked properly at her face and his jaw dropped. "Lady Rosaline? What in the world!" Rosaline made no reply, merely tried to push past him. He stopped her with a hand on her elbow. His eyes narrowed as he saw the book she carried. "Ah, that way goes the game. Stop, thief!" he shouted, reaching to grab it away from her.

And then his grip went slack, falling away. Rosaline glanced at him, and realized he'd spotted her other prize, clutched against her chest: his drawing.

"Father—"

"Go." He pressed a trembling hand to his eyes and stepped out of her way. "Go."

She started past him, and then turned back, pressing the drawing into his hand. Then she ran straight down the stairs, out the back door, and into the stables. And she and Silvius rode once more toward home. She prayed with all her might that they would reach it this time.

"Livia! What dost thou hereabouts?"

Livia's heart swelled at the concern on Paris's face. He was seated behind a small desk in the middle of a military tent, where the two guards who had found her had dragged her. "I had to see you," she said. "I know 'twas foolish to fly the city all alone, but when I heard yesterday that you were nearby I could wait no longer. I rode all day. Ay! That hurts, you joit-head." She tried without success to shake off the grip of the two guards holding her arms.

Paris jumped to his feet with an impatient gesture to the two men. "Take your hands off my lady, louts, or I'll cut them off."

"You said not to allow anyone into camp," one of them protested.

Paris waved them off and snapped, "This is your lady. Obey her as you would me. Leave us." The two men bowed and withdrew.

"I told you you'd be in trouble," Livia called after them.

Paris turned to Livia, smiling. "My dear Lady Livia." He took her hands in his, brushing his lips over one set of knuckles, then the other. "Aghast though I am to find thee here among these rough men I command, I must admit my heart leaps for joy to see thee."

"And so does mine," Livia said. "How I longed for thee! It feels an eternity since I watched thee ride away."

"Oh, my love. I shall never leave thy side again." Paris pulled her into his arms and kissed her sweetly, and for a moment Livia lost herself in the touch of his lips and the joy of his words. He loved her.

But reality intruded in her thoughts and she pulled back, laying her hands against his chest. "My lord, what is all this? I expected perhaps a half-dozen men when I came to seek thee, and instead I find an army! Why are they here? And where is my sister?"

His smile vanished. "Thy sister was here. We had a disagreement, and though I begged her to remain in my protection, she would depart. But I assure thee, she was whole and well when last I saw her."

Livia frowned. Rosaline certainly preferred to keep her own counsel, but wandering the countryside alone? "Did she say when she would return home?"

"I do not believe she intended to return to Verona," Paris replied vaguely. "But, sweet Livia, thou wilt understand my aims better than she could. Thou must do so, for they concern thee too." He took her hand and pressed it to his heart, and told her what he intended to do.

Livia's eyes went wide as Paris described his plans to overthrow their sovereign. "You intend to seize Escalus's throne? You cannot! 'Tis madness!"

He smiled. "All great plans appear mad at first. Canst thou not see, Livia? Just as thy gentle hands cleansed my wound each day till I was sound, so shall I rid Verona of the pestilence that brings it low again and again." He drew back, taking both of her hands in his. "And once I've the crown, there shall remain only one thing necessary to be perfectly happy evermore. A prince needs a princess by his side. I can think of no one better to be my help and comfort than she who restored my very life. Before I left Verona I asked and received thy good aunt's blessing, so the choice is thine—Livia, wilt thou be my wife?"

Livia's heart seized in her throat. Paris's eyes were wide and smiling, boring into hers, and she found she could not look away. *Princess of Verona*. Paris meant to raise her above all other ladies in the city. To *marry* her.

Dazzling visions swam in front of her eyes. A crown on Paris's head . . . Paris taking her hand before the bishop, making her his wife, eyes lit by love . . . standing with him on a palace balcony, waving to cheering crowds . . . children with his warm eyes and her honey-colored hair . . .

"Dearest, sweetest Livia." He kissed her again, and again, as though he could not have enough of her. "Say thou wilt stand with me."

Benvolio's head was throbbing when he woke.

His vision swam with vague, muddy shapes and colors that slowly drifted back into focus. He winced, trying to raise his hands to scrub the haze from his eyes, but found his wrists shackled.

The last two days had passed in a miserable blur. Paris's

army had moved out the morning after Rosaline's escape, but because of their numbers they moved more slowly than he and Rosaline had, and they had only just arrived outside the city walls—he hoped that meant she was already safe at home. Paris had kept him chained in a supply wagon when they were on the move, and in a tent when they were not. Occasionally one of his captors would come in and knock him around a bit, trying to learn what he knew of Rosaline's flight. He was able to take those beatings in fairly good spirits, because as long as they continued, it meant Paris's men had not found her. Now he was in yet another tent, curled in the mud with several men talking over him, and though a series of blinks failed to bring their faces into focus, their voices could not be mistaken.

"He will not say a word of Rosaline," a voice he recognized as Paris's said. "Prepare yourself, cousin. He will no doubt spin you a heartbreaking tale of his innocence, and may even lay all his crimes at my feet. I have never met so skilled a liar."

"That's to be expected," said a cool, amused voice. "The prospect of imminent death is often a great inspiration to the imagination, I have found."

Benvolio's fingers flexed against the damp grass beneath him. The prince.

A hand gripped his arm, hauling him to his knees. "The dog stirs. What have you to say for yourself, cur?"

Benvolio squinted, forcing his eyes to obey him. Before him stood the captain of Paris's guard, Paris himself, and the prince. After all that he had been through—hell, all that

Verona had been through—Benvolio found it odd to see the prince looking just as usual, his hair combed smoothly back, his fine doublet unspotted by mud or blood.

Even the day Mercutio had died, the prince had been ever spotless.

"Your Grace," Benvolio said, forcing the words like jagged glass through his aching throat. "You are not safe here. He means to kill you! Run!"

The prince's eyebrow shot up. "Kill me?" He exchanged a glance with Paris. "Why should my kinsman kill me, when he has delivered me the knave he tracked down at my behest?" He shook his head. "Why did you kill young Gramio? Was it for revenge? Did your temperate face hide hotter hate toward the Capulets than the basest of your breed?"

Benvolio shook his head. "Upon my honor, 'twas not I."

The prince knelt down before him. Those cool, assessing eyes held an unaccustomed glint of anger. "I am aweary of making excuses for the vicious things your families have wrought upon each other," he said quietly. "Of believing there are honest men among you, only to be proven again and again that you are naught but dogs. Of seeing innocents fall victim to your enmity." A muscle in his jaw twitched. "Knowest thou the sycamore grove to the west of the city walls? Even now, my men are preparing the highest hill for the executioner's work. Every gate to the city shall stand open, so that every merchant, lord, and vassal may come and see what becomes of a traitor to the Crown. I offer thee one last time the mercy thou hast never shown. Tell me what thou didst to Lady Rosaline or thou wilt be dead by tomorrow's sunset."

Benvolio glanced up. Paris was smiling faintly. He looked back to his sovereign, endeavoring to show him with his gaze that he was in earnest. "Listen to me, Your Grace," Benvolio said, trying to keep his voice low. "I speak as one who was ever your honest and true servant. I will go to the grave as such, even if 'tis your own hand that dispatches me. Paris means to depose you. Why think you he raised such a massive force? Would it take a thousand men to find one Benvolio? You must flee *now* and close the city gates behind you, if you value your life and wish to guard our city 'gainst his tyranny."

Paris laughed. "A thousand men? Though Benvolio speaks, 'tis his cowardice that babbles with his tongue." He swept open the entrance to the tent, and with a nod, beckoned his guards to haul Benvolio outside.

Benvolio blinked as the sun stabbed into his eyes. As the scene before him swam into his sight, he thought he must be hallucinating. There were but two other small tents. No more than a dozen men. That was all.

"They are coming," he said, turning to the prince. "He has left them over the next hill, or hidden them in the forest, but they are coming. I saw them, Your Grace, and so did Rosaline—"

"Stop this raving!" the prince said sharply. "Rosaline! Where is she? My cousin says she was raving when he rescued her, unable to tell friend from foe—that she fled his men when they tried to help her. What did you do to her?"

"Answer him!" the captain growled, and cuffed him across the face, sending him sprawling into the dirt. He raised a foot, about to bring it down on his ribs, but a sharp gesture from the prince made him fall back.

Benvolio shook his head to try to clear the ringing from his ears. "She— I made her flee."

"Where?"

"I know not, and if I did I would not reveal it in such treacherous company. I pray she will never return."

A ripple of anger passed across the prince's face. "Wherefore? So she cannot tell the tale of her ravishment at thy hands?"

"How I— No! I never—"

"Silence, you dog." The prince knelt before him, and for the first time, that cool mask cracked, revealing a fury such as Benvolio had never seen him show. "No word you can say now will save you from the executioner's blade."

"I never touched her," Benvolio said. "She came with me willingly, to prove I was falsely accused."

The prince looked up at Paris. "Art thou certain thou knowest nothing of where she's gone?"

"She was raving when we found her. Her sojourn in his clutches had quite destroyed her wits. I know not where she may have gone. I shall never forgive myself for letting her wander away," Paris said sadly.

The prince shook his head. "I thought you the most honorable of men, Benvolio. Never have I been so mistaken in placing my trust. To think I nearly forced her to marry you." He drew a sharp breath in through his teeth. "And now you have ruined her."

"No man could ruin her," Benvolio said. "She is the wisest, bravest, best of ladies. I had rather cut off my hand before using it to outrage fair Rosaline—"

The prince barked a bitter laugh. "How speak you so of the lady you destroyed, Benvolio? Is't possible that e'en as you betrayed her trusting spirit for your own foul ends, she's won your heart?"

Benvolio's eyes widened as he stared up at his sovereign's impassioned face. "My lord," he said, "has she won *yours*?"

The prince's hand dealt him a fierce blow to the cheek. Benvolio crumpled to the ground, his head ringing again.

"Make your peace with God, Benvolio," the prince said over his shoulder, turning to leave. "You die at dawn." Benvolio tried to move, to cry out, to warn him once more, but darkness drew him inexorably into its embrace.

The stars' unchanging gleam mocked him tonight.

Escalus held the palace balcony in a white-knuckled grip as he stared up at the Verona sky, as he had often done before. Usually it soothed him, but there was no comfort to be found in the stars this night; their stately progress across the sky only served to highlight how little of such serenity could be found here on earth of late.

There was a cough behind him. "The streets are clearing, my lord," Penlet said. "As you ordered, Benvolio's capture has been announced. On learning of his coming execution, the Capulets and their allies have ceased their sallies and returned home. They pledge to be at the judgment place at dawn. The Montagues have withdrawn to mourn. All is calm."

"For the moment." The prince smiled mirthlessly. "My thanks, good Penlet. That is all."

Penlet nodded, and with a bow and a cough, he retreated, leaving Escalus alone with the stars.

What would his father think of him now, to see Verona citizens slaughtering each other in the streets like animals? To see him forced to draw arms against his own subjects? Such shame he'd brought upon the crown!

Not he alone, of course. Those damnable Montagues and Capulets had given him generous aid in rendering Verona's gray streets incarnadine.

Escalus let his head fall. Sometimes he was tempted to let them slaughter each other. Any essay he made to soothe their struggles only worsened things; any man of them he thought he could trust would only betray him. At least he still had Paris at his side. He shuddered to think where he would be without his cousin now.

I' faith, how could he have been so wrong about Benvolio? True, he'd been a close friend of Romeo and Mercutio, hotheads both—but Escalus had truly thought him a wiser man than they. One who could be worthy of Rosaline's hand, unwillingly given though it was. The stab of pain that went through him at that thought took his breath away. He'd thrown Benvolio and Rosaline together, forced them into one another's company.

And thus, he'd unwittingly sentenced the lady he loved to hell at the hands of a villain.

Where was she? What had Benvolio done to her? Something horrible enough that she'd lost her wits, according to his cousin. Sickening images flooded his mind and he gritted his teeth. It nearly made him want to throw himself off the balcony to imagine such things happening to her. Why had Benvolio done it? Why abduct her, ravish her, only to throw her away? Even at their worst, neither family had ever targeted a maiden so. For a moment Escalus's mind returned to Benvolio's wild tale of an army waiting to attack the city. There could not be any truth to it, could there?

But no. It was as Paris said—Benvolio was a liar. Why trust a man whose sword was found buried in a young Capulet's heart—whom Livia had seen making off with her sister—over his own flesh and blood? And he had also claimed that Rosaline fled with him willingly—why would she do that, after what had passed between herself and Escalus? No. Paris was his kinsman. Escalus was certain he would not betray him so. While Benvolio betrayed as easily as he breathed. Escalus's momentary whim to believe Benvolio's wild tale stemmed from one thing—if he spoke the truth, it meant Rosaline might still be unharmed. But though his heart longed to believe it, his reason knew better.

The Prince of Verona laughed, burying his head in his hands. The woman he loved was destroyed, and he would probably never see her again. There was naught he could do to help her. Except to make certain that her offender never saw another sunset.

Benvolio's sleep was ended by a kick.

He groaned, jerking away from the guard's prodding foot. "Up, villain," the man said. "Thy judgment is at hand."

Benvolio scrambled to his feet, but not quickly enough for his companion, who gave him another vicious kick to the ribs. "There's one would see thee, ere thou meet'st thy maker."

Benvolio craned his neck eagerly beyond the guard. "Rosaline? Is she returned?"

"No, nephew." Lord Montague stepped through the door. He nodded to the guard. "Leave us."

The guard gave a reluctant bow and withdrew, closing the tent behind him. With a sigh, Benvolio's uncle turned to face him. Though he was facing his own death, Benvolio felt a twinge of pity for him—the lord of the Montagues had grown even older in the days since Benvolio had last seen him.

"Uncle." Benvolio bowed to him; with palsied hands, his uncle drew him to stand once more. Benvolio steadied his shaking hands with his own, wondering as he did so whether it could be long before his uncle joined his wife and son in the grave. "Good day, sir." He opened his mouth again, then shut it. What else was there to say, when one was minutes from death?

"Oh, Benvolio. My poor child. What we are fallen to." His uncle shook his head.

"Listen well, Uncle. I am innocent of all that they claim, do you hear? 'Tis Lady Capulet and Paris who are the authors of all."

"'Tis no use. I have pled with the prince for mercy these three hours, begged him to sweeten thy sentence from death to banishment, but he is steadfast. I did remind him of your rank, of the suffering you have endured at the Capulets' hands, but 'tis no use. He says you shall die this morn."

Benvolio grew cold as he listened to his uncle's words. "My rank? My suffering? Why did you move him thus to pity me, and not beg for an innocent man?" And then it dawned on him, and he felt sick. "You believe I am guilty."

"I believe thou hast cause for whatever thou hast done."

"Think you I would slay young Gramio? Would hurt a *woman*? When Lady Rosaline comes home—"

"Paris believes she is dead. He says she wandered raving into the woods, there to fall prey to wild beasts, or drowned in the river."

"She lives." Benvolio shook his head. "She lives, she *must*. Uncle, listen well. *Do not* trust County Paris, nor Lady Capulet. Friar Laurence knows of their guilt. I saw it written with his own hand." His uncle's watery eyes were filled with pity. Benvolio looked to the heavens in frustration. Paris's army would be here long before anyone could send for Friar Laurence. "Soon, very soon, Verona shall have need of you and Capulet both, you must prepare House Montague to repel Paris's invasion—"

But Lord Montague shook his head, his watery old eyes

fixed sadly on his nephew. "I have done all I can. 'Tis the hour to pray. Unburden thy soul of whatever weighs upon it."

Benvolio glared at his uncle. His heart was beating fast, his hand twitching at his side for his sword. But his blade was gone; there was nothing to fight. So he did as his uncle asked, and fell to one knee, hands clasped.

God in heaven, he thought, *I pray thee now in my darkest hour, deliver me. Bring the truth to light. Let me not die today.*

And if 'tis thy will I should die upon these false accusations, I pray that thou wilt watch over my family. Save my house and my city from destruction.

And, Lord, watch over my Rosaline.

Rosaline was close to passing out.

Silvius carried her on through the night, the rocking of his gait lulling her exhausted body to sleep. Twice she nodded off and managed to jerk awake just in time to keep herself from tumbling off his back.

She knew she needed rest, but she'd allowed them only an hour—enough for Silvius to eat and recover, that was all. She could die of exhaustion later, if it kept Benvolio from the executioner's blade and kept Escalus's rule safe. Though they rode swiftly, she had to keep to the back roads to avoid Paris's search parties, which delayed them for most of a day, and the delay terrified her.

And so she forced her fingers to keep their aching grip on

the reins, kept her eyes on the road stretching toward the two men she cared for above all others, and prayed.

She was perhaps four leagues from Verona's walls when she crested a hill and pulled Silvius up short. There they were beneath her: Paris's army. She supposed he had left them encamped here while he diverted Escalus's attention. Now they stood between her and Verona. She thought quickly. There was another path that would take her home, but it meandered through the hills. Could she make it in time? She looked to the east. The sun was beginning to stain the sky. It soon would be dawn.

The morning breeze blew back Benvolio's hair.

He closed his eyes, letting it wash over him one last time as the guards at his elbows hauled him up Executioner's Hill. His hands were not tied—a small mercy, or maybe they thought that in his current state he posed no threat. He tried to focus on the cool air caressing his face, ignoring the bruising grip on his arms and the sickly pounding of his heart and the crescendo of the crowd as he was dragged before them.

Behind him thundered the river, swollen with the recent rains. His blood would slake Verona's thirst tonight, he thought grimly.

The sight that greeted his eyes when he opened them was enough to make him fight for control of his features. Though the day was young, nine tenths of Verona's nobility and great families had made the trek outside the city walls, all shouting and jeering and straining to catch a glimpse of him.

"Murderer!"

"Knave!"

"Montague cur, you'll burn for what you've done!"

Such a prominent execution would usually be held in the town square. But perhaps the prince had decided to keep the spectacle where its audience could not spill over onto Verona's streets. It was easy to see why. At Benvolio's appearance dozens of harsh Capulet snarls had broken the air, shouting insults. The Montagues roared back, the two sides kept apart by the prince's guards. Had they not been surrounded by the prince's men, it could have easily become a riot.

As for Benvolio himself, an odd peace stole over him. The voices raised in strife by friend and foe seemed to fade to a distant, wordless sea that he floated on as the guards hauled him by the elbows to a raised stone platform at the top of the hill. He was surrounded by the sycamore trees where he and Romeo used to play as children. Where he had seen Romeo, just days before his death, wandering before dawn. Pining, he remembered, for Rosaline. A smile touched his lips. Fate did like its little jests.

I come, cousin, he thought. There was nothing else to be done. His pleas of innocence had fallen on deaf ears. His family's influence had no power to sway this case. The one woman who could save him was gone.

The platform held but two occupants: the prince, and a masked man holding an axe. His executioner. As the guards led Benvolio up onto it, he caught sight of faces in the crowd:

his uncle, looking bereft; Lady Capulet on her husband's arm, a soft smile on her graceful features; Paris, mounted at the rear of the crowd, regarding him stone-faced; his young cousins, lost and unsure. Though he would not for all the world desire her to see this, he could not help but wish to behold Rosaline's fair face once more.

As Benvolio was thrust onto the platform, the prince raised his arms, calling for quiet, and the courtyard grew still.

"Benvolio of House Montague," the prince said, "for thy crimes against our Crown and our people, including the murder of Master Gramio of House Capulet and"—the prince's jaw clenched—"the abduction and ravishment of a good lady of Verona, we sentence you hereby to death. Have you anything to say before you leave this world?"

Benvolio drew a deep breath. "I am innocent of these crimes, Your Grace, but was ever your honest and true servant. If I must die, I pray that my death may at least bring peace to my family and to the city I have always tried faithfully to serve, for no justice shall be done in slaying me. Heed my dying warning: Treachery is afoot, and all men of Verona, no matter their houses, must be prepared to defend their sovereign with their lives."

He turned to face the crowd. He sought out his uncle's face, and his young cousins'. "Someday it shall be clear that I was slandered," he called past the lump in his throat. "When that day comes, I pray, do not venge yourselves upon House Capulet, but only ensure that those who wrought my death meet the Crown's true justice."

Against his will, his eyes sought out Lady Capulet's face in the back of the crowd. Her soft, satisfied smile did not alter. "For those whose cunning hath ensured I die for their crimes, my death shall fall heavy on you, in this world or the next."

With that, he fell silent. The prince's hand fell on his shoulder. "On your knees," he said.

Benvolio sank down before the chopping block. The prince raised his arms. "See, Verona!" he called. "Thus your grudges must end."

A firm hand pushed Benvolio's head down on the block. The courtyard grew deathly quiet, the only sound the gentle rush of the morning breeze. Benvolio closed his eyes.

"Halt!"

Instead of the swift agony of the blade, Benvolio felt a soft body hurl itself atop his. Struggling upright, his eyes went wide at what he saw.

"*Rosaline?*"

The proper, modest maid she was when last he saw her had been replaced with an entirely new Rosaline, from the wild look in her eyes to the mannish style of her hair to— He shook his head and blinked. Was she *wearing his clothes*?

Hang all that. She was alive. Alive, and whole, and there had never been a more welcome sight in his life.

"Hear me, Verona!" she shouted. "Benvolio of Montague is innocent!"

The prince's air of solemn majesty was broken. "Rosaline?" he cried, pulling her away from Benvolio. "Oh, my lady. What has befallen thee? Why art thou so wildly attired? Art thou unhurt?" His hands trailed over her hair and shoulders. Benvolio clenched his jaw. "You must remove from this place. 'Tis no sight for thee."

"'Tis no sight for any honest soul," Rosaline returned, stilling his hands with her own. "My lord, upon my honor, Benvolio is belied."

The prince sighed, pulling her gently to her feet. "Sweet, 'tis he who hath made assault 'gainst that honor you swear by, and left your brain in this confusion."

"I am not mad!" Rosaline said. "My madness and Benvolio's wickedness are both inventions of they that truly committed these crimes." She pointed toward the rear of the courtyard. "Paris and Lady Capulet."

The thundering in her ears was deafening.

Rosaline had felt as though her heart would burst when she saw the executioner's axe raised. She had not even thought before hurling her body over Benvolio's.

If they wanted to kill an innocent today, they would have to kill two of them.

Now, though her voice was strong, her stomach fluttered in fear. The clamor of her heartbeat was soon joined by the roar of the crowd as she made her accusation. She was shaking, near to swooning with exhaustion, but a look at Benvolio's bloodied face was enough to give her strength.

"Benvolio never offered me the slightest discourtesy," she called. "I left Verona in his company of mine own free will." She ignored the flash of surprise and hurt that crossed

Escalus's face at that. "We journeyed to see Friar Laurence, who we believed had some intelligence regarding the latest mischief between our houses." She exchanged glances with Benvolio. "And he did."

Reaching into her bag, she pulled out Friar Laurence's book. "Behold the good friar's diary," she said to Escalus. "Listen to what he says." The crowd grew quieter, straining to hear her voice. She opened the book to the page she'd marked and began to read.

"'I have had a confession today from one I shall call A. She is a servant of long standing of the house of C, and furthermore, she and I shared the burden of the terrible events this summer. The good soul is troubled in her heart, for her mistress L, believed by all Verona to be felled by grief, instead channels her sorrow in a shocking direction. I can scarce write these words: P lives still. He is recovering under the roof of C, though L's lord has no notion of his unexpected guest.'" She heard her uncle Capulet huff at that.

Lady Capulet raised an eyebrow and called in that silken voice, "All Verona knows I did succor him. How is this proof of your accusations, child?"

Rosaline flipped forward several pages to the day of the friar's departure from Verona and read, "'Even as I quit Verona, its bloody tendrils still reached out once more to ensnare me. If P's return from the dead filled me with joy, these new tidings give me nothing but sorrow. Three more youths of Verona lie dead, two this night alone, and I know their killer. For early this morn, just as I was about to depart, A came to confession. She tells me that she came upon P's chamber empty this morn—just at the early hour when Truchio was killed. What is more, she found a bloody raiment P had hidden. Sweet A, though deeply troubled, will not see the thing I fear must be true: 'Tis P who slew them. And at Lady C's direction. Verona has receded down the road behind me, and I pray my troubled heart shall at last know peace when I reach the abbey. But I fear it never shall, for I cannot tell a soul what these murderers have done, and I am sure that their thirst for blood will not be satisfied with these few deaths.' "

"Lady of C? Sir P?" Lady Capulet gave a rueful laugh. She had threaded through the crowd, and now she approached the prince, sweeping him an elegant curtsy. "Your Grace, I apologize for my niece's addled babblings, and the indecent state in which she comes before you. 'Tis plain Paris speaks true—Benvolio's abuse hath robbed her of her wits. Let us take her home." She put an arm around Rosaline. "My poor sweet." Her grip was like iron.

Rosaline shook her off and looked toward the prince, whose face was set into a deep frown. "This *is* Friar Laurence's diary," she insisted. "You must believe me. Verona is in danger. Paris's army is fast approaching. I have seen it with mine own eyes!"

"Eyes addled by madness," Lady Capulet snapped, losing her grip on her motherly tone. "Your Grace has no need to attend to fairy stories. Besides, 'tis not Orlino's death we are here to avenge today." She turned to her husband, who still stood out among the crowd. "My lord, you were to marry Paris to your daughter. Tell the prince he is no traitor."

Lord Capulet's face was red, his brow furrowed. "I know not what the truth of this is," he called gruffly. "But, wife, if you want me to attest to the character of our guests, you will have to tell me when they are under our roof."

Escalus raised his hands. "Enough!" he roared. "Each speaker is more fantastical than the last." He turned to Rosaline. "If this be Friar Laurence's book indeed, how came it to thy hands?"

She swallowed. "I—I stole it." Better she be sanctioned for that than let the prince know that Friar Laurence had willingly violated the sanctity of confession. The crowd murmured at that. She continued quickly, "Punish me for that crime if need be, but, Escalus, you know well that I have never lied to you. I did only what was necessary to save an innocent life. If you believe me a liar now, I shall regain your trust most bitterly before the day is out, for Paris's army is poised to attack."

"Cousin?" Escalus called to Paris, who had not moved from the rear of the crowd. "What say you to these accusations? Pray defend yourself."

"I shall make his answer," a voice replied from behind them. "He is guilty of every word, and worse."

Rosaline turned and gaped. There, behind her on the dais, blue eyes filling with tears and slim shoulders set, was Livia. In her hand she held a small bundle of cloth. She ignored Rosaline, ignored everyone, to stare over the crowd's heads at Paris.

Paris looked as surprised to see her sister as Rosaline herself. "Love, why art thou here?" he demanded. "Thou wast to wait for me back at camp—"

Escalus's eyebrows raised. "Camp?"

"Aye," Livia said. Her voice rang out over the crowd, her hands clasped behind her back. "The camp where he imprisoned Benvolio *and* Rosaline, before she escaped. Where he gathered enough men to storm Verona in an hour." She drew a deep breath. "And where—"

"Livia—" Paris pleaded, his voice high and panicked.

"I'm sorry, my love," Livia said, and then, turning to the prince, "Where he promised to make me princess of Verona."

There was a long, shocked silence. Livia seemed frozen, staring at the dumbfounded Paris, as a tear slipped down her cheek. She unfolded the black scrap in her hands and held it aloft. It was a black mask. "This was among my lord Paris's things in his tent," she said. "He was the man in black. He slew Orlino, Gramio, and Truchio, all three."

Lady Capulet screamed, "Traitor!" and before anyone could move to stop her, she plucked a dagger from her bosom, lunged across the executioner's dais, and plunged it to the hilt into Livia's side.

Time seemed to slow down, shattering into a thousand pieces. The surprised little *uht* that fell from Livia's lips as the blade slid into her. Her body wilting toward the ground. Benvolio leaping at Lady Capulet, wresting the knife from her. Rosaline screaming, "Livia!" as her sister crumpled, racing to catch her in her arms.

"Livia?" she demanded frantically. "Livia?"

His greatest sacrifices. All for naught.

Escalus grimly drew his sword as chaos erupted around him. Paris had wheeled his horse about and was racing away from the city. No doubt returning to this army of his, whose existence Escalus could no longer disbelieve. The crowd was roiling with shock and suspicion; they had not turned on each other yet, but they soon might, if he knew his subjects. To his left, Rosaline cradled her sister, shrieking her name; behind him, Benvolio struggled to keep Lady Capulet from escaping. Escalus rushed to his aid to subdue her. She fought like a wild animal, and it took several of his men to wrestle her to the ground. Escalus growled, "I want her in irons in my dungeon straight away."

She faced him with a crazed grin. Her sleek hair had fallen halfway out of its pins, and her fine gown was stained with mud and her niece's blood. Escalus wondered how he could have looked at her and ever thought her anything but mad. "I shall not pass the night there," she taunted. "By sunset 'tis thou that shall be a prisoner, Escalus, while I stand by the throne."

"Take her away. We've no time for her ravings." He turned to Benvolio. "How now, Montague?"

Benvolio, dirty and bruised and pale, managed a smirk. "In better health than I expected to be ten minutes ago."

Escalus clapped him on the shoulder. "Good. I've need of thee."

Benvolio nodded, took a deep breath, and knelt to the man who, moments before, had been planning to have him executed. "I am Your Grace's to command."

Escalus gave him a nod and turned to the assembled crowd, raising his arms. "Hear me, Verona!" His subjects quieted. "I am betrayed," he called. "*We* are betrayed. If we cannot fight as one, Verona will fall by sundown. For generations, we men of Verona have shed each other's blood—can we now unite against those who would slay us all? Tell me, city of mine, can we fight side by side with our countrymen—*all* our countrymen?"

Numb shock glazed the faces of the crowd. Montagues and Capulets glanced at each other uneasily. Escalus gritted his jaw. Even now, they feuded.

"Aye," Benvolio's harsh voice called beside him. He glared at his young cousins until they too muttered, "Aye."

"Can we face the enemy as one?"

"Aye." This time it was old Capulet—white-faced, shaking like jelly, still staring at the spot where his wife had disappeared, but raising his sword in a trembling salute.

"Can we prevail, Verona?"

"Aye!"

"Can we win the day!"

"*Aye!*"

Every sword was raised, every throat roaring out in unison. The threat of imminent destruction, at least, was enough to unite his fractured people. "Capulet, to me," he called to Lord Capulet. "And Montague."

The two old enemies mounted the platform to the prince's

side. Giving each other wary nods, they stood some distance from each other. "Together, you will look to our defenses," Escalus said, telling them with his glare that he would brook no disagreement. With a sigh, old Montague stuck out a hand and Capulet took it.

"I've ten score men, all told," Capulet said gruffly.

"I've about that number. Paris's forces will likely dwarf us—his lands are vast and his purse vaster. But we shall be better armed than his mercenaries. . . ."

As they conferred, Benvolio tapped Escalus's shoulder. "Where am I to go?"

Escalus looked Benvolio over properly for the first time. He'd lost weight, and was covered in cuts and bruises—some of them, he realized ruefully, likely dealt by Escalus himself— and he was swaying slightly where he stood. He had been through enough at Verona's hands.

But Benvolio, apparently reading his mind, scowled and said, "I shall not be mewed up in chains of safety while my kin and countrymen are abroad. No one has suffered more at these villains' hands than I; no one deserves more to face them."

Escalus nodded. "In that case, you know what I will ask of thee, Benvolio."

Benvolio's gaze followed Escalus's up the hill. "Paris."

Paris's army was in sight by noon.

Rosaline watched them crest the hill with a shiver. A team

of the prince's men had borne Livia back within the city as gently as they could, but her moans of pain would haunt Rosaline's dreams.

Now they were ensconced in the topmost tower of the palace, where Escalus had insisted on installing them. "If the city should fall, every guard in this palace shall fight to the death to protect you."

Hardly comforting, since that would mean that everyone they knew was dead, but Rosaline was glad of a safe place for Livia, and for the prince's physicians, who were currently clustered about her sister's bed.

Livia gasped her name, and Rosaline flew to her side, grasping her hand in hers. "Shh, shh. Rest."

Livia shook her head and said in a dry whisper, "I'm sorry—should have—known—should have said—"

Rosaline shook her head. "Hush, little one. 'Tis no fault of thine."

A pale hint of her usual humor crept into Livia's eyes. "Always—think I'm a child."

It was true. Rosaline had paid little attention to Livia these last weeks. It never would have occurred to her that her impish little baby sister could have involved herself in trouble such as this—or that she could have kept it secret from Rosaline for so long. She pressed Livia's fingers to her lips. "No child could have been as brave as thou wast today."

"Paris told me—" Livia coughed, and with an effort continued, "He told me thou hadst fled Verona forever. 'Tis how I knew he lied. Thou wouldst not leave me so without a word."

A tear slipped over Rosaline's nose. "No, nor may'st thou leave me."

But if Livia had a retort to that, Rosaline was not to learn it, for she fainted once more. Escalus's chief physician took Rosaline's arm, drawing her from Livia's bedside.

"Let her rest now."

"Will she—" Rosaline could barely force the words past the lump in her throat. Livia's breathing was shallow, her cheek nearly as pale as the pillow where it lay. "Will she live?"

"While she breathes, there is hope." But the man's face was grim. Rosaline gripped his arm as the room seemed to swim around her.

There was a little cough. "Lady Rosaline?"

Rosaline took a deep breath until the world solidified, and turned to find Chancellor Penlet hovering in the doorway. He gave another little cough, then said, "His Grace would speak with you." His gaze swept over her. "My . . . lady." The following cough was rather distressed. Rosaline realized she was still wearing Benvolio's clothes, now thick with grime and blood. She offered Penlet a manly bow just to irk him further, then slipped past him and down the stairs.

Benvolio and Escalus were waiting for her in the chamber below. She paused on the landing, regarding them. Both were armor-clad, Benvolio in a breastplate with a Montague crest, the prince in a shining silver helmet surmounted by a stylized golden crown. She shivered. The handsome prince who'd begged to win her heart, the young man who'd mocked and goaded and kissed her—they were going to war.

Both looked up as she descended to them. The prince's gaze was solemn, but questioning. Benvolio, on the other hand, offered her a quick grin and winked behind the prince's back. "Your Grace," she said. "Signor Benvolio."

Escalus took her arm and drew her a little ways away from his companion. "Verona owes you a debt, lady," he said stiffly. "Our city's gates would never have been closed in time without you. Your bravery puts my boldest men to shame."

She winced. Such rigid formality, she knew, masked hurt. "I did but what I must, for you, and for Verona."

"And for Benvolio," he said softly.

She ducked her head. "He needed my help."

"And so thou didst flee with him, under the cover of night." He drew a shaky breath. "I thought he'd killed thee."

She turned tear-filled eyes up to his. "Escalus—"

"Nay." He pressed two fingers to her lips. "Now is the hour for war, not the heart." He took her face in his hands, heedless of their audience, and kissed her forehead. "I am glad thou liv'st, lady. All else shall keep till after we have prevailed in battle."

"Ahem."

"Ay, by and by, Penlet." Escalus kissed her hand in farewell and took his leave, Benvolio at his heels. Rosaline waited for him to bid her farewell too, but he said not a word, and her cheeks flamed as she realized he had overheard what had just passed. She mouthed his name, but he merely jerked a bow and then he too was gone. They had not spoken a word to each other since that night in Paris's camp.

Turning, she flew back up the stairs, pelting into the tower and throwing herself halfway out the window. Far below, two armor-clad figures rode toward the gate. One of them stopped to look back up at her. On impulse, Rosaline pulled out her handkerchief and let it flutter from her fingers down to the courtyard below.

She did not see who caught it.

The Battle of Verona was soon joined.

As Benvolio's uncle had surmised, Paris's forces were mercenaries for the most part. They had expected a rich prize, easily won; many of them turned and ran the moment they saw Verona's forces massed and waiting for them. But even so, Paris remained the commander of an immense horde, and they had come prepared for battle, while Verona's men had only scant hours to make ready. The plain that lay to the east of the city, usually dusty and quiet, was soon a-clang with sword against sword and awash with blood.

Benvolio patted his mount's neck—not the exhausted Silvius, but a steady enough creature of the prince's—and raised his sword, guiding his company to draw in and shore up its flank. The prince had put him in command of a small force of Verona's best warriors. They darted from one knot of fighting to the next, offering what aid they could. Benvolio was glad to be of service, for Verona's beleaguered forces needed every scrap of aid they could get. He just hoped he lived long enough to fulfill the task the prince had set him.

A broken cry to his left drew his attention, and he looked

over and saw a slight Verona youth struggling with a much larger foe. Wheeling his mount about, he bore down on the pair. One swipe of his blade effectively drew the enemy's attention from the boy to himself. The mercenary, a man of forty with mismatched armor and a long brown beard, snarled a gold-toothed grin and aimed a jab at Benvolio's side, which he neatly parried. A few more passes, and the man realized he was overmatched and withdrew, leaving Benvolio to bend over the boy, who was hunched with his hands cupping his side.

"How now, sir knight?"

The boy shook his head. "'Tis but a scratch."

Benvolio pulled his hands away and suppressed a hiss. Quite a scratch. "Marry, Signor . . ."

"Lucio. Of House Capulet."

"Signor Lucio, thou hast done a man's work today. 'Tis time to retire. Hie thee back to the city."

"Nay. I'll not withdraw a coward." Young Lucio had a familiar stubborn chin. Over his shoulder, Benvolio caught the eye of another young Capulet, this one slightly older. Valentine, he thought. The youth had much the look of his cousin Tybalt. He offered Benvolio a slow nod. Benvolio had no time to do more than return his salute before their attention was called back to the battle before them.

Old Montague was fighting for his life.

His arms, once strong and terrible, trembled under the

brunt of yet another blow. He spared a glance behind him, but there was no path to take in retreat—nothing but foes, as far as the eye could see. Years of practice kept his sword arm moving, parrying, avoiding his opponent's blade, but it was only a matter of time. He would see his wife and son before the day was out.

"Yahh! Back and back, you misbegotten swag-headed puttocks!"

The weight on Montague's sword arm was suddenly relieved when a mountain of flesh and steel surged between him and his opponent. He knew that vast form. Lord Capulet wore a helmet and shoulder guards, but no breastplate—doubtless it had grown too small for him in the years since he'd had need of it. He shed drops of sweat as he swung his sword in a great arc over his head with a roar. Montague would not have thought his old rival could move half that fast—was fairly certain that the man had not done so these twenty years—but corpulent though his form had grown, it seemed a warrior's grace and zeal had not entirely deserted it. Well, a warrior's zeal, at least. The invader, taken by surprise by the behemoth suddenly hacking at him, faltered under his swift attack, and after a moment wheeled about and retreated toward his own forces.

"That's right! Tell them 'twas Capulet that sent you hence!" Lord Capulet yelled after him. "By God, there's vinegar in me yet!" He turned to Lord Montague and said, "Well met, sir, whoe'er you may be, for all men of Verona are as brothers today— Oh it's *you*."

Montague had raised his helm, revealing his face, and he

could not help but laugh at the look of dismay on his old foe's face. "Brothers indeed, for you have saved me, sir," he said. "A sweeter revenge you could not have than to put me in the debt of my most loathed enemy. I pray I shall have the chance to return the offense before the day is out."

Capulet, after a moment, harrumphed a laugh as well. "Come, you old scoundrel, let's play out our fury 'gainst our foes and not each other for this day. With luck, one or both of us will fall to the enemy, and none need tell of this shameful passage." Together, they wheeled their horses and charged back into the fray, roaring out their battle cries.

"For Montague!"

"For Capulet!"

"For Verona!"

His city and his crown, he feared, were lost.

Verona's forces fought on bravely, and never had Escalus felt more fierce pride in the city he ruled. But Paris's army was simply too numerous. Little by little, they were slicing Escalus's army away, forcing them back toward the city walls. The ground was littered with Verona's dead. The northern gate had briefly been breached, and though only a small force had made it into the city proper, repelling them had cost many lives.

Escalus surveyed the field with a lump in his throat. His own life was nothing, compared to the safety of the city. To protect it, he would do the unthinkable. He would surrender.

"Ready a white flag," he told his page, who looked astonished. "We'll go to Paris to parley."

The boy shook his head in horror. "My lord, my lord, you cannot surrender yourself to him. Surely we can still prevail."

But even as the boy spoke, a fresh wave of troops came pounding onto the field from the east. There was no way his weary countrymen could withstand yet another onslaught. The devil take his cousin! Where had Paris gotten so many soldiers to follow him? He must have bankrupted his estates. Of course, he soon hoped to replace them with a city.

Although oddly, this latest force did not appear to be mercenaries, nor did they wear the colors of Paris's house. In fact, their blue-and-white livery was that of—

Of Arragon.

Before his battle-numbed brain could fully comprehend the miracle before him, the figures leading those blue-and-white saviors peeled off and came galloping toward him. "Hail, brother," one of them said, raising his helmet. "How goes the day?"

Escalus closed his gaping mouth and saluted his brother-in-law. "Hail, Don Pedro, and well met. The day went ill indeed until your heaven-sent appearance. How came you here?"

"By luck only. Whilst on the road for Arragon, my princess Isabella and I met a man who hoped to enter my service. He was one of County Paris's men by birth, and he told us the count was raising a great army and making for Verona." He nodded to his forces. "I came here forthwith to offer what aid I could. My friends Sir Claudio of Messina and Sir Benedick of Padua have joined their forces to mine." The two men at his side nodded.

"How knew you that we needed your aid?"

"I know something of traitorous kinsmen," Don Pedro said drily. "Besides, your sister can be most persuasive."

Escalus would never chide Isabella's unladylike yelling again. "Where is Isabella?"

"Safe at Benedick's estate in Padua. I have promised to send her word the moment Verona is saved."

Escalus grinned. Already, Don Pedro's forces were pushing Paris's army back from the wall. "We shall send for her ere nightfall."

"Well, Montague, your short reprieve is done."

Paris wore that faint smile again. Benvolio longed to wipe it off his face. He'd grown to so detest that look. But the two men in Paris's livery had a firm grip on his arms. He hung nearly limp from their hold, his face toward the ground. Nearby, the sounds of battle could still be heard, but they were fainter than they'd been an hour ago. Here in this grove, there were only Paris, Benvolio, the men at his arms, and Paris's captain. "Surrender, Paris," Benvolio gritted out. "Your mercenaries are in flight. Your house's men are slaughtered. The day is Verona's. Throw yourself on your cousin's mercy and he will spare your life."

Paris laughed. "Bold words from a man who's spent his

strength and fallen in the grip of the enemy. Half dead you are, and still a-snarling, like a dog with its entrails torn out that still bites. No wonder your family's so hated. Your claws are never sheathed."

"My lord," his captain said urgently at his elbow, "you're needed on the field—"

Paris waved a hand. "Take care of it. I must dispatch the Montague first. It will not wait. Go and marshal our forces."

"My lord, I must advise retreat—"

"I said take care of it!" Paris yelled. "The day will be ours!"

The captain looked as though he had more to say, but instead he closed his mouth, bowed, and withdrew. Paris drew his sword, advancing on Benvolio. "Not the first Montague I have put down, but the first whose death I may freely claim with pride," he said. "Last words, Benvolio?"

"Aye," Benvolio panted. "A bit of advice. For Verona's future sovereign, if so you shall be."

"Advice?" Paris looked amused. "Let us have it, then."

"There is more to being a prince than conquest. Escalus may have his faults as a ruler, but attention to his people is not one of them. He meets his subjects' eyes. He knew the names of every Montague or Capulet slain, and no matter how we vexed him, he grieved for each senseless death as though it were the first."

"So your advice is . . ."

"Learn your servants' faces. Now!" he roared, and Lucio and Valentine released his arms, Lucio tossing him the sword he'd hidden beneath his livery. They'd taken their cloaks off some of Paris's captured men, and the county had not given them a second glance.

He did now, though, recovering from his shock with his usual feline grace. His own sword was up and dancing with Benvolio's before he could blink. "Three against one, Montague?" he said. "I knew you were honorless."

Benvolio shook his head. His weariness and pain were rippling away from him like a discarded cloak. He knew it was just the elation of facing his enemy at last, that the respite would be short, but that was all he needed. One way or another. "My Capulet friends here are longing to let their blades taste your blood in repayment for yoking their family name to your treason, but they have kindly agreed to cede the field to me. They'll not interfere with our sport. 'Tis you and I, Paris."

"Then let's have at it." And Paris lunged.

Benvolio had known the night Paris slew Gramio with his sword how skilled a swordsman the murderer was. And that had been when he himself was uninjured and at his full strength. Now, as he and Paris whirled about the grove, their boots kicking up clods of mud with the speed of their passes, he feared his own skill with the blade was no longer enough. Paris was swift, and skilled, and strong. Benvolio reflected grimly that he'd once defeated five men at once, but it was quickly becoming clear that he was hardly a match for one Paris. Indeed, judging by the flashes of panicked faces he saw whenever he was able to spare a glance for Lucio and Valentine, he was no match for Paris at all.

His only hope was to outthink him. Paris might be a natural with a sword, but as Lucio and Valentine had just proven, he did not deal terribly well with surprises. Benvolio would have to catch him off guard. To that aim, he began to talk.

"Wherefore your betrayal?" he demanded when they drew apart briefly, circling each other. "Your cousin loved you. He might even have made you his heir."

Paris was scarcely out of breath. "He let Juliet die. That will not stand."

"All this for your sweet lost love, then?" Benvolio taunted. "She gave not a fig for you."

Paris's face twisted with rage. "She would have, had you Montagues not warped her. Her parents had given her to me. I would have given her everything." His features resumed their accustomed smoothness. "But no. Not just for her. I've a new love now. You Montagues may have confused her sweet young mind too, but I shall correct her. You shall not steal another wife from me, though I have to tear your house stone from stone to prevent it."

Benvolio had nearly forgotten Livia had somehow entangled herself with Paris. God, nothing in Verona was ever simple, was it? "She seemed not bewitched when she denounced you."

"She is misled. Henceforth she shall be led by me. Livia will be my wife."

The fanatic devotion that lit Paris's mad face as he thought of his love was shudderingly familiar. Was this how Romeo had looked as he pined?

No. That was not it. Subtract the mad sneer from Paris's

face, and you had his kinsman the prince, gazing at Rosaline before they rode off to war.

He had been avoiding dwelling on what he'd seen in the prince's tower. After the battle, he'd thought. After this bloody day was done, he could admit to himself what he'd seen, when he had leisure for his heart to break. But now his traitorous mind thrust the knowledge to the forefront. Rosaline, his Rosaline, was beloved of the prince.

In the moment that Benvolio realized that his own love was lost to him, he had a sudden, wild thought of how he was going to defeat Paris: by depriving him of his.

But then his foot, clumsied by exhaustion, caught on a root as he stepped back, and he stumbled. It was only a split second of weakness, but for a swordsman as skilled as his opponent, it might as well have been an hour. Paris's eyes lit up and he drove forward, sword flashing so fast Benvolio could barely see it, let alone parry it.

"Did you not hear, County?" he wheezed. "Your new love is lost to you too. Did you not see your friend Lady Capulet's blade pierce her heart?"

Paris's eyes tightened. "'Tis a lie."

"'Tis none. Your treachery has killed her."

Paris faltered, his eyes wide, and Benvolio prayed with all his might. *Half a minute of strength, Lord. 'Tis all I ask.*

It was enough. As the enraged Paris rushed at him, leaving himself open, Benvolio leapt like a coiled spring. The force of his body drove Paris back, throwing him off balance, and then Paris was on the ground, Benvolio's blade at his throat.

For a moment they stayed frozen, Benvolio's panting breaths his only movement. The red haze of fury had once more dropped over his eyes.

"Kill him, Benvolio!" young Valentine called.

"For Gramio!"

For me, Truchio's shade seemed to whisper.

For House Montague. Romeo's face was grim.

For Verona. Mercutio's grin was far more bloodthirsty than usual.

Paris met his vanquisher's eyes with a defiant snarl. "Well, whoreson cur? I'll beg not for my life. No life is life if I be vanquished by such."

I thought you wished to end this cycle of death, Benvolio.

The memory of Rosaline's wide, pleading eyes was enough to drown out the maelstrom of voices in his head calling for revenge. He withdrew his blade a few inches. "Yield."

"Never." Paris's elegant features were twisted in a sneer. His hand darted to the ground, retrieving his fallen blade, and with a broken cry he threw himself at Benvolio.

Forgive me, Rosaline.

Epilogue

A glooming peace this morning with it brings.

—Romeo and Juliet

$\mathcal{F}$RAIL LIVIA HAD WANDERED off alone.

Rosaline closed her eyes in relief as her carriage came round the bend and she saw her sister sitting by the river-bank. Though two weeks had passed since Paris's forces had been defeated, and Livia's strength was beginning to return, she was still ill and weak. Rosaline had been frantic when she found her gone from her bed. With her sister's death filling her nightmares, Rosaline could scarcely stand to allow Livia out of her sight, but she had managed to disappear the moment her back was turned. Luckily, one of their servants had seen her walking toward the east gate.

Servants. Now that was a change indeed. House Capulet had suddenly granted their household a generous allowance. She could not say for certain, but she saw the prince's hand in it. Now that Lady Capulet was imprisoned for life, the rest of the Capulet clan were eager to prove they were not traitors. Rosaline suspected that Escalus's first suggestion was that they take better care of her and Livia. Their little cottage was growing more elegantly furnished by the day.

"Shall we go and get her, my lady?" the coachman asked, but Rosaline shook her head.

"Nay. Bide you here awhile, sirrah." She stepped out of the carriage, a footman helping her down.

She sighed at the sight before her. Her sister was seated on the riverbank in a gown of the pure black that she'd once so despised. Her complexion, even paler than usual thanks to her fortnight a-bed, was rendered ethereally white against the black of her mourning gown. Her lap held an armful of wildflowers, which she dropped one by one into the water. She did not look up when Rosaline approached, but when she was a few paces away, Livia smiled.

"I thought 'twould take thee longer to seek me out."

"'Twas not hard to find thee, once I knew thou didst depart through the east gate." Bending down at Livia's side, she took one of Livia's flowers and tucked it into her sister's golden hair. "Thou shouldst be yet in bed."

Livia took the flower from behind her ear and dropped it in the water. "'Twas here Paris died."

"I know." Rosaline focused on the flowers to banish the image of the grim young Montagues and Capulets bearing Paris's slain body back to the palace. No face grimmer than Benvolio's, though 'twas he whose blade had pierced the traitor's heart. "I am sorry."

Livia laughed, a bitter sound, and Rosaline's heart twisted in her chest. Her merry little scamp of a sister was gone forever, leaving behind a much sadder woman. "No, thou art not. No one is sorry for it. Except for me. And I killed him."

"Oh, dearest, no."

"Pray coddle me not."

"Thou didst but what thou must. Paris was a heartless wretch. Hadst thou not stopped him, God only knows what would have become of us all."

Livia shook her head. "Not heartless. For he loved me. I know he did."

Rosaline did not know what to say to that. So she just took her sister's hand and squeezed.

Livia's gaze strayed to the carriage patiently waiting in the road. "Another fine gift from the prince?"

Rosaline ducked her head, pretending to focus on the little flowers she was plucking to hide her blush. "He has been most generous. To our house and to Benvolio too, I hear."

"Generous." Livia gave a snort.

"He's very grateful," Rosaline said. "To thee above all. Hadst thou not warned him in time, Verona never would have prevailed against Paris's forces. He would give anything in Verona to make thee happy."

"I fear nothing in Verona could."

"Livia—"

"Hush. Pray do not try to comprehend. He whom thou lov'st yet lives."

Rosaline just stared out over the sun-dappled water.

In the end, she was able to bundle her sister back into the carriage, though she suspected it was only because Livia was too fatigued to refuse.

The next few weeks were busy ones for all, as the city in general, and Houses Montague and Capulet in particular, began repairing and rebuilding. The riots after the nurse's death had left extensive damage, as had those of Paris's men who had managed to fight past the city walls. The Duchess of Vitruvio was one of the lucky ones whose estates had been largely untouched by the rioting. She sent her servants to help the other Capulets rebuild, but she herself stayed mostly at home. Rosaline supposed that was only natural. Her daughter's treason must have come as quite a shock. She had gone up to her great-aunt's house to visit once or twice, but the old woman did not seem to welcome her company more than she ever had, so Rosaline left her to her solitude. She had an uncomfortable feeling that the duchess knew she and Benvolio had suspected her of the treachery that turned out to be her daughter's.

She saw none of Benvolio, who had been sent to nearby cities to do business on House Montague's behalf. The prince was more often in her company. He had her to dine at the palace several times, officially to thank her for her service to the Crown, and when he walked through the city to observe the rebuilding efforts he often took her with him. He was sweet, and attentive, and generous, but they had not spoken of what had passed between them before he went into battle. She often caught him looking at her, though. Had his feelings changed? She could not bring herself to ask.

But he continued to shower them with gifts, although Livia seemed entirely indifferent, and Rosaline herself protested mightily. At least his gratitude helped distract her from the little hurt she was nursing about Benvolio's silence. Busy though he might be, he could at least write to her and let her know he was all right.

After a few weeks, Livia's health had improved greatly, though her spirits were no higher. Rosaline's relief at her recovery gave way to disquiet. Verona gossip told her that Benvolio had returned several days prior. But she'd had no word from him—and, after all, what right had she to expect any? They had worked together to end their betrothal. Well, it was ended, and while Houses Capulet and Montague were not exactly the best of friends, they had agreed to a chilly peace that seemed likely to hold. Perhaps he was content now to be free of her company.

Perhaps his kiss had meant nothing.

Then one day there was a clatter of horses outside. When Rosaline opened the door, several servants in the yellow and white livery of the prince's men stood on the threshold of the cottage. With cursory glances at Rosaline, they took up positions by her door. A third stopped on the new carpet and, after a self-important pause, spoke.

"His Grace the Prince and Her Grace the Princess of Arragon wish to speak to Lady Rosaline of House Tirimo," the man said.

Rosaline stared. "Both of them? Here? Isabella is returned?"

The man looked pained, and Rosaline gave herself a mental shake. "Please, I'd be honored. Let them in."

The next moment her old friend was striding through the door, her smile as merry as ever. "No turnips today, I am afraid," said Isabella. Rosaline had scarcely given her a curtsy before she found herself engulfed in Isabella's embrace.

"Your Grace, well met. I did not know you were back in Verona." She returned her friend's hug.

Isabella pulled back and gave a good-natured groan. "I'd have been here sooner, but my husband is overcautious, and he bade me stay away until he was sure there was no one else in this conspiracy, lying in wait for impetuous princesses."

"He is wise. You missed Verona's worst hours."

"I always seem to."

Rosaline curtsied to Escalus, who nodded in return, but remained back by the doorway. "To what do I owe the honor of this visit?" she asked.

Isabella said, "Oh, I'm not here for thee. Where is thy sister?"

Rosaline blinked. "Livia? What—" She stopped herself. "Livia," she called over her shoulder. "We've visitors. Wilt thou come?"

"By and by," her sister's weary voice floated down.

"Ah, nay, now, an it please thee . . ."

After a few moments Livia appeared at the top of the stairs, clinging to the banister. Her eyes widened when she saw their guests, and she sank into a curtsy. "Your Grace. Your Grace."

"Hello," said Isabella.

Escalus nodded. "Livia. Thou look'st much better."

"Thank you, Your Grace." She shot a puzzled glance at Rosaline, who shrugged. "Why are you here?"

Rosaline smiled as it was the prince's turn to look flustered. At least Livia had lost none of her accustomed directness. But it was Isabella who answered. "I've a quarrel to that sister of thine, Livia. Rosaline promised me two Verona ladies to go back to Arragon with me, but gave me none. I've come to collect on the debt, in part at least."

Livia's brow wrinkled in confusion. "My lady . . . you mean . . ."

"I mean I need a lady-in-waiting," Isabella said. "Wilt thou come with me to Arragon, Livia?"

Livia went very still, her eyes wide. "Arragon."

"Yes."

"'Tis very far from Verona."

"Yes."

For a long moment, Livia stood frozen. Then, for the first time since Paris had died, Rosaline's sister burst into tears.

The prince stepped forward in distress as Rosaline took the sobbing girl in her arms. "My lady—we did not mean to give offense—"

"I do not believe you did," Rosaline said, patting Livia's shuddering back. "Hush now, Livia. He thinks they've upset thee."

"Arragon," Livia sobbed. "I can go. I can *leave*."

"Yes, dearest."

Livia pulled back, swallowing her sobs in great gulps. "No. I cannot. How can I leave thee?"

Now Rosaline was close to crying too. "You can. You must, if you cannot be happy in Verona."

"Oh God, never," Livia breathed. "I cannot stand the sight of this accursed city. I mean no offense, Your Grace." Escalus nodded gravely.

"So thou wilt come?" Isabella asked.

But Rosaline shook her head. "No, wait. Livia is still too weak to make this journey."

"How now if she make it with a kinswoman?" the Duchess of Vitruvio asked. She had joined the prince at the base of the stairs.

Rosaline and Livia looked at each other in surprise. "Aunt?" Rosaline asked cautiously. "We could not ask you to accompany her—"

The duchess waved this off. "Please. Even were she hale and well, I'd not allow her to go unchaperoned. Secret elopement, consorting with traitors, wandering about dressed as men—Capulet maids are turned terribly wanton of late. Besides, the young lady's right. Verona is intolerable. My wits are grown soft as pudding here. I knew my daughter was up to no good, but I said nothing. Travel will sharpen me."

Livia gasped. "That is why you were trying to get into Paris's chamber."

"Aye." Her sharp gaze turned on Rosaline. "This one thought I was behind it, I'd wager. I should have told thee, girl, when thou cam'st to see me, of my suspicions. If we'd been less deceitful, we might have saved a great deal of strife." She sniffed. "But thou hadst that *Montague* with thee."

Rosaline laughed in surprise. "You cannot still think the Montagues to blame."

The duchess sniffed again. "You cannot deny that where they go, trouble follows. But no matter. Shall I relieve thee of this sister of thine or no?"

Rosaline opened her mouth to refuse, but she looked at Livia and was surprised to see a glint of her old mirth lurking deep in her eyes. "I thank you, Aunt," Livia said. "I believe I shall find it most amusing to travel with you."

Rosaline hid a smile. She foresaw barrels of wine in her aunt's future. No prospect could have pleased her more. "Very well, Aunt."

"Come, ladies. Let's discuss thy gowns. Fashions are rather different in Arragon." With a sly look at Escalus, Isabella swept the duchess and Livia upstairs, leaving Rosaline and the prince to stand in awkward silence.

He clasped his hands behind his back, turning a circle, taking in the new furniture. Some had been gifts from him; some she'd bought with her new allowance; a few had even been sent by House Montague, who could not choose but be grateful that she'd saved their heir. Altogether, the cottage was much grander than it had been. His servants stood unmoving at attention, for all the world as though this were his house, and Rosaline an interloper. The majesty of his person made the finery Rosaline was so proud of seem shabby by comparison.

Then he grinned at her, and Rosaline felt ashamed of her momentary resentment. "Beautiful," he pronounced. "The finest home in all Verona."

Rosaline shook her head, even as a pleased smile grew unwilling on her lips. "You flatter yourself, for any beauty is due entirely to you—as is the fact that the roof no longer admits rain."

"To my aid, perhaps, in persuading the Capulets to give you your due. But if my men could produce such beauty under mine own direction, the palace would be a much more welcoming place. So lovely an abode requires a woman's touch."

Rosaline smiled her thanks. An awkward silence fell once more. Rosaline found her hands twisting in her skirts and forced them back to her sides. The prince turned, admiring a shelf of small statues he could not possibly care about.

"May I offer you something to eat?" she offered, casting her mind wildly into the kitchen, trying to imagine what she might serve that was worthy of royalty.

He held up a hand. "No, no. There's no need."

"As it please you."

They lapsed into silence again, and Rosaline wondered what in the world he was doing here. It occurred to her how few conversations like this Escalus must have—not to hear a complaint or issue a command, but simply to talk. That disquieting, awe-inducing air of majesty he wore about him discouraged easy conversation. How lonely that must be.

"I've a gift for thee," he said.

Rosaline shook her head. "No, please, Your Grace has already been too generous—"

He waved a dismissive hand at the finery that now bedecked her house. "No gifts they were, but well earned, for you saved the city." He took her hand, tugging her toward the door with a smile. "Now, this—this is a gift."

He opened the door and she gasped when she saw what waited outside. There, tied at her door, was a stunning white mare—a far finer horse than even her father had ever owned.

"By this day, she's beautiful!"

"She is thine."

She turned to Escalus. "No, no—"

"Yes. By order of your sovereign. Take her."

She ought to refuse. He had already been far too generous.

Oh hell. "What's her name?"

Escalus grinned. "Tomasina, and a prettier piece of horse-flesh there never was. Come, wilt thou ride with me? The day is fair for a gallop through the hills."

Wildly tempting, but Rosaline shook her head. "Your sister, and Livia—I cannot."

"They will be all right. Please, I crave thy company." He gave her his most charming smile, but when he saw that she still wavered, he added, "Perhaps thou think'st I've not done penance enough for the trouble I have caused thee? Thou think'st not right, for look."

Taking hold of Tomasina's bridle, he drew her aside, revealing his own stallion. Rosaline clapped a hand to her mouth, but could not restrain a laugh. The poor horse's mane had been shaved.

"Since there were no small maidens about to teach me my lesson, I did it myself."

Rosaline shook her head, stroking the embarrassed horse's neck. "You will be the silliest-looking prince in all of Italy till it grows back."

"'Tis worth the humiliation, if it makes thee smile, sweet Rosaline." There was an unaccustomed warmth in his eyes.

"Let me don a clean gown," she said.

They rode south and west, along the river. Once they were out of sight of the city walls, Rosaline gave him a saucy look over her shoulder and tried to scandalize him by throwing Tomasina into an unladylike gallop, but he merely gave a boyish whoop and came racing up behind her. At last, laughing and windblown, she reined Tomasina in on a ridge overlooking the forest. Escalus drew up next to her, blowing out a breath.

"By this day, I hope no one saw that," he said.

"Always so proper."

"We cannot all go flitting about the countryside in disguise."

Rosaline shuddered. "I hope I ne'er again have cause to do so."

"Come," he said. "Let us walk awhile."

He dismounted before offering a hand to help her down too. After all that had passed, it felt strange to be treated so gently. Benvolio had been chivalrous to a fault, but he'd treated her as a comrade. Escalus made her feel as delicate as a bit of porcelain.

He kept hold of her hand and threaded their fingers together. For a few minutes they walked in silence as the horses grazed nearby. Rosaline let her eyes drift over the countryside below them. Summer was ripening into fall, and the farms and fields were rich with crops soon to be harvested. Strange to think that all she could see owed fealty to the man beside her.

"I thank you," she said finally. "For Livia. 'Twas your idea to send her with Isabella, was it not?"

"I hope thou wilt not mind."

Rosaline shook her head. "I shall miss her desperately,

but I knew not what else to do for her here. I think if she stayed, she would pine herself to death."

"We'll have no more of that," the prince said fervently.

"Amen."

"That night you fled," he said. "You left no sign of where you were going. Left me no sign."

His voice was as calm and polite as it always was, but she could tell he had been thinking about this. "I am sorry for the pain I caused you," she said. "More sorry than I can say. I should have woken Livia, or left a note, but I had to leave in all haste—Benvolio was pursued, and we knew not how much time we had before he was discovered."

He smiled to himself. "Benvolio."

"Your Grace—"

But he put a finger to her lips, just as he had the day of the battle. "Sweet, I have not asked thee what passed between thee and Signor Benvolio, and I never shall. But I confess I have thought much of that night in these weeks since. Why didst thou need to go at all? Why not come to me?"

"To thee?"

"Just that afternoon I swore I loved thee. Why not come to me for help, when Benvolio sought thee out?"

It was just the question she had asked herself of late. But the truth would hurt him, so she kept silent.

But Escalus had already arrived at it. "Thou didst not trust me."

"*Thou* didst force me to broker my freedom for my virtue," she snapped back before she could stop herself.

"I know. And if thou wilt forgive me that transgression,

I'll forgive thee thy flight." He stopped, taking both her hands in his. Escalus took a deep breath. "Verona must return to peace and quiet. To do that, my people must know that my reign is stable. I believe 'tis time I took a wife. Rosaline, you are one of Verona's most eligible daughters. Your beauty, your character, and your lineage are all beyond reproach. What is more, you are well known to me, and I know you will occupy my mother's throne with the utmost wisdom and delicacy. Your loyalty has proven itself a thousand times over." He drew another shaky breath. "And you know well how I love you. I do not believe another could make me happy. Sweet, I do love you. I hope you will believe me this time."

He smiled at her, nervous but sincere, and she remembered how gingerly he'd patted her little back as she wailed over his abandonment when they were children. She knew Verona's prince, inside and out, as perhaps no other soul could claim to. This time he meant every word he was saying. Framing her face in his hands, he leaned in and kissed her, slowly and delicately, like a sunbeam kissing the face of an upturned flower. Rosaline sighed against him.

"Well, my love?" he asked, taking both her hands in his and pressing them to his chest. "Will you be mine?"

Rosaline gazed at the expectant face of her sovereign. The man she'd longed to marry for most of her life. Finally, the turmoil she'd felt for so long whenever she thought of him was calm. She knew her answer.

"Nephew, are you quite sure that you must go?"

Benvolio winced internally as he looked at his uncle's pleading face. The old man stood next to him at the city gate, one restraining hand at his elbow. He knew that he was being dreadfully irresponsible as House Montague's heir. He ought to stay in the city, let one of his cousins undertake this long trading journey.

But with all Verona telling him that the prince was on the point of announcing his betrothal to Rosaline of House Tirimo, he knew he could no more stay at home than he could stab himself in the heart. "Right well you know that House Montague has need of a champion abroad, Uncle. Our fortunes at home in Verona have suffered a grievous blow. We must do what we can to augment our properties elsewhere."

He worried that his uncle would order him to stay, but the old man only sighed and shook his head. "Very well. Write when thou canst. I hope to see thee before a year is out." He nodded beyond Benvolio's shoulder. "Look, here's another to bid thee farewell."

Benvolio turned around to find none other than Rosaline, mounted on a fine white horse and wearing a sour expression. Benvolio turned back to his uncle, planning to avoid her gaze, but his uncle gave him a dry look and a bow and withdrew, heading back into the city.

"Good morrow, Montague." She slid from her horse. "So 'tis true. You aim to quit Verona."

He nodded to her mount. "Pretty. A gift from your prince?"

"He is your prince too, unless you've turned the traitor you were once believed to be."

He had not been so close to her since the day of the battle. It had been even longer since they'd conversed privately. The weeks of recovery had done wonders for her. She was arrayed in a fine gown of pale green—another gift from the prince, surely—with matching ribbons in her hair, just as she'd been the day they were betrothed. He had seen many women in similar hues of late—Rosaline, it seemed, was setting Verona's fashions. Not surprising, in a future princess. But it was not just her new finery that made her look so lovely. The strain that had marked her face during their travails was gone; the weight she'd lost had returned. She was as lovely as a breeze off the water on a summer day. He turned away, preoccupying himself with Silvius's bridle. "Wherefore are you here, my lady?"

"Merely to bid you adieu. You saved my life. I've not had the chance to offer my thanks."

"'Twas thanks enough when you saved mine in turn."

"Still, you deserve to hear it."

"Very well. I am thanked." And he shut his jaw with a snap. They stared at each other in sullen silence, but she did not move to leave.

Rosaline bit her lip. "Why came you not to see me?"

He barked a laugh. "Why should I wish to do that?"

"Bare courtesy, perchance?" she muttered, then fished about in her sleeve. "Here. I made this for you. 'Twas finished weeks ago. I should have known better than to expect your attentions when you had no further need of me." She thrust a scrap of cloth at him. "Here."

He took it. It was a handkerchief, embroidered with the Montague crest. "Thanks."

"You're welcome. Go choke on it."

What did she expect from him? Was she so vain as to demand he hang about and pine for her as she made ready to wed his sovereign? He went to shove the cursed thing to the bottom of his saddlebag, but her hand shot out and seized his wrist. "It is customary, when a lady makes you a gift, to wear it upon your person," she said icily.

God in heaven, she would be the death of him. He gave her a mocking bow, then took the handkerchief and began to tuck it into his sleeve. He tried to turn his back slightly, but when he drew his sleeve up she drew in a sharp breath. Benvolio closed his eyes. Caught.

Her fingers were gentle now as she turned his wrist over and brushed his sleeve up to reveal that he already carried a handkerchief—one embroidered by the same hand. She stayed like that, dark curly head bent over his hand, fingers tracing the stitches she herself had worked. Benvolio clenched his jaw against a shiver.

"I knew 'twas thee who had it." She raised her face, her big green eyes clouded with hurt and confusion. "Why didst thou keep it?"

"Thou knowest right well why." He turned away, fussing with Silvius's buckles again until the horse nickered in protest.

"Then wherefore hast thou in all outward behavior seemed to hate me?" she cried. "How have I fallen so from thy favor?"

He whirled on her, incredulous. "What claim to my favors hast thou when thou art to wed the prince?"

She frowned. "Wed the prince? Who told thee so?"

"'Tis all Verona speaks of."

"As usual, Verona speaks not right."

He shook his head in disbelief. "Rosaline. He has scarce been seen out of thy company for a fortnight."

She ducked her head, a blush staining her cheeks. "He—he asked me," she admitted. "I had to refuse him."

His chest began to fill with shaky hope he hardly dared to feel. One disbelieving hand drifted up to her shoulder, then hesitated, hovering without touching her. "Refuse him."

"Aye."

"Why?"

A slight smile graced her lips. Her eyes darted up to his. "Thou knowest right well why."

He swallowed hard, and gripped both her shoulders. "Rosaline. *Please.*"

"I could not wed him when I love another," she said. Her eyes were tender now, softer than he'd ever seen them, as she shook her head and mouthed, "Benvolio."

"Oh thank *God,*" he said as he drew her to him.

If he had been asked before this moment, he would have said that nothing in this world or the next could improve upon the previous kisses he'd stolen from her. But he had to admit that subtracting rain and mud and mortal peril from the equation was even better. She was eager and soft and sun-warmed in his arms, and he felt that he could quite happily live out his life right here, running his fingers down her spine and feeling her sigh and smile against his lips, with only the hoots of passing peddlers to distract them.

They continued that way for quite some time, until Benvolio pressed her a little too enthusiastically against Silvius's side and he shied away in protest, sending them both stumbling. Laughing, he grabbed her waist to right her, and she pressed her forehead against his.

"If I once more broach the subject of marriage," he murmured, "wilt thou scream to the heavens and march off to a nunnery?"

Rosaline laughed. "After thieving through Montenova in your clothing, I am quite certain no decent nunnery would have me."

"Good," he said, and kissed her again. "Friar Laurence will have another Montague and Capulet to marry, then."

"Montague and Tirimo."

"Of course." He bent to kiss her once more, but she drew back.

"What of thy yearlong exile from Verona?"

"I'll send Marius." His lips found hers again, muffling her laughing protests.

"We'd best go now and tell our families. If we carry on so in public, House Montague will not allow thee to wed such a scandalous jade."

He raised an eyebrow. "Didst thou not just say thou art a confirmed wanton? Where's the harm, then?"

"Benvolio!" Laughing, she placed a hand to his chest to hold him at bay.

He gave a mighty sigh. "As you wish." He stole one more

kiss, then they mounted their horses and turned back from the gates. Benvolio grinned as they rode up the street. His city had not seemed such a beautiful sight in months. It was as though the burden that had been lifted from his shoulders had relieved all Verona too. The streets were crowded with merchants, nobles, and servants, the color and clamor of the city overwhelming as it returned at last to life. On such a fair day, it was impossible to imagine that even the dead could slumber through it. A group of young men were bent over a dice game, and he imagined that he saw Gramio's and Truchio's slim young forms among them—that Mercutio's lanky form flashed him a mile-wide grin in the corner of his eye.

And, at the crest of a distant hill, he thought he saw another young Montague, hand in hand with a slim, dark-haired maiden, both of them smiling down at the newly betrothed couple. Beside him, Rosaline reached over and laced her fingers through his. And they smiled too.

Author's Note

The wonderful thing about Shakespeare is that we all feel like he belongs to us. We've heard his words our whole lives, but his stories still feel as fresh and moving as they must have when they were first performed. In some plays, the settings he creates feel very self-contained—it's hard to picture Elsinore after Hamlet, for example—but with *Romeo and Juliet,* he created a world so bursting with life that it's impossible not to imagine what happened afterward.

That's what inspired me to write *Still Star-Crossed.* Since Shakespeare himself borrowed liberally from other stories, I trust that his spirit will forgive me for borrowing the characters and setting I love so much. But to further my hope that he and I will one day have a less strained meeting up in writers' heaven (lots of coffee, no writer's block, chairs with lumbar support), let me lay out which parts of *Still Star-Crossed* are borrowed from Shakespeare's works and which are my own creation.

First, a note about the setting. *Still Star-Crossed* doesn't take place in Italy—it takes place in Shakespeare's Italy, an imaginary country where the geography is slightly different and everyone speaks English. Thus this book makes no claim to historical accuracy for any period of Italian history. I did my best to keep the characters' speech true to Shakespearean diction and vocabulary, but I felt it was more important to channel Shakespeare's love of language than to painstakingly replicate his style. His vocabulary is famously vast; I didn't want to make mine smaller than usual, so there are doubtless plenty of anachronisms. You may have also noticed that each section begins with a line or two on its own; those are in iambic pentameter, which is the usual rhythm of Shakespeare's verse. *Romeo and Juliet* contains some of the most beautiful examples of it.

Most of the major characters from *Still Star-Crossed* either appear in *Romeo and Juliet* or are mentioned there. Benvolio appears throughout the first half of *Romeo and Juliet*, usually teasing Romeo about his infatuation with Rosaline. His very first line is "Part, fools! Put up your swords. You know not what you do," but seven lines later he's dueling Tybalt himself, which is a mixture of maturity and stab-happy impulsiveness that really inspired me as I wrote my version of his character. He disappears from the play after Mercutio's death, but as far as the audience knows, he survives.

Prince Escalus appears throughout *Romeo and Juliet*, but aside from his increasingly short temper with the feuding Montagues and Capulets, we aren't privy to a great deal about his inner emotional life. His relationship with Rosaline is entirely invented.

Friar Laurence, the nurse, Lord Montague, and Lord and Lady Capulet all appear in the play. Lady Capulet's characterization is probably the most different in *Still Star-Crossed*—in the play, she's kind of a piece of work, but not actually evil as far as we know.

Probably the greatest liberty I took was with the character of Paris. In *Romeo and Juliet,* Romeo kills him outside Juliet's tomb, and he does not live on to become a secret villain.

Rosaline never appears onstage in *Romeo and Juliet,* but she is frequently mentioned in the first couple of acts, most often by Benvolio, who is sick of hearing the lovesick Romeo moan over her. We learn very little about her, except that she is Capulet's niece, that she is beautiful, and that she steadily refuses Romeo's ardent advances, preferring to "live chaste." These three pieces of information went remarkably far in the creation of my grumpy, independent heroine.

This is a list of party guests that appears in act one, which I found useful when naming Capulet types.

> Signior Martino and his wife and daughters
> County Anselmo and his beauteous sisters
> the lady widow of Vitruvio
> Signior Placentio and his lovely nieces
> Mercutio and his brother Valentine
> mine uncle Capulet, his wife, and daughters
> my fair niece Rosaline; Livia
> Signior Valentio and his cousin Tybalt
> Lucio and the lively Helena

As you can see, both Livia and the Duchess of Vitruvio appear on this list. I decided that Lord Capulet was the kind of guy who would refer to his noble mother-in-law not by her full title, but as "the widow," probably to get on her nerves.

Penlet, Tuft, Lucullus, the gravedigger, and all the other Montagues and Capulets are my creations. Their names are mostly drawn from other plays or are made up, although my friend Graham Moore's book *The Sherlockian* contains a character named Melinda who (spoiler alert) also dies a violent death, so I named Gramio after him in revenge.

Shakespeare superfans will have noted that I introduced a couple of small crossovers. The gravedigger alludes to a cousin in Denmark in the same profession—that's a reference to *Hamlet* (the "Alas, poor Yorick" bit). Princess Isabella is my creation, but she's married to Don Pedro of Arragon, who is a character from *Much Ado About Nothing*. She was going to be Hermione from *A Winter's Tale*, but I woke up one day and remembered Hermione's father was the emperor of Russia. I'm still annoyed about that.

Acknowledgments

This book would never have been written without the help and support of many wonderful people. My agent, Jennifer Joel at ICM, has been with the book from the very start, and I can never thank her enough for all her insight, faith, and patience. My editor, Michelle Poploff at Delacorte Press, also made this book a hundred times better.

Every day I worked on *Still Star-Crossed*, I referenced an electronic copy of the complete works of Shakespeare compiled by Project Gutenberg, which was an endlessly useful tool.

I'd like to thank all the other friends who have helped me through this process. The Upright Citizens Brigade taught me to write and helped me get paid to do it. UCB and all my friends there mean the world to me. For three months, Avi Karnani, Matt Wallaert, and their company Churnless gave me a desk in their office to write. It was one of the greatest creative windfalls I've ever gotten. I will also always be grateful to Graham Moore; Will Hines; Charlie Baily; Ayesha Choudhury; Nick Sansone; Terry Figel; Marysue Foster;

Patty Riley; my parents, Bart and Barbara Taub; my sister Hannah Taub; my brother, Nathan Taub; all the other friends who put up with me muttering in iambic pentameter; and most especially, my sister Amanda Taub, without whom this book would not exist.

Finally, I would like to thank William Shakespeare, for Cordelia, for the forest of Arden, for "exit, pursued by bear," and above all for the surpassing beauty of *Romeo and Juliet*.

About the Author

Melinda Taub got a Trapper Keeper for her seventh birthday and sat right down and wrote her first story in it. The Trapper Keeper is long gone, but the writing never stopped. Her work has appeared on FUSE TV's *Billy on the Street*, on the Onion News Network, and at the Upright Citizens Brigade. Her Internet videos have been viewed by more people than the population of Fiji.

Melinda lives in New York City. She likes biking, running, eating Peking duck, and seeing every Shakespeare production she can.